FROM THE EMBERS

ALY MARTINEZ

To Mo Mabie
Thank you for suggesting pure brilliance like steel-toed boots.
And also for making sure I never wrote it down.

AND

To Corinne Michaels
For all the nice things I've done that you never remember.

CHAPTER ONE

EASON

"Hey," I breathed, catching Jessica's arm as she tiptoed out of the nursery.

"Stop, Eason. I'm not in the mood."

She was never in the mood. And not the kind of mood that happened in the bedroom. Though, coincidentally, she was never up for that, either.

I gave her arm a warm squeeze. "Come on. You have to talk to me."

"No, I don't!" she yelled, spinning around to face me.

Bracing for war—and defeat—I silently shut the door to our daughter's bedroom. "Quiet or you'll wake her."

"You don't have to remind me of that. *I* was the one who got her to sleep in the first place while you were out in the garage, pretending to be Billy Joel on that fucking piano."

Yep. She was absolutely right. Though, I was actually trying to be Eason Maxwell and force lyrical blood from my fingertips in order to string together a damn chorus that would allow me to keep our home out of foreclosure.

"There is no winning here, Jess. If I spend all day trying to create even the biggest pile-of-shit song that I can sell to keep us afloat take a hunk of my flesh. She acted like I was the only adult who lived in the house. She'd wanted to be a stay-at-home mom like Bree. I'd wanted that for her too. But when things got tough and my savings dwindled to nothing, Jessica never once stepped up to ask what she could do or how she could help our family. And yes, I was bitter about it, but you didn't see me taking that shit out on her.

Above and beyond that, I wasn't leaning on Bree for shit.

Luckily—or unluckily depending on how you looked at it—Jessica's best friend, Bree, was married to my best friend, Rob. This meant I'd phoned the closest thing I had to a brother and asked *my* best friend if I could drop our daughter off to stay with *his* sitter.

He'd of course said yes. Then, after hearing the shame and frustration in my voice, he'd spent the next fifteen minutes on a pep talk, reminding me he and Bree had also struggled after their oldest had been born. To hear him tell it, everything we were experiencing was perfectly normal. I had a feeling that his wife wasn't giving Jessica the same encouragement.

It could be said that Bree wasn't my biggest fan. It could also be said that I'd puked on her shoes the night we'd met. But hey, stomach acid under the bridge, right?

We weren't mortal enemies or anything. Bree and I got along just fine—on the surface. Deep down, she was a touch…uh, *difficult.*

And judgmental.

And snobby.

And…well, high maintenance.

I was learning some of that applied to my own wife too.

I'd been moving heaven and earth to work my way back into Jessica's good graces. My hopes were high that a double-date night would at least bring her smile back. There was no way I could afford dinner and drinks at whatever five-star restaurant Bree would deem worthy of her presence, so Rob had suggested we make it a game night. With the kids at their place, the four of us could hang out at our house, free from little ears and responsibility. Everyone would BYOB. I'd drink the remnants of the Scotch Rob had given me when Luna was born, and I'd buy Jessica whatever giant bottle of wine I could find on sale. The good news for me was she wasn't picky when it came to drinking away her troubles.

Gripping the back of my neck, I held her icy stare. "Can we just not do this tonight? Please. I'm so sick and fucking tired of fighting all the time. You're pissed. I get it, okay? We'll figure it out." Reaching out, I hooked my pinky with hers and gave it a gentle tug.

She inched closer, stopping before her chest touched mine. "You've been trying to figure it out for months now, and nothing has changed. The mortgage company is blowing up my phone like I can magically produce four months of payments if they just keep calling. Every morning, I wake up terrified that it's going to be the day they finally turn off the water or the power or—" Her voice cracked. "Or…I don't know. *Something*."

My stomach wrenched. Shit was bad, but arguing about it all the time wasn't doing anything productive other than driving a wedge between us.

I moved into her, wrapping her in a hug, and kissed the top of her head. I didn't let her stiffness faze me. "I'm not going to let them turn the water off. Or the power. Or anything else you can think of."

"How?" she croaked, her lack of faith as insulting as it was justified.

I sucked in a deep breath, my chest filling painfully. Dammit. It was time. I couldn't put it off any longer. Not for pride. Not for what-ifs. Not for all the "maybe one days" in the world. It was our only way out. I was a father and a husband who had responsibilities that didn't involve chasing a dream.

CHAPTER TWO

BREE

"H E'S SELLING '92?" I WHISPERED WITH UTTER shock into the phone.

Jessica blew out an exasperated breath on the other end of the line. "Well, he said he was. The real question will be if he actually follows through."

I peeked around the corner of the kitchen to make sure Rob wasn't within earshot. My husband hated when Jessica and I talked about his closest friend. Rob always thought we were ganging up on the poor guy, but it was literally at the very top of my best friend job description to make sure Eason was taking care of my girl. My concern was more than warranted. For the last few years, he had been failing in spectacular fashion at that task.

When I was sure Rob was still in the garage, probably whispering sweet nothings to his precious Porsche, I walked back to the oven to check on dinner for the kids. "But he brought up selling the album all on his own this time, right? That has to mean something."

She scoffed. "Yeah, it means he's sick of sleeping on the couch and not getting laid."

"Well, whatever the case. As long as it ends with you and Luna not being homeless, I'm good with it." I paused and chewed on my bottom lip. "You know if you need anything until he's able to sell—"

"Nope. Don't even start with that crap. This is not your problem."

I let out a sigh. Jessica and I had been friends since our college waitressing days. She was stubborn, hard-headed, and so damn full of pride that she wouldn't accept a helping hand even if she was flat on her ass. Which wasn't too far from her current situation.

"Jess, stop. Just let me give you a little—"

"Champagne," she finished for me. "The only thing I'm accepting from you is champagne. We're celebrating tonight."

"This is technically the first time I've been away from the kids since Madison was born."

"Wow. Your first outing is to my crappy living room. What a lucky girl."

"Hey, I'm just happy to get a night out that doesn't involve a diaper bag." This wasn't totally true. I'd been stressing about leaving the kids all week.

It drove Rob crazy that I'd been shutting down date night after date night for almost ten months. We had a great sitter in our neighbor, Evelyn. She was crazy sweet and patient, with four teenage boys of her own. Rob and I both trusted her with Asher, but Madison was different. She had been a preemie who spent over a month in the NICU. At ten months old, she was thriving, but in my eyes, she would always be that tiny three-and-a-half-pound baby covered in wires and struggling to breathe.

It was time though. Mentally and emotionally, this mama needed a break.

"I'm calling bullshit." Jessica laughed. "You've been pacing the house all day, haven't you?"

I peeked out of my kitchen window for the sixth time in so

many minutes to check on Evelyn and Madison playing on a blanket in the grass. "What? No. I haven't."

"Liar."

Movement at the door to the garage caught my attention. Rob's deep-brown eyes immediately found mine, and a mischievous smile grew across his face. It was the way he always looked at me—rapt and awestruck.

My cheeks heated as he prowled toward me, his gaze sliding down my body, lingering in all the right places.

"Jess, I need to go."

"Fine, but Eason should be there any minute to drop off Luna. Chances are Rob already knows about the album, but don't mention to either of them that I told you."

"Mmhm," I hummed, biting my lips. My husband's muscular body swayed as he made his predatory advance. "See you tonight." I didn't say goodbye before hitting the end button.

Rob plucked the phone from my hand and set it on the counter, hooking one arm around my hips to draw me close. "Wow," he whispered, his breath ghosting across my lips. "You look gorgeous."

"Let's not get carried away. It's just a sundress," I replied, smiling against his mouth. More specifically, it was my least favorite sundress. Yellow-and-brown floral had never been my friend, but I was still on the uphill climb of losing the last ten pounds after having Madison, so it was one of the few dresses I had that fit.

Once upon a time, I'd been a businesswoman—pencil skirts and blazers had made up the majority of my wardrobe. Now, I was a stay-at-home mom of two. On a good day, I wore pants with a waistband.

Sneaking his hand under the hem of my dress, he cupped

my ass. "Don't say the word *just* about anything when it comes to you in this dress."

"I take it you like—"

"Mom!" Asher yelled down the stairs.

Rob let out a groan and tipped his head back to stare at the ceiling. "I swear that kid has some kind of sixth sense for when I'm trying to make a move on his mother."

"That's what you get for creating your mini-me. He knows when you're up to no good."

The side of his lips hiked in a breathtaking smirk. "Oh, it would have been good, Bree. Real good."

"So you always tell me. Though the jury is still out on your follow-through."

His mouth gaped in feigned offense, but that damn twinkle in his eyes told me I was in for a long, much overdue night after we got home.

Laughing, I replied to our son, "Yeah, buddy?"

"Is dinner almost ready? Starving kids is illegal, ya know!"

Yep. That was my boy. Five years old and hangry just like his mama.

"Two minutes!" I shouted back just as the doorbell sounded.

Rob arched an eyebrow. "Jesus, did he call in reinforcements?"

"I think it's Eason. Jessica said he was on his way."

His smile returned and he dipped low for another kiss. "In that case, he can wait. Now, where were we?"

I dodged his mouth. "You get the door for your man child and I'll feed our actual child before he calls the cops."

"Hey," Rob scolded. "Be nice tonight. Eason's been planning this for a while."

"What? I'm always nice."

He frowned and headed out of the kitchen, saying, "Right. Of course. Calling him a man child is the pinnacle of kindness. Your invitation to sainthood is probably already in the mail."

I rolled my eyes even as a small seed of guilt sprouted in my stomach.

Fine. No. I wasn't always easy on Eason. I didn't hate him though. He was a good guy, the kind who opened doors and made a point to include everyone in whatever conversation he was animatedly dominating. With all of his sandy-blond hair, warm brown eyes, and a sly one-sided smile that made women lose their minds, he'd hypnotized Jessica right off the bat. Factor in that Jessica was gorgeous with a sharp wit and Eason never stood a chance.

In theory, your best friend marrying your husband's best friend was every high school girl's dream.

But not with these two.

Jessica had had a hard life, and whoever was destined to end up with Eason was going to have it even harder while he tried to chase a nearly impossible future. At first, they had been all laughter, longing stares, and wild nights. But a positive pregnancy test and the crash and burn of Eason's career had put them on thin ice—right where I'd always known they'd end up.

However, their relationship was none of my business—or so my husband loved to tell me.

Using an oven mitt, I retrieved the homemade heart-shaped nuggets from the oven and set the cookie sheet on a trivet to cool.

"Dinner's ready," I called up to Asher. "Wash your hands before you come down."

I assumed he'd heard me when there was a telltale thud from him jumping off his bed the way I'd told him not to eighty-seven million times. Rough estimate of course.

Eason strolled into the kitchen, wearing a huge smile on his face and my second favorite baby girl on his hip. "Hey, Bree," he greeted, pulling me into his customary hug, and it wouldn't have been Eason if he didn't finish it with a tight, lingering squeeze. "How ya been?"

"I'm good," I chirped, awkwardly inching out of his hold. Turning my attention to my goddaughter, I clapped and extended my hands in her direction. "Come here, sweet girl."

Eason passed her off with pure fatherly pride beaming from his eyes. For all of his struggles in the professional and financial departments, he did love his daughter something fierce.

"Well, you look pretty. Is this new?" I asked Luna, straightening the ruffle on the sleeve of her pink monogrammed outfit. I shuddered to think what maxed-out credit card Jessica had used to buy it.

Eason smoothed down the front of his gray Henley. "Aw, shucks, Bree. Thanks for noticing. You look good too. Is that Jessica's dress?"

"Uh, no. It's my dress that Jessica borrowed, and I had to do an entire Tom Cruise *Mission Impossible* thing to get it back last week. Your wife is a clothing thief, but I stole these wedges while I was there, so it evened out."

Chuckling, Eason plucked a nugget off the tray and popped it into his mouth. I made no extraordinary efforts to warn him that they were still hot. Yeah, my sainthood was definitely on the way.

"Shit, shit, shit," he panted, chewing with his mouth open.

Mildly amused, I bounced Luna on my hip and watched his struggle. "You want another?"

"Mmm. Thanks, but I think I'll pass on the molten lava chicken nuggets."

"They're veggie nuggets."

He curled his lip. "That explains the grassy aftertaste."

I shook my head, because honestly, it was all I could do with him most of the time.

"Uncle Eason!" Asher jumped down the last three stairs, giving me my daily heart attack.

"What's up, lil man?" Eason asked, dropping into a squat.

After the elaborate handshake they'd been crafting since my son was three days old, they finished with a behind-the-back high five.

"Guess what?" Asher asked.

Eason didn't miss a beat. "You found a fossil in the backyard that unearthed a new species of dinosaurs. With no teeth, it appears this dino could have been friendly, so scientists have decided to use its DNA to bring them back to life with hopes of taming them and using them as a new form of transportation, thus saving our precious...well, fossil fuels."

Asher's freckled nose crinkled adorably. "What? No!"

"Dang," Eason breathed, his face filled with wonder as he stared off into the distance. "I was really looking forward to riding an Asherosaurus."

My son howled with laughter, a common reaction when his favorite and only "uncle" was around. Eason laughed right along with him, complete with the abridged version of their secret handshake.

"All right, you two," I interrupted. "Go sit at the table, Ash."

"Don't do it," Eason whispered from the corner of his mouth. "They're veggie nuggets that may or may not be laced with grass clippings."

"Yessss! I love veggie nuggets."

Eason cut him a side-eye. "Boy, you aren't right. That's it. Tomorrow when I pick up Luna, I'm bringing you some good old-fashioned Mickey D's Chicken McNuggets. You'll never grow hair on your chest eating this veggie stuff."

With his father's nearly black hair and eyes, he argued, "Gross. I don't want hair on my chest!"

"You will one day."

"No, I won't. Dad doesn't have hair on his chest."

"Well. That's weird. Every man has hair on his body. Maybe check his butt next time he's in the shower."

"Ewwwwwww!" Asher shouted, causing Luna to startle in my arms.

"Ohhh-kay," I drawled, passing Eason back his daughter. "That's enough hair and butt talk for one day...and possibly ever." I grabbed a plate from the cabinet and called out, "Rob! Please come save me!"

Eason, doing the universal step-step-sway baby-soothing dance, used his free hand to pull the neck of his shirt down, revealing his neatly trimmed chest hair before mouthing to Asher, "*McNuggets.*"

Right on cue, Rob walked into the kitchen and slapped his best friend on the back. "Quit harassing my wife." He too snagged a nugget off the tray. It was still hot. So he also did the panting bit before curling his lip. "Oh God, what is this crap?"

"It's a vegetable, honey. Be careful or your body will go into shock." After prepping Asher's plate with nuggets, a handful of baby carrots, and half a banana, I handed it off to Rob.

He carried it over to the table. "Okay, I got Luna's Pack 'n Play all set up in the guest room. I feel bad. Maybe we should put her in with Madison so she doesn't get lonely?"

"Not if you want them to sleep." I propped my hip against the counter. "Two babies-slash-future-best-friends will never sleep if they can see each other."

He stopped in front of Eason and gave Luna's belly a tickle. "You sure Jessica's okay with leaving her here tonight?"

Eason chuckled. "If she isn't, the twenty-seven outfits, bibs, bottles, and a winter coat in the middle of May that she packed was a real waste." He looked at his watch. "And on that note, I need to get out of here. I still have to stop at the store to get a few things." After kissing Luna on the head a dozen or so times, he reluctantly passed her to Rob and then looked at me. "Jess told me to grab the *good* champagne from you."

The shame in his tone was clear to every ear in the room.

And damn if that seed of guilt in my stomach didn't grow. "Oh. Yeah. Sure. Let me just grab—"

"Take the Dom," Rob interrupted.

Eason scoffed. "I'm not taking that for game night. Save that for—"

Rob slanted his head in challenge. "I said take the P3 Rosé. Oh, and grab the Bollinger too."

My eyes flared. Holy shit. That had to have been at least three thousand dollars in champagne.

Rob and I did okay ourselves—more than okay if I was being honest. My once-small side gig sewing custom comforters for the girls in my dorm to earn beer money had taken off shortly after I graduated. Armed with a business degree, I'd rebranded Bree's Blankets into Prism Bedding and moved to mass production and distribution to department stores all across the country. I loved my job, but the minute I laid eyes on my baby boy, my heart wasn't in it anymore. Keeping it in the family, Rob took over as CEO and not long after landed us an eight-figure deal with the biggest hotel chain in North America to exclusively supply all five thousand of their hotels with private-label bedding. We'd spent that night celebrating in a penthouse suite in Vegas with a bottle of each Dom and Bollinger.

However, unless Jessica had left out some seriously important details about this celebration we were having for Eason, I wasn't sure Dom and Bollinger were necessary.

I assumed Eason shared my thoughts when he nearly choked on his tongue. "Have you lost your mind?"

My husband shook his head. "My best friend is a musical genius who has decided to grace the biggest artists in the world with his songs before eventually writing more and dominating the entire industry as a solo artist. I did not spend a summer with you in a nineteen ninety-two Ford Aerostar van, taking two showers a week—combined—to celebrate your future successes with shitty champagne. End of discussion." With that, he patted Eason on the shoulder and carried Luna out the back door to Evelyn.

"Jesus," Eason breathed, pinching the bridge of his nose. "As if taking champagne from you guys wasn't bad enough, now I have to add half a million dollars of bubbly to my infinite debt."

I offered him a tight smile. "It's not that expensive, but should you find yourself the biggest artist in modern history like he expects you'll be, we'll be happy to accept half a million dollars as repayment."

He huffed. "I wouldn't hold your breath on it."

I wasn't, but if Rob had that kind of faith in him, the least I could do was walk down to the wine cellar and get the champagne.

CHAPTER THREE

EASON

I WAS DUMPING THE LAST OF THE CHIPS INTO A BOWL JUST as the doorbell rang. "Jess?"

"Yeah, I got it."

Wiping my hands on a towel beside the sink, I surveyed my handiwork. Chips with homemade salsa and some random cheese that the lady at the grocery store had promised would be delicious along with a plate of fancy crackers, each one looking about as appetizing as a piece of cardboard. It wasn't perfect. All in all, it had cost less than twenty bucks. But it looked good and that was more than enough to appease my wife.

"How's it going?" Rob asked, walking in carrying a bottle of wine, as if the champagne hadn't been bad enough.

"What's that?"

"A gift for our hosts."

I leveled him with a glare. "Seriously?"

Laughing, he shook his head. "Don't give me shit. Bree insisted. Besides, a little extra wine never hurt anyone." He arched an eyebrow and turned a pointed gaze on the ladies who were already huddled around the sofa table I'd converted into a makeshift bar.

Jessica was sporting a massive grin, so I gave up being annoyed at my best friend's gratuitous generosity, took the bottle, and put it in the fridge.

"Can I get you a Scotch?"

He quirked a dark eyebrow. "Are you expecting me to play Pictionary tonight?"

I chuckled and started toward the bar. "Right. I'll make it a double."

Together, we walked over to the ladies, where I went in for the hug on Bree. "Hey, long time no see." As usual, her return embrace was short and stiff, but I'd long since given up on reading into it. "How were the kids when you left?"

Rob coughed. "Don't." Another cough. "Mention." He cleared his throat. "The kids." He grinned at his wife. "Champagne or wine, sweetheart?"

Bree rolled her eyes. "I'm fine. Stop making such a big deal about it."

"Of course you are, my love," Rob crooned, shooting me a wink. "Champagne?"

After the pop of a cork that cost more than my mortgage and a quick toast to me with some bullshit about new beginnings and a bright future, we migrated in different directions. Jessica took Bree to Luna's nursery to show her the new letters we'd hung over her crib while Rob and I meandered into my fortress of solitude that I shared with Jessica's car—the garage.

Long before he'd worn Dolce and Gabbana suits and started driving a Porsche, Rob and I had grown up together, playing pickup basketball at the park while our parents worked late to keep food on the table. He'd made fun of me when I found an old keyboard at a yard sale and spent hours teaching myself piano in high school. He'd also given me hell when I began singing and writing my own music. But once I started gigging in college, he became my biggest fan.

The summer after our second year at the University of Georgia, Rob borrowed his grandmother's decrepit '92 minivan and booked my very first tour. Okay, the so-called "tour" consisted of fifteen open-mic nights around the state, many of which had Rob and the bartender as the only faces in the audience, but dammit, that was the summer I truly discovered what I wanted to do with the rest of my life.

Not long after, I dropped out of college and threw myself into writing and playing anywhere that would have me, and my album *Solstice in the '92* was born.

Rob had always believed in me, even when I was ready to throw in the towel. Which was exactly why I side-stepped the truth when he finished bitching about a new guy he'd hired at Prism and asked, "So, how are you really feeling about selling the songs?"

Avoiding eye contact, I swirled the Scotch in my glass. "It's good for the family."

"And what about what's good for you?"

I shrugged. "There's been a lot of what's good for me happening the last few years. It's not my turn anymore."

His lips thinned, a motivational speech no doubt poised on the tip of his tongue. I wasn't in the mood though. This was supposed to be a night of fun and freedom. A few hours of laughs to distract us all from the real world.

Or, in my case, drown them in a bottle.

"Let's go find the ladies. Jess and I have a game of Pictionary to win."

He barked a laugh, clearly reading my escape. But Rob being Rob, he didn't call me on it.

Just like in the game of life, Jessica and I lost the first round.

I had a strong suspicion Bree was either cheating or had become a telepath. There was no way she got *apple picking* from Rob drawing a damn tree that honestly looked more like a shrub, not a single fruit in sight. It did make for some good old-fashioned trash talk and upped the ante for round two, so I let it slide.

"Walking. Floating. Doing magic!" Jessica yelled.

"No. This." I stabbed the marker at the very skillfully drawn stick figure jumping rope.

Bree giggled from the couch as my Pictionary-challenged wife threw her hands up in the air.

"I don't know! Draw something else."

Grabbing Jessica's arm, I dragged her closer to the board as if the three feet between us were somehow distorting her vision. "This. This thing." I pointed at the jump rope.

"No talking!" Rob chided, holding the tiny hourglass to his face, already smiling in victory, waiting for the last grain to fall.

Ignoring him, I cleared the frustration from my voice. "Baby, sweetie, honey, *look* at the—"

That was all I got out before time expired on us all.

With a deafening boom, the entire house exploded.

I didn't remember falling, but in the next blink, I was on the floor, covered in debris. My ears rang and my vision blurred as I fought to gain my bearings, but nothing made sense. As I rolled to my back, the ceiling was wide open, insulation and wires hanging, flames covering the support beams like lightning streaking the sky.

"Shit," I breathed, gripping my head as though I could manually slow my thoughts. "Jes—" I coughed, smoke scorching a path down my throat. "Jessica." Suddenly, a single terrifying thought pierced through my foggy brain. "Luna!" I sat bolt upright.

No. Wait.

I shook my head again, memories flooding my subconscious. Luna wasn't there. She was at… Fuck.

"Rob! Bree!"

It was eerily silent.

No cries.

No screams.

No pleas for help.

And in that second, it might have been the most terrifying sound of all.

Desperation collided with a surge of adrenaline in my veins. With a strained groan, I managed to climb to my feet. Heat licked at my face as I staggered to catch my balance amongst the wreckage. It was somehow simultaneously dark and yet blindingly bright. In the shadows of the dancing flames, I made out the empty space where the couch Bree and Rob had been sitting on had once been.

It was gone.

Everything was fucking gone.

"Jessica!" I roared into the nothingness. She'd been standing right in front of me. She couldn't have fallen far. Panic engulfed me and I dropped my knees, frantically digging through the rubble. Blood poured from my hands as broken pieces of God only knew what slashed through my skin.

I had to find her and get her out of there and then come back and find Rob and Bree and somehow get them out too.

In the first few seconds, everything seemed possible. I still couldn't wrap my mind around what had happened. It was bad, but losing the people I loved didn't seem like a realistic outcome. Though, as the fire grew, so did my fears.

Smoke invaded my vision until I was searching blind, furiously patting around the floor where I thought she might have been.

Where I *prayed* she might have been.

Where I really fucking *needed* her to be.

A wave of relief hit me like a tsunami, nearly knocking me to my ass, when I finally felt her hand. "Jessica!" I choked, coughing and gagging.

I had no idea if she was injured or breathing, but I'd found her. Now, I had to get her the hell out of there. In one fluid motion, I scooped her into my arms and took off toward the door, forging a path by memory alone through the pieces of a home that no longer existed.

We'd almost made it to the front door when I tripped over something, nearly dropping her. Pure determination alone kept me upright.

One step farther, one second later, one wrong move and I would have missed her completely. Her body was hidden beneath a pile of broken furniture, but her dark hair cascaded across the dirty floor.

Oh, God. Bree.

I froze for a beat, juggling Jessica in my arms while trying to squat down to grab Bree too. At six-two, I was a big guy, but one lifeless woman was hard enough to blindly carry from a burning house, much less two. Panic screamed inside me. The smoke was getting thicker by the second. The more I tried and the longer we stayed, the more dangerous it became for all of us.

Everything changed in the next second.

My life.

Jessica's life.

Bree's life.

Rob's life.

Luna's life.

Asher's and Madison's lives.

One decision in the middle of the unimaginable and the world as we knew it was irrevocably changed.

It all came down to one single decision.

"I'll be right back," I choked out.

Using my arm to block my face, I continued to the door. The knob seared my palm as I yanked it open, but the pain didn't even register through the adrenaline. The sound of my feet pounding down the driveway echoed in my ears as the fire crackled behind me. Our closest neighbor was over half a mile away, but there was no way they hadn't heard the explosion. The fire department would be there soon.

I'd get Bree out. They'd find Rob. Everyone would be okay.

"Eason," she croaked in my arms.

My feet were still moving as I sprinted away, but time stopped as her voice permeated my senses.

No.

It wasn't possible.

She was covered in soot, and my eyes were caked with ash and what I would later learn to be blood, but I could still make out the large flowers on her yellow—

"Uh, no. It's my dress that Jessica borrowed and I had to do an entire Tom Cruise Mission Impossible *thing to get it back last week."*

Oh, God.

I kept running until the wind changed direction, clearing the smoke. With my heart in my throat, I prayed that my still ringing ears had deceived me. Then I set her down and used the inside of my shirt to clear my face.

"Eason," she croaked.

But once again, *she* wasn't my wife.

"Oh, God," I breathed, watching as she rose on unsteady legs. Tears carved twin riverbeds through the ash on her cheeks.

"What happened?" Bree asked, her green eyes focused on the blazing inferno behind me.

Acrid guilt devoured me. "I…"

I saved the wrong woman.

I left the mother of my child in a burning building.

My final broken promise to the woman I'd vowed forever to was, "I'll be right back."

Bile crawled up my throat. "I don't know."

I glanced back at the house, the heat of the roaring fire scorching me even from yards away. Overwhelming grief hit me as I realized there was no way I could get back through those flames.

Oh, God. Jessica.

In the middle of tragedy, it's strange the things that become engrained into your memories. Years later, I wouldn't be able to tell you how long it took the firetrucks to get there. I couldn't tell you what time it was or what I had been wearing. But I would never be able to forget the absolute devastation on Bree's face when she realized we were the only two standing outside the burning house.

"Where's Rob?" she rasped, her voice sounding like it had traveled over a mile of gravel before exiting her throat. "And Jessica. Where are they?" She took an urgent stride toward me.

"I tried…" I doubled over into a fit of coughing. It was probably for the best. There was no way I could have finished that thought.

Grabbing the front of my shirt, she shoved me back upright and gave me a hard shake. "Are they in there?"

"I don't know!" I shouted, fear and failure mingling into one soul-crushing emotion.

There was a pause. Neither of us breathed. We desperately tried to rationalize our way out. She'd been unconscious when I found her. She hadn't seen the inside of that house.

The destruction.

The carnage.

The hell we'd both narrowly escaped.

No. Bree hadn't experienced any of that.

And it showed, because she still had hope.

"Rob!" she cried, darting past me. She slipped on the grass and fell, the brutal heat like a forcefield stopping her in her tracks. "Help me!" she screamed, giving up on standing altogether. She began crawling one inch at a time. "Eason, help me. We have to get them out."

It took every ounce of strength I had left to hook her around the hips. "Bree, stop."

She tore at my arms, kicking and flailing. "Let me go! I have to get them." Her voice echoed off the trees, each reverberation slicing me to the core.

"You can't go in there!" I barked. "You won't make it out."

"Then you go." Her chest shook with broken exhales. "You did this. You did all of this. Now you go in there and get my husband and you fucking fix it."

I was in a state of shock, running on nothing more than adrenaline. I couldn't feel the third-degree burns on my hands or the six-inch gash on my head, but her verbal jab hit me like a TKO. "What?"

"Get him!" she screamed, her face vibrating with a pain so visceral it rattled my bones. Her anger broke into sobs, but her words were no less venomous. "You left him in there. You have to go get him. He never would have done that to you."

I drew in a deep breath, desperate for oxygen I couldn't seem to absorb. My mind spun in a million different directions, a frantic sprint of my neurons to make sense of the world on fire around me. "I didn't do this," I gasped, glancing over my shoulder at the towering inferno, the weight of gravity suddenly more than I could carry. "I barely got you out. I thought you were Jessica. I was going to go back for—"

That was all I got out before our entire lives exploded all over again.

Maybe she was right and this was somehow my fault.

Maybe I'd failed them both.

But as blinding orange and red flames shot high into the sky, there was only one person left that I could save.

"No!" Bree screamed as I dove on top of her, pinning her to the Earth. Fiery fragments of my life rained down over us, each one feeling like a rusty blade slicing the heart from my chest.

She fought beneath me, biting and clawing at me.

She cried his name and cussed mine.

As sirens screamed in the distance, she had air in her lungs and a beat in her chest.

And through it all, no matter how hard I prayed, *she* never magically became Jessica.

CHAPTER FOUR

BREE

Numb, alone, and utterly lost, I stared at his side of the bed. With my hands under the pillow, I angled my legs to where only three days ago he would have let out a playful hiss when my cold feet touched his calves. He would have grabbed my hip and dragged me toward him with a growled, "Get over here, woman."

And then he would have held me.

Talked to me.

Grown old with me.

"Come back," I whispered, squeezing my eyes shut, desperate to feel him again. I could still smell his signature scent of crisp lemon and cedarwood on the sheets. His dirty clothes were still in the hamper. A bag of his dry cleaning had been delivered since he'd taken his last breath. Yet my husband, the father of my children—*my Rob*. He was gone. "Please just come back," I choked out around the inescapable sadness that had defined my every waking hour since the fire.

It's going to be okay. I heard his voice in my head. *You and the kids. You're going to be fine. Let's be honest, you were always the four-hundred-horsepower engine behind this family. I was just the hood ornament.*

A sob bubbled in my throat. It was such a Rob thing to say. I swear the man could have convinced a mud puddle it was an ocean. He had a way about him that was so calm and rational it soothed my insecurities and left me with a smile in the process.

God, I needed a smile.

But most of all, I needed him.

"How?" I begged. "How am I supposed to do this without you?"

That was where our imaginary conversations always ended. The ghost in my head never had any answers. I couldn't wrap my mind around how I'd ended up in this situation in the first place, much less how to carry on in the aftermath.

Everything immediately before and after I'd woken up in Eason's arms was splotchy. I remembered the panic and confusion. The anger and resentment. The absolute frustration that the world kept spinning and it was all I could do to hold on. But I'd never forget the earth-shattering pain as a police officer stood in my hospital room, informing me that Rob and Jessica's bodies had both been recovered—or at least what was left of them. He'd asked me a dozen questions. I'd answered them as best I could, but nothing felt real anymore.

Not the emptiness in my chest.

Not the jagged ache in my soul.

Not even the absolute devastation swirling in my stomach.

Rob was gone.

Jessica was gone.

And people just expected me to carry on without them.

I'd spent two days in the hospital, crying myself into a state of nothingness.

The doctors diagnosed me with a concussion. They gave me oxygen for my lungs, antibiotics to prevent infections in the burns on my arms and legs, and even a sedative to help me sleep.

Nothing eased the pain.

Nothing ever would.

It was an accident. While the four of us had sat upstairs, laughing and drinking wine, a faulty pipe had filled the basement with enough gas to take out the entire house. The second explosion was from Jessica's car catching fire in the garage. According to the well-meaning but completely tone-deaf fire inspector, we'd been lucky to survive.

I didn't feel lucky. Though maybe Eason did.

Eason.

Jesus…Eason.

We'd been whisked away in different ambulances to separate hospitals and hadn't spoken since.

There was no rulebook on behavior in the middle of a catastrophic tragedy. Desperation doesn't come with courtesy or kindness. But it shouldn't have come with this much blame.

Yet, even as I lay in that bed, there was a conflicted part of me that wanted to rage at the world for what it had taken from me. A lot of the anger was aimed at Eason.

He was always the loser in my little what-if games.

What if we hadn't been there that night?

What if he hadn't been trying to get back into Jessica's good graces?

What if he hadn't bought that house in the first place?

Of all the people, why did *he* have to survive?

Why wasn't it Rob?

Why wasn't it Jessica?

Why…*Eason?*

Still, he'd saved my life. Even through my heartbreak, I knew I should have been on my knees, thanking him. My kids still had their mom because of him. I still had a chance to watch them grow up—graduations, weddings, grandkids.

Because of Eason, I still had a future.

Though being trapped in a spiral of grief didn't afford me many opportunities to focus on the silver lining.

Our neighbor Evelyn, the incredible woman she was, had taken a few days off work to stay with all three of the kids while Eason and I were in the hospital. None of us had a lot of family support. My parents had been dead for years, and Rob's mother was elderly with dementia. Eason had no one. He'd grown up without a dad, and his mom had died of breast cancer a few years back. Jessica's family was beyond worthless. They would no doubt show up at the funeral, sobbing dramatically over her casket, but they would be gone again before she was even laid to rest.

It had never been an issue before. *We* were the family. Me, Rob, Jessica, Eason.

And then there were two.

As if he'd been summoned from my thoughts, the doorbell rang and my stomach knotted.

I'd gotten home from the hospital the day before, and after I'd told Asher about his father and had a nervous breakdown in my bedroom, Evelyn had insisted on staying one more night. The woman was amazing. I didn't know what I would have done without her.

Over a somber breakfast where Asher sat in my lap, absently pushing his food around his plate, and Luna and Madison sat in highchairs playing tug-of-war with a sippy cup, Evelyn had told us Eason had been released from the hospital. She'd smiled and tickled Luna's stomach, saying something about how excited he was to come get his baby girl.

And that was how I'd ended up upstairs, lying in bed, having a conversation with my dead husband rather than sorting through the myriad of warring emotions that accompanied the idea of seeing Eason.

The doorbell rang again.

"Shit," I sighed, rolling out of bed, a staggering combination of guilt and panic colliding in my chest.

Grief was a complex emotion. My brain told me it was just Eason. Rob's best friend. Jessica's husband. I'd spent countless Christmases, birthdays, and summer vacations with the guy. But the dark and bitter parts inside my shattered heart told me he was the man who had survived while the charred fragments left of my husband and my best friend lay in a funeral home across town. Yes, he'd saved my life, but in doing it, he'd sentenced them both to death.

It wasn't fair and it wasn't right. But don't worry—I hated myself for surviving too.

Be nice, I heard Rob say in my head as I made my way down the stairs.

"I'm always nice," I replied, fully aware it was as much a lie as it was unnecessary. There was no one left for me to convince.

Taking my time to mask my emotions, I slowly walked to the door. I assumed Evelyn had already let him in when I heard his deep, raspy voice in the entryway.

"Hey, baby," he cooed. "God, Daddy missed you." His voice broke at the end, and as much as I didn't want it to, it cracked in my heart too.

Eason clung to his daughter, shoulders shaking, his bandaged hand cupping the back of her head. But as soon as my feet hit the bottom stair, his sunken, red-rimmed eyes jumped to mine.

I froze, unable to so much as breathe under the weight of his gaze. I'd never witnessed such raw desolation before. Not even when I looked in the mirror.

Dark circles hung under his eyes, which were barely supported by his hollow cheeks. I hadn't been eating, either, but Eason looked like he'd lost significant weight. Had I not known it was him, I would have had to do a double take. His sandy blond hair, which was usually messy on the top, had been shaved, and a long line of stitches started above his eyebrow, disappearing somewhere at the top of his skull. The sleeve of colorful tattoos on his left arm was covered in bandages, but scabs and burns were prominent on his neck and face.

Eason had always been larger than life. But as he stood in my foyer, holding his daughter, his whole body sagged as if it were too much for his skeleton to support.

"Hey," he rasped.

The knot in my stomach twisted painfully. "Hey."

We stared at each other for a long second, a million words hanging in the air between us, but we both knew that none of them would change our reality.

My nose stung as I watched him shift Luna to his hip.

He'd lost his wife.

His house.

His closest friend.

All of his possessions.

That little girl in his arms was everything he had left.

I was as far as one could get from the sainthood my husband had teased me about, but grief, bitterness, and devastation aside, I was still a human looking at another human who was lost in the pits of despair. I didn't have much to offer him in the way of emotional support, but I had resources Eason didn't.

"What are you planning to do?" I asked, crossing my arms over my chest as though the chill were in the room and not inside me.

He looked down at the tile floor. "Ah, that's a good question. A guy I used to gig with is going to let us crash in his guest room for a few nights. I need to get in touch with the insurance company and see what my options are for housing, but I haven't made it that far yet. Luckily, Jessica overpacked for Luna to stay here and my buddy brought me a bag of clothes he'd collected."

He paused and drew in a shaky breath. "It's like this domino effect, ya know? I don't have my wallet. Which means I don't have my debit card. But I gotta have an ID to get money from the bank. Not that cash really does you any good these days. Without a credit card, I can't get a new phone, which is what I need for the insurance company to call me back. Meanwhile, I have no car, no way to get a car, and somehow during all of this, I have to figure out how to bury my wife."

He let out a guttural groan filled with more agony than any cry he could have produced. His chest heaved as he lifted his head, those desolate brown eyes once again meeting mine. "Jesus fuck, Bree. How is any of this real?"

I couldn't answer that. Part of me still hoped it was just a nightmare I would eventually wake up from.

"Evelyn," I called, coming unstuck.

She quickly came around the corner as though she hadn't been far—wisely so. Searching his face for permission, I took Luna from his arms and then passed her off to Evelyn. "Can you do me a favor and take the kids outside for a little bit?"

"Of course," she replied.

"That's not necessary," he said, reaching for his daughter. "I just need to get her stuff so we can get out of here. I have a lot to do today." His tone became increasingly agitated. "I don't have time to—"

I stepped between him and Evelyn. "Eason, stop."

"I can't stop. I can't stop any of this," he snapped. "Look, I've got a buddy waiting in the car, I just need to get her stuff."

"You're not going anywhere," I whispered. "You and Luna are going to stay here for a while. In the pool house. It's what Rob would have wanted."

"Yeah, well. Rob's dead, right? Lets you off the hook there."

My back shot straight. It was a fact, yet it still felt like a punch to the stomach. "That's not fair."

"And what part of this is fair?"

With a chin jerk, I signaled for Evelyn to go, and without further objections from Eason, she hurried Luna from the room.

We stood in silence until I heard the back door close. "You need to take a deep breath and relax. I know you're hurting but—"

"Hurting?" he laughed. "Having my arms torn off would be *hurting* compared to the shit that is happening inside me right now. I can't fucking close my eyes without those flames consuming me again. I can't eat or sleep." He lifted a trembling hand out in front of him. "I just fucking shake all the time, like my soul is trying to tear free from my body. And sometimes I wish it would, even if that meant I went with it. But then there's Luna and I know she needs me, but how do I look that little girl in the face knowing I let her mother die?"

I swallowed hard. "You didn't let—"

"Bullshit," he hissed. "Don't you dare stand there and act like you don't blame me for this. Rob wouldn't have left me in that house, right? Isn't that what you said? This was all my fault, right, Bree?" He took a long stride toward me, crowding me in

35

the otherwise empty foyer. "You already said it once. Seeing how I haven't heard one fucking word from you, I'm not guessing your opinion has changed all that much since then."

Guilt swelled in my chest, but I stood there with my mouth clamped shut, unable to argue the truth.

"Right," he whispered. "So, thanks, but no, thanks. I already blame myself enough without staying here, knowing you blame me too."

He turned on a toe and marched toward the back door.

Jesus, what was happening?

Rob and Jessica would have hated us arguing like this.

In the wake of tragedy, it's easy to withdraw into yourself. After all, you can't fathom how anyone else could adequately understand the misery you're going through.

But Eason did. We filtered our pain in our own ways. Our hearts would work their way through the stages of grief differently. But whether we liked it or not, with every step, Eason was beside me on that same trip through hell.

The realization that I wasn't completely alone in this eased the pressure in my chest in unimaginable ways.

"You thought I was Jessica," I told his back.

He froze mid-step.

"I saw your face that night. You were devastated that it was me you'd carried out. And honestly, I don't blame you for that."

"Bree," he whispered, slowly turning around, his face pale and filled with shame.

"It's okay to hate me for not being her."

"I don't hate you. I'm just so fucking—"

"Mad," I finished for him, a tear sliding down my cheek. "Bitter. Terrified. Heartbroken. Lost. *Confused*."

He slanted his head, pained understanding crinkling his forehead. "Yeah. All of it."

"Me too." A heart-wrenching sob I could no longer contain ravaged my body, but in the next beat, I was in his arms.

"I'm sorry," he whispered, his strong arms wrapping around me. "I'm so fucking sorry. I wish I could have saved all of you."

He had nothing to apologize for. Rationally, I knew that. Getting to a place of acceptance would be a ways off though. Much like him finding a way to look at me without the regret of that night devouring him.

But I was willing to try if he was.

"Please stay here with us," I cried into his chest. "Just until you get on your feet. You can hate me and I'll hate you, but we can do it together, okay?"

"Yeah," he rumbled through an onslaught of emotion. He gathered me closer, his chest vibrating with silent tears of his own. "I can do that."

We didn't say anything else.

Eason and I stood in the foyer, crying together for what felt like an eternity. Two people who had lost everything finding solace in familiarity.

When he finally released me, I didn't feel better. Having company in hell didn't change the fact that you were still actually *in hell*.

Then again, I didn't feel worse, either. And that in and of itself was progress.

CHAPTER FIVE

EASON

WE BURIED JESSICA TEN DAYS AFTER THE FIRE. IT could have been a thousand days after and I wouldn't have been ready. Her funeral was small—only about fifty people in attendance. A few of her family members had made the trek from Florida, her father notably missing even after I'd sent him money for a plane ticket.

Despite the gaping hole in my chest, I did everything I could to make that day as special as Jessica deserved. Orange roses, the kind she'd carried at our wedding, covered her ivory casket and a huge memorial of hundreds of photos I'd painstakingly constructed from the cloud storage on our old cell phones created the backdrop to say goodbye to my wife.

A preacher who had never met her spoke about celebrating her life and honoring her memory.

Bree attempted to tell the story of how they met, but she broke down about halfway through and had to be ushered back to her seat.

I played the Rolling Stone's "Wild Horses" on the guitar. There were supposed to be lyrics, but it was all I could do to find the right chords.

Through it all, Evelyn stood in the corner, bouncing my fussy daughter, who would never remember her mother.

I hugged people I didn't know.

Caught up with old friends I hadn't seen in years.

Consoled family members she'd hated.

Bree was generous enough to open her house for lunch after the funeral. It was a kind and thoughtful gesture, especially since the wasteland that had once been my home was still roped off with police tape.

By the end of the day, as I retreated to the pool house with Luna, I was so physically and emotionally exhausted that I somehow managed to actually sleep. Which was amazing, considering first thing the next morning, I had to wake up and do it all over again.

"Does Dad have to wear work clothes in heaven?"

Squatting in front of Asher, I stopped buttoning his shirt and looked him in the eye. "What?"

"Like suits and stuff. Does he have to wear those or can he wear weekend clothes?"

My throat got thick. "It's heaven. I guess your dad can wear whatever he wants."

He half smiled. "He'll probably wear weekend clothes, then. He had this one shirt he wore all the time with a hole under the arm. Mom hated it, so she used to poke her finger in it and tell him to go change." He slanted his head. Everything from his straight, dark brown hair to his expressive eyebrows looked just like a younger version of Rob. "I wonder if he took that shirt with him."

Familiar pain wrenched my stomach. Madison and Luna were one thing. They were too young to truly understand what had happened to Jessica and Rob, but Asher was a vortex of curiosity. In the span of a week, he'd gone from a wild child to a Jeopardy contestant stuck on the category *Afterlife*. I couldn't blame him though. Death was an abstract concept even to adults, much less a five-year-old.

I didn't know how Bree did it. I could barely talk to Luna about Jessica and she was usually slapping me in the face and blowing spit bubbles through the majority of our conversations.

"I don't think he got to take anything with him, buddy. But maybe you can keep the shirt. You can wear it anytime you're missing him."

His eyes flared comically wide. "Is that what you do with Aunt Jessica's clothes?"

The laugh sprang from my throat before my constant state of misery had the chance to tamp it down. If I'd given it a second to really sink in, it would have been a bullet through my heart. I didn't have any of Jessica's clothes. Nothing to cling to on the darkest nights. Nothing to pass down to Luna. Short of the photos I'd recovered, nothing from our lives together had been salvageable after the fire.

However, right then, as I stared at a brave little boy getting dressed for his father's funeral, I lived in the moment.

"What? You don't think I'd look good in one of her outfits?"

He shrugged. "Not really."

"I'll have you know that I look spectacular in a crop top."

"A crop what?" He curled his lip—again, just like Rob.

I stood up and patted my stomach. "A crop top. It's a shirt that shows off your stomach. Surely you've seen my abs."

"No, but I've seen your chicken nugget chest hair."

I barked a laugh that I swear traveled through my entire body. *Well, hello there, Endorphins. So nice of you to join me again.*

"What's going on in here?" Bree asked.

I spun like a kid caught with my hand in the cookie jar and found her standing in a long, black dress, her wavy, brown hair pinned back and her makeup flawless—such was her personal brand of excellence.

"Oh, hey," I greeted with an awkward grin.

Things with Bree were still, um, for lack of better terms, *fucking weird*. I mostly kept to myself in the pool house. However, with food being dropped off by the truckload, Bree had set an open invitation for dinner. Okay, so it wasn't so much of an invitation as a demand.

"Dinner will be ready at six. Be there so I know you haven't gone off the deep end and drunk yourself into a coma, leaving me with three children under six and another funeral to plan."

Oh, that woman had a way with words. And to think, *I* was the songwriter. Then again, her harsh words were just how she was coping, and her brash honesty was at least something normal in my chaotic existence.

The first night, we ate in silence. Well, eating was a bit of a stretch. I fed Luna a bottle while staring at a pasta dish Rob's secretary had delivered. Bree sat in front of Madison's highchair, feeding her from an untouched plate.

Night two, she silently cried through dinner, swirling around the kitchen and making any and every excuse to avoid Asher's scrutinizing gaze. I attempted to distract him with questions about his birthday, which was three months away. It seemed to work. He wanted an Iron Man cake and a piñata. Oh, and for his dad to come back from heaven for the day, which immediately sent Bree up to her room to grab her phone charger—for twenty minutes.

For two people who still couldn't decide if we liked each other or not, we quickly became tag-team champions with the kids.

If I was having a bad day—like, say, when Jessica's mom called to ask if she could pick up a check for half of Jessica's life insurance from me at the funeral (a policy my wife did not have, and even if

she had, I sure as hell wasn't giving a portion of it to that woman)—
Bree would come outside and, without a word, pluck Luna from
the blanket on the grass, leaving me to cuss and rage in private.

Then, on the day Rob's mother with Alzheimer's called looking
for her son and Bree was forced to tell her for the fifth time that
he had passed away, she'd walked out to the pool house, delivered
the kids without so much as a request, and then left for over an
hour. Asher and I were tight, so that was easy, but Madison wasn't
quite as fond of ole Uncle Eason. Luckily the mini chocolate chips
plucked off some cookies had seemed to do the trick—as long as
Bree didn't find out.

Bree smiled warmly at Asher. "Something funny?"

He tugged at the neck of his white dress shirt. "Uncle Eason
wears crop tops when he misses Aunt Jessica."

Her eyebrows shot up her forehead as she turned a suspicious gaze on me.

I quickly waved him off. "No. We were kidding. It was a whole
story. You had to be there." I bumped Asher with my hip, sending
him stumbling to the side. He laughed before retaliating with a kick
to my ankle. Ignoring the Karate Kid, I looked at Bree. "Anyway.
You almost ready to go?"

She hadn't been smiling, but somehow, her face still fell. "No."

And just like that, anguish washed over me again. "Me either."

Drawing in a deep breath, she rolled her shoulders back and
lifted her chin. "But if we don't leave soon, we'll be late."

"Right, of course."

"Get your socks and shoes on, Ash. You've got five minutes."

"Five minutes!" he whined, though I had no idea why. The
kid had no concept of time. He'd once told me he hated mashed
potatoes because it took an hour to chew them.

Leaning over, I grabbed his navy socks off the floor and chucked them at him before following Bree into the hall.

"You're not wearing a tie," she said, more of a statement than a question.

I looked down at my black suit and white button-down with the top button left open. My clothing options were limited to what I'd picked up on my two-hour sprint through the mall during Luna's afternoon nap. It was literally the exact thing I'd worn to Jessica's funeral the day before and Bree hadn't said a peep about a tie then. "I wasn't planning on it. You think I need one?"

"Up to you," she snipped.

"Oh-kay, let's try that again. Do *you* want me to wear a tie?"

"No. I just figured, since today is for Rob, you might try actually looking the part for once."

I blinked at her. What did that even mean? It was definitely an insult—there was no mistaking that. But when I had been the best man at their wedding, Rob hadn't asked me to wear a tie. Why the hell would she think I'd wear one now?

I raked my teeth over my bottom lip, trying and failing to dodge the verbal blow. "And what part might that be?" I clipped more roughly than I'd intended. "Because honestly, if I showed up in a tie for the first time in twenty years, there is a strong possibility Rob's going to sit up just to see if I've suffered a stroke." I regretted it before the last syllable cleared my lips. And not because it was rude and insensitive—which it absolutely was. For fuck's sake, the woman was burying her husband and I was slinging an attitude.

But I hated myself that much more when tears welled in her eyes.

"If that's all it takes to bring him back, then maybe I should wear a fucking tie too." She turned on a toe, her heels clicking on the wood floor as she marched away.

I had options. None of which were going to pry my foot from my mouth. Also none of which she probably wanted anything to do with.

I could chase her down and hug her. It'd worked when she hugged me in the middle of my nervous breakdown. Though going to Rob's funeral with her palm print across my face would likely raise more questions than I wanted to answer.

I could apologize—for, oh, the hundredth time—because, clearly, that was working out so well for me.

Or, because I too was a fucking mess who had the emotional bandwidth of a cinderblock that day, I could let her walk away, pissed off and fuming.

Though only one of them would make it so Rob didn't haunt me for the rest of my life.

"I'm sorry!" I called after her, jogging to catch up. "I'll put on a tie. Hell, I'll put on three ties. I'm not trying to be a dick. Just tell me what will make today easier for you and I swear to God I'll do it."

She stopped and dabbed at her tears, careful not to mess up her makeup. I expected more anger, a few curse words, and a lecture on God only knew what. But when she finally opened her mouth, it was a plea toppling out.

"Then help me figure out a way so I don't have to go." Her desperate, green eyes collided with mine. "I can't do this, Eason. I know I'm supposed to be strong for the kids, but I can't do this. I'm not like you. You were amazing yesterday. Talking to everyone and thanking them for coming. I'm not built like that. He was my *husband*. If Tommy No-Name who went to kindergarten with him and hasn't seen him in thirty years comes up to me crying about how much he's going to miss him, I'm going to end up in jail."

"Okay, let's not do that."

She dragged a large teardrop diamond back and forth on the chain at her neck. "I don't understand why we have to do this whole circus to begin with. He would have hated it. Don't get me wrong—yesterday was beautiful. Jessica would have loved the attention, but Rob wouldn't have lasted five minutes before sneaking out the back to find the nearest bar. But now, because of some fucked-up social construct, I have to go stand there alone and listen to a priest who has never even met my husband talk about what an amazing human being he was."

She drew in a sharp breath, and always aware of her proximity to her children, she whisper-yelled, "Was! As in past tense. And then what? Let's pretend I somehow manage to keep it together and don't do something crazy like cry too loudly because God knows all eyes are going to be on me. But let's just say, hypothetically, I don't tell everyone to fuck off, what happens then? When this funeral is over, Rob is *gone*. Truly gone. But I'm still going to be here with no idea how to do this without him. So maybe it makes me a bad wife or just an all-around bad person, but I really just don't want to go." By the time she finished, she was panting with tears dripping from her chin.

"You won't be alone," I vowed, clueless of what else to say.

"I know. I know. You'll be at the funeral too. I appreciate it. I do. I'm just overwhelmed." Her shoulders sagged as if she'd been expecting me to pull a piece of sage wisdom out of thin air to magically quell all of her anxieties.

I had none to give though, or I sure as shit would have kept some for myself while breaking down in the shower that morning.

The feel-good chats were never my specialty. Advice? Please, I could barely take care of my own life. Now if someone needed a one-liner, I was the guy. And if the situation was awkward enough and someone didn't need a one-liner, I unfortunately was still usually that guy too.

It was the worst thing I could say. I knew it before I even opened my mouth. But right or wrong, it was better than saying nothing at all.

"Oh, I was saying you won't be alone in jail. Tommy No-Name is by far my least favorite of all Rob's kindergarten friends. If that fool takes one step out of line, you and I will be sharing a cell in the slammer."

She didn't laugh.

She didn't even smile.

She did, however, stare at me like I had two heads, so I took it as progress from yelling at me about the whole tie thing.

"Right," she murmured. "We should get going before we're late." She started away.

I caught her hand and pulled her back. "Look. I'm a shit fill-in for Rob or Jessica in this situation. But I promise I'm here for you today. You get overwhelmed or feel like you can't take any more, just say the word and I'll drive the getaway car. Don't for one second think that it makes you a bad wife or a bad person. Whatever you do or don't do today, that's for you and your heart. Rob doesn't need you to suffer through any *social construct* to prove how much you love him. And that's *love*, Bree. Present tense."

She stared at me for a long second, her cheeks still damp, but the tiniest flicker of light hit her sparkling green eyes. "Thank you," she whispered, using her other hand to cover mine on her forearm. "I needed to hear that."

"Good. Then I'll write it down for future use because I feel like I might have just peaked."

She shook her head, the corner of her mouth rising almost imperceptibly. "Probably."

"At least we're in agreement."

That time, she laughed. It was quiet and sad, but on the darkest of days imaginable, a laugh was a laugh any way it came.

Rob's funeral was a far cry from Jessica's quaint affair. The cathedral downtown was packed, standing room only. I wasn't surprised. Everyone who had ever crossed Rob's path considered him a friend.

But nobody had known him like I had.

Nobody had failed him like I had, either.

In a black skinny tie, I never left Bree's side. She'd highly underestimated herself that morning. Bree was a rock star during the funeral. I waded in and redirected conversations when it looked like she was waning, but for the most part, she was the epitome of grace and strength. I even played a few sneaky games of Rock, Paper, Scissors with Asher when it looked like he needed a distraction. But make no mistake about it, the agonizing guilt was still there, rotting the very core of my existence from the inside out.

Just as I deserved.

CHAPTER SIX

EASON

"Open up," I said with the spoon catapult poised in front of my face.

Asher giggled, his mouth so wide it was a wonder his jaw didn't come unhinged.

"You ready?"

"Ha ray uh tow et," he said in a language only dentists could understand, but I assumed he meant yes.

Ever competitive, I spread my legs and bent at the knees to center my balance. The shot could be make or break, and there was no way I was going to be the weak link. "Okay. Okay. Here we go. One, two, *three*!"

The waffle sailed through the air with nearly perfect aim, but of course, just like the last four pieces I'd flung, it bounced off his nose before landing on the floor.

"No!" he yelled, pounding his fists on the white marble bar. "I was so close."

I went back to cutting up tiny bites of Bree's famous sweet-po-tato-and-spinach waffles. Trust me, I used the word famous lightly. My tastebuds had all but declared mutiny the first time I'd tried one, but she made them in bulk and kept them in the freezer for the kids to eat throughout the week. When it came to juggling breakfast for three children, I was never one to complain about quick and easy.

Over the last month, life had moved at lightspeed yet also in slow motion. Bree and I were still emotional zombies, going through the movements for the sake of the kids, no closer to peace or acceptance, but pretending had gotten easier.

The fire still haunted me. Obsessing over all the things I could have done differently became a nightly staple in my routine. "If I had just…" followed by a fill-in-the-blank with whatever ludicrous and impossible superhero act of the day my mind had conjured up was how I passed the time until my brain finally gave up and allowed me to slip into what could only loosely be described as sleep.

Sometimes I raged. Sometimes I dropped to my knees and cried. Sometimes I just stared into space, resigning myself to a life lost in sorrow.

But each morning, I put one foot in front of the other for my daughter. That little girl, with her honey brown eyes and wispy hair, was my reason for existence.

I'd started therapy—for Luna.

Diligently taken the antidepressants my doctor had prescribed me—for Luna.

And I was currently reading my second parenting book for widowers—for Luna.

People told me to take care of myself, and I guessed in a way I was, but only because Jessica would have wanted our daughter to have the very best in life. Unfortunately, I doubted Jessica, wherever she was, would agree that the "best" was me.

But I'd try anyway.

I wasn't a big believer in the old adage that everything happened for a reason. I'd never be able to accept there was a purpose in Jessica and Rob being stolen from us. But you'd never be able to convince me it wasn't a miracle Luna hadn't been in the house that night. Whether it had been because of habit or circumstance, Jessica and I hadn't gone out much. And since the day she'd come home from the hospital, Luna had never slept anywhere other than her crib. In her room. In her house.

Until that night. That tragic, horrific night.

So, yeah, I was still struggling to breathe most days, but at night, when I fell asleep staring at my daughter in a portable crib next to my bed, I had a reason to wake up. I clung to that even in my darkest hours.

And trust me, there were a lot of those.

"One more time," Asher begged from his stool at the bar. "I can catch it this time, I know it."

Smiling, I scooped the diced waffle onto the tray of Madison's highchair and glanced over to Luna as she played in the activity saucer. "What do you think? Should I do it again, Lunes?"

"Please, Luna. Say yes, say yes!" Asher yelled.

My daughter bounced twice before shooting me a gummy, slobbery grin.

"All right, buddy. That sounds like a yes to me!" I cut the corner of the puke-green waffle. "Get your choppers open. Incoming in, ten, nine, eight—"

"Absolutely not," Bree said, walking into the kitchen, empty coffee mug in hand and exhaustion on her face.

"Mooom!" Asher whined.

She pressed a kiss to the top of Madison's head before moving to her son. "I know. Worst mom ever." She paused, her gaze snapping to mine. "Is that *syrup?*"

Shit!

"What? Where?" I snatched Asher's plate and quickly scraped it into the sink.

"Hey! I was still eating that."

Strategically avoiding the lasers shooting from Bree's eyes, I gave the plate the old rinse-and-scrub routine before stashing it in the dishwasher. "No, bud. That was my plate, not yours. Ya know. With all-natural *honey*. There's no syrup in this house." I not-so-sneakily slid the bottle of Hungry Jack behind a canister.

"Nuh, huh. You poured it on my plate and said, 'Here, Ash, let's make this edible. Just don't tell your—'" He snapped his mouth shut so fast that I could hear his teeth clink. "Oops."

Bree's lips formed a thin line. "When he's bouncing off the walls and playing airplane from the top of the stairs later, I'll be sure to send him out to the pool house."

"Fair enough," I mumbled sheepishly.

Shaking her head, she helped him off the stool. "Go brush your teeth. Like six times. And then never eat anything Uncle Eason feeds you again."

Wise like the owl, he didn't argue as he bolted up the stairs.

No sooner than he disappeared, Bree's shoulders sagged, and she sat down on his stool. "Hit me, bartender."

I forked the last two waffles onto a plate and slid them her way. "How'd your call with Prism go?"

"Like I need to pour a tall glass of red wine at eight a.m." Using the footrest on the stool, she stood up and leaned over the bar, grabbing the not-so-hidden bottle of syrup. Then she began drowning her waffles.

"Amateur. Morning drinking is dominated by vodka or Irish whiskey or—" I stopped and lowered my head before letting the word *champagne* trip out of my mouth. I doubted either of us would ever touch the stuff again. "So, Prism…" I led her to continue.

51

"It's a mess. Like a genuine grade-A disaster over there." She tore into her breakfast, a small moan escaping with the first bite of forbidden syrup. "This is better than wine."

"Why? What's going on?"

"Well, let's see." She shoveled in another fork-load of breakfast and then talked around it in the least prim-and-proper Bree way possible. "For some asinine reason, Prism contracted a new manufacturer a few months back. Not only did the fabric fail our quality inspections, but they only sent half our order. Meanwhile, the hotels are breathing down our neck for products they've already paid for, and we have nothing to send them. Oh, except for pillowcases. We seem to have two full warehouses of those and not one single buyer requesting them. There's apparently a maintenance guy, some guy named Barton, who hasn't shown up for a month or been officially terminated. So I guess I'm paying employees to just stay home. Oh, and the best part is I've spent all week reaching out to every connection I'd ever had and can't get anyone to call me back. And in a rather interesting turn of events, HR called today to tell me that I would no longer be covered by Rob's health insurance because he is no longer employed with Prism, as if I don't own the entire freaking company myself."

I headed for the coffee pot. I was on cup number three for the day, but Bree had a strict morning routine. Two-mile run, yoga, protein shake, and only then did she allow herself a perfectly portioned eight ounces of coffee—black no less. However, since she was downing syrup like she was drinking directly from Willy Wonka's chocolate river, I figured we were making exceptions that morning. I filled her mug and she didn't hesitate before lifting it to her lips.

"What does all of that mean?" I asked.

"It means I have to go into the office and see if I can figure out what the hell Rob was thinking. Did you know he downsized the comforter division to the point that I could quite literally go back to sewing them in my dorm room and make more profit?"

"Fuck," I mouthed, very aware that Madison was done with her banana and watching our interaction like a ping-pong match.

"My thoughts exactly." Bree shoved another sugary bite into her mouth, chewing as though it had wronged her.

"Relax. I'm sure he had a plan."

"Yeah. But I'm assuming it wasn't dying and leaving me with a company I don't even recognize anymore." Her voice hitched, but she quickly covered it with a cough before turning to her daughter. "Hey, baby. You want to go to the office with Mommy for a few hours?"

"Why don't you leave the kids with me? I don't have anything going on today." I didn't add that I was hoping the noise and mayhem might distract me from reality for a while.

Bree laughed and stood up, sliding the tray off the highchair before unbuckling Madison. "Thanks, but it's fine. She can play with Asher while I make calls. Besides, don't you have an interview this afternoon?"

"It's not an interview. The job's mine—I just needed to fill out the new-hire paperwork." After over a decade, I was going back to the same dueling piano job I'd hated in my twenties. But much like then, I was desperate and needed a way to pay the bills.

My agent had a few leads on selling the songs from *Solstice in the '92*, though it would take time before I got paid. Bree had been generous to let Luna and me stay with her for the last month, but it was high time we found our own place.

The insurance company was rebuilding the house Jessica and I had shared; however, there was absolutely no chance in hell I was moving back there. If I was lucky, I could sell it and use any profit

I made after paying off the mortgage to put a down payment on something small. Until then, I needed a steady source of income to show a future landlord.

I had zero clue what I was going to do with Luna on the nights I had to work. Daycares didn't exactly operate at three a.m. But much like I was doing with the rest of my life…I'd figure it out as I went.

Somehow.

There was no other choice.

I handed Bree a wet rag to clean Madison's face and hands. "Come on. I've been keeping them all week while you take calls upstairs."

"Yeah, but I was upstairs. And this time, I would be…at the office."

"Which is ten minutes away."

She laughed again.

I did my best to not be offended—but let's be real, that shit stung. "Look, you know as well as I do, if Madison doesn't get her morning nap, you won't be making any phone calls that don't involve a baby screaming in the background. Plus, I heard that someone who shall not be named gave Asher sugar for breakfast. How much work do you think you're going to get done with him doing parkour off the desk?"

She slanted her head. "Did you plan this?"

"No. But I would have if I'd thought of it in advance. Come on. Let me keep the kids for the day. You can put Madison down for her nap before you go. I'll put Luna down too. Then Asher and I will run laps around the living room for two hours." I snapped a few times when I thought of a way to sweeten the deal. "While practicing his multiplication tables."

I was greeted by another Bree Winters specialty glare, but

thankfully, this one held slightly less heat than when she'd seen the syrup. "He's five, Eason. He doesn't know multiplication."

"Well, not yet anyway. You'd be surprised how much math there is in music. There's all those twos and fours and threes and sixes. Sometimes a wild eight here and there." I moved around Bree and picked up Madison. As usual, she whined and reached for her mother, but it was nothing a little Superman spin couldn't fix.

Madison giggled and I'll be damned if it didn't stretch a rare smile across Bree's face too.

"Traitor," she whispered to her daughter. Just as quickly as it had appeared, her flicker of happiness faded. "I don't know, Eason. Nothing against you, it's just, after everything…"

Knife.

Heart.

Twist.

But I just kept on grinning. It was less awkward that way.

Our whole *I'll hate you, you hate me, but we do it together* agreement hadn't come into play often over the last month. And the truth was, I didn't ever actually *hate* Bree.

I hated myself. For not being able to save Jessica or Rob. For not knowing about the gas leak. And a myriad of other things that factored into us being in the house that horrible night.

Clearly, my grin didn't hide everything though.

"I mean, it's not that I don't trust you," she rushed out. "I do. It's just… I have a hard time leaving them with anyone."

"No. I get it. No explanation needed." I gave Madison's belly a tickle—anything to avoid Bree's gaze.

She rested her hand on my forearm. "I appreciate the offer though."

"Yeah. Of course." I forced a smile. "Anytime."

Bree extended her arms and Madison all but leapt to her,

leaving me standing there empty-handed and wondering how I'd managed to both embarrass myself and shatter whatever progress we'd made toward comfortably coexisting.

"Hey, uh, I'm going to take Luna out and get her changed. Looks like she used that banana I gave her as a hair gel instead of breakfast." I squeezed past Bree, careful not to touch her, and scooped Luna out of the activity saucer.

"Eason…" Bree trailed off, cleared her throat, and then smiled. She wasn't as good at faking it as I was, so it was closer to a grimace. "Thanks again. For everything. Except the syrup."

I jerked my chin and winked. "What syrup?"

Without giving her the time to respond, I pulled the back door open and slid through it, my baby girl babbling the entire way.

CHAPTER SEVEN

BREE

"Y OU SURE I CAN'T GET YOU ANYTHING ELSE?" Rob's secretary, Jillian, asked, cleaning up the remnants of snack wrappers and juice boxes she'd magically produced from her Mary Poppins desk drawer. I guessed being a sixty-five-year-old grandmother to nine meant you learned a few tricks about being prepared.

I held the phone between my ear and my shoulder, offered her a tight smile, and lied, "No, I think we're good. Thank you."

Truthfully, I was drowning. Just setting foot in Rob's office had been a herculean task. He should have been there. Sitting behind the huge mahogany desk, welcoming us in with a smile—or, if it had been me without the kids, a mischievous glint in his dark-brown eyes.

Without him, the massive corner office filled with bookshelves and a six-person sitting area was too empty. I'd told myself this was just a quick stop. I'd grab what I needed, take the rest home, and work on it at night when the kids went to sleep. Though actually locating the things I needed in his messy cabinets was something different altogether. For as clean and tidy as Rob had been in virtually every other facet of his life, his filing system made my eyes twitch.

Jillian had known where most of the contracts I needed were, the majority of those being digitized, but there were quite a few orders I couldn't locate. So, rather than the quick stop I'd hoped for, we were on hour number two of me calling our vendors all around the world.

Jillian nodded, her orthopedic shoes squeaking against the wood floor as she backed out of the door. "Well, if you need anything, just give me a holler."

"Will do," I once again lied. Accepting help was still a foreign concept to me.

Rob had been an amazing husband, but he'd worked a lot. I couldn't fault him for trying to take care of his family. The majority of the time, it was just me and the kids. That was my job. A job I'd picked. A job I'd dearly loved. A job I should have been able to do without relying on everyone around me. I understood the whole *it takes a village* concept, and when someone was in need, I was the first one to offer a helping hand. But being on the receiving end of that help was a slightly harder pill for me to swallow.

People meant well; I knew they did. But letting go of that kind of control did not give me comfort. Especially since it felt like every portion of my life lately was up in the air, flying around in a state of upheaval. I needed to grab on to anything I could and rein it in. Even if at that moment all the help I needed was something as simple as asking Eason or Jillian to watch the kids for a few minutes so I could actually get work done. I just couldn't do it.

With the click of the door, Jillian disappeared, leaving me alone, the way I feared I would always be.

"Asher, stop!" I whisper-yelled as my son dragged a six-foot-long paperclip chain across the floor.

Madison squealed with delight as she crawled after it like a baby Olympian. Using my foot, I lifted it out of her reach before she had the chance to grab it—and no doubt put it into her mouth.

"Hey!" Asher objected—which I would like to note was not a whisper-yell. Half of Prism's employees must have heard it.

"Mr. Winters?" A man's voice finally came through the line.

I quickly switched the phone to my other ear, nearly dropping it in my frenzy. "Yes. I'm here. Well, I'm not Mr. Winters. But I am his wife." I cut my gaze to Asher. He had already moved on to shredding the paper I'd given him to color on. Damn Eason and that syrup. Giving him my back as if it could shield him from the truth, I finished, "My husband passed away last month." The slice through my heart was just as sharp as ever.

"Rob? Really? What happened?"

None of your fucking business.

"An accident."

"I'm so sorry to hear that. Rob was a good man. But I can't help you with this order, Mrs. Winters. I'm going to need to speak with someone at Prism."

This had been the general consensus of everyone I'd spoken to that day. And it was all I could do not to lose my ever-loving mind each and every time I heard it.

I'd built that business from the ground up. Rob had taken over as CEO, but I had hardly fallen off the face of the Earth in the five-ish years since then. I still attended board meetings and maintained final approval when it came to creative control. Sure, most of these decisions were cast over dinner or on the sofa with a glass of wine at night after the kids had gone to bed, but I was still very much a part of the company.

"Then you're in luck. I'm the owner. And I need those purchase orders emailed over by the end of day."

"Uhhhh..." he drawled.

But I did not have time to paint the man a damn flowchart of Prism's leadership team. Especially not when I turned around and saw Madison sitting at Asher's feet as he removed the top off a crystal decanter Rob had kept in his Mad Men-esque corner bar.

Snapping twice to get his attention, I hissed, "Put that down."

Being the obedient child he very seldomly was, he immediately set it down—directly in front of his sister.

"No!" I shouted, abandoning the phone altogether as she knocked it over, causing it to shatter all over the mahogany floor.

Madison screamed as I raced over, but it wasn't until I saw the blood drip from my baby's palm that the adrenaline hit me.

The cut was small. But the wave of panic that slammed into me was towering.

It was too much. Too familiar. Too consuming.

An onslaught of raw emotion stormed the gates of my brain. With trembling hands, I scooped her up and then hooked Asher around the hips, carrying him away from the glass before depositing them both on to the leather loveseat. My head spun as I dropped to my knees in front of them and tried unsuccessfully to slow my breathing.

Three drops of blood.

A wound so tiny that it barely required a Band-Aid.

Yet my body reacted as though the world were ending all over again.

"I'm sorry! I'm sorry!" Asher screamed hysterically at the sight of his sister bleeding.

Amid the chaos, Jillian came rushing into the room. "Is everything okay?"

No. It was safe to say everything was not okay.

My husband was dead. My heart was broken. And I was

realizing that, no matter how much I wanted to be, I would never be superwoman.

In that moment, there was only one person who could possibly understand.

Clearing my throat, I dragged both of my children into my lap, holding them as if they could ground me. I desperately fought back tears so I wouldn't scare them more than they already were and asked in a shaky voice, "Could you please call Eason Maxwell for me?"

∽

It was cool for June in Atlanta. Pulling my cardigan around my shoulders, I sank deeper into the corner of the wicker sectional I'd had custom cushions made from my favorite blue damask after Rob had surprised me with a raised deck and firepit overlooking the pool and transforming our backyard into my own private oasis.

"Winter and Summer. We have it all covered now," he'd said, knowing how much I loved to spend my nights under the stars. Sometimes he'd join me, reading a book or playing on his phone, but for the most part, I'd sit outside alone, absorbing my day while planning the next.

Yet, that night, as I stared at the lights dancing in the pool, I couldn't find the peace I so desperately longed for.

"You in the mood for company?" Eason asked, appearing at the end of the couch, a glass of red wine in one hand, a beer in his other.

I couldn't exactly say no. Not after he'd dropped everything and spent the day taking care of the kids while I'd stared into space like a robot with a dead battery.

"Sure," I replied, taking the glass from his hand. "Thanks."

He pulled two video monitors from his back pockets, passing

one my way before settling on the far end of the couch. "Kids went down pretty easy. Ash had a lot of heaven questions about Rob tonight, so I thought he might need a distraction for a while. I told him he could use his flashlight to read a book until nine. He's holding the book upside down, but I figure reading's never a bad thing." He took a sip of his beer while pulling the side chair in front of him, resting his bare feet in the seat. "Ahhh," he moaned, stretching out between the two pieces of furniture, his lean muscles sagging with exhaustion.

A pang of guilt struck me hard. Of course he was tired. Eason had enough of his own problems without shouldering mine as well.

"I'm sorry," I whispered. "I shouldn't have called you today, and then—"

He tilted his head my way, his warm, brown eyes snapping to mine. "Yes, you should have. I'm exactly who you should have called, and I'm glad you did."

Jesus, why did that make the guilt grow?

"No, it's not okay. I'm a single mom now. I'm going to have to start figuring these things out for myself. I can't expect everyone around me to put their lives on hold because I'm having some kind of mental breakdown." My nose stung, but I took a sip of the wine to hide the tears.

At what point did I get to stop crying all the damn time?

"You're not having a mental breakdown, Bree. You lost your husband and your best friend a month ago. Give yourself a little grace. You're allowed to have bad days. You're allowed to be overwhelmed. You don't have to keep it together twenty-four-seven just because you have kids."

"It shouldn't bleed over into your life too though. You lost your wife and your friend too. You have a child of your own to focus on. Eason, you missed the meeting for your new job because of me tonight."

He suddenly sat up, planting both feet on the ground. "And thank you for that. I've been dreading taking the job all fucking week. I hated it there when I quit ten years ago, and I'm pretty sure I'm not going to feel any differently about it now. Honest to God, I was having nightmares about playing 'Sweet Caroline' again."

"What?" I gasped. "You told me you were excited about getting back behind a piano."

"Bree, I'm a thirty-four-year-old man living rent-free in my best friend's pool house—*with my daughter*. Beggars and choosers and all, I needed that job."

I set the wine on the edge of the firepit and turned to face him, curling my leg on the cushion between us, anxiety creeping into my voice. "Right. And now you don't have it *because of me*."

"I didn't lose it. I can still go fill out the paperwork tomorrow if I want." He dropped his head but looked at me from the corner of his eye, a playful smile twitching the side of his mouth. "*Or you could reward me for wrestling Madison into a pair of pajamas tonight by not kicking me out for another week so I can search for a job that doesn't require me to play Ginuwine's 'Pony' every time a bachelorette party comes through the door.*" He punctuated it with a sly smile that somehow defied the laws of grief and guilt by making me laugh.

"I'm not kicking you out."

"You should. I'm a terrible freeloading tenant who punched a hole in your bathroom wall last week."

"What!" I laughed again.

He shrugged and took a pull of his beer before replying, "Apparently my bad days come with slightly more aggression than yours."

"Mmm." I nodded with understanding. "I get those too. I just scream into my pillow."

"I'll give that a try next time. Probably safer considering I'll need two hands to play the incessant dueling of the Georgia and Georgia Tech fight songs."

I rolled my eyes. "Don't take the job, Eason. Find something you want to do. You and Luna can stay here as long as you need. Or want. Or any combination of the two."

"Honest to God, I don't know how I would have made it through the last month without you." He blew out a ragged breath. "And the kids."

"Well, that makes two of us." My chest warmed as I lifted my glass in his direction.

He met it halfway with a clink of his beer.

Madison stirred on the screen of the monitor, momentarily stealing my attention. She had rolled to her side, fussing for a brief second before falling back asleep pressed up against the wooden slats. But that wasn't why I leaned in close to the small screen.

Pink-and-white-striped pajamas covered her arms, but the rest of her body was secure in a zip-up sleep sack. Her crib was empty—the blanket and two stuffed animals that were strictly for decoration had been removed, and her princess castle nightlight illuminated the corner of the room. The glow of her cool mist humidifier next to the bed let me know it had been turned on, and with a single stroke to turn up the monitor's volume, her sound machine whooshed in the background.

I hadn't told Eason to do any of that. Not once had I mentioned she stripped naked at night without the sleep sack. Or how the blankets and pillows were a suffocation hazard, so I removed them every time I laid her down. I didn't explain to him how she'd been congested recently, so I put the humidifier on to help her sleep, and the nightlight made it easy for me to check on her. Nor did I tell him that, without the sound machine, Asher woke her up in the mornings.

While I had been sitting outside, lost in a sea of pain and reliving flashbacks of the night of the fire, Eason had done it all. He was a good dad who had a daughter of his own; it shouldn't have been a surprise that he knew how to put a baby to bed.

Madison wasn't his daughter. Though he loved her and cared for her as if she were.

I clicked the button and switched the screen to Asher's room. He wasn't reading. A dozen action figures surrounded him while a fireman and dinosaur fought so fiercely that it would have made Tyler Durden proud.

He wasn't crying that he missed his father as he'd done so many times over the last few weeks. I was unsure what questions he had asked about Rob in heaven, but whatever Eason had answered quelled his curious soul at a time when I was so distraught that I hadn't even been able to soothe my own.

Eason hadn't dropped everything and raced up to Prism that day when I needed him the most out of responsibility or duty. He was there because, whether I realized it or not, Rob had been right.

Eason was one of the best.

I set the monitor on my lap and turned my attention to the man casually sipping his beer beside me. "What do you want to do with your life?"

Twisting his lips, he shifted his eyes from side to side. "Is that a serious question?"

"Completely."

"Music," he stated, those two syllables lighting his entire face.

"Yeah? I noticed you haven't replaced your piano yet."

He chuckled. "Pianos aren't cheap. Right now, I'm focused

on the little details like a job, a place to live, furniture, and maybe buying more than a funeral suit, three pair of jeans, and a pack of shirts." He pointedly smoothed down the front of his plain black tee.

I took another sip of my wine and then twirled the stem of the glass between my fingers. "And what if I could take care of three out of four of those things for you?"

His mouth tipped in a wry smile. "As nice as it sounds, I think I'm going to take a pass on more handouts. I'm all maxed out."

Resting my arm on the back of the cushion, I turned my upper body to fully face him. "Things at Prism are worse than I thought. Nobody knows what the hell is going on. We have no product. No reliable manufacturer. Suppliers I'd had in my back pocket before stepping down to raise the kids won't even return my phone calls."

"Damn," he breathed. "You have enough on your plate. That's not the kind of shit you need to be dealing with right now."

"Actually, it's exactly what I need to be dealing with right now. Because if I don't, Prism is done. I need that company, Eason. My *family* needs that company."

He raked a hand over the top of his hair. His blond fuzz was still too short to style from his hospital buzzcut. "Shit. Okay, what can I do to help?"

There it was.

The reason why everyone I loved—Rob, Jessica, Asher, Madison, and Luna—all adored Eason Maxwell.

"Move in," I said bluntly.

He started to open his mouth, probably with some smartass comment about already living there, but I cut him off.

"Permanently. The pool house is yours. I'm going back to work full time. And if it works for you, I'd rather not hire a stranger to keep the kids, rocking their lives all over again. They could stay here with you and Luna during the day. When I get home from work, I'll take over and keep Luna too. You can go out and play shows or just lock yourself away and write. Whatever pursuing music looks like for you, nights and weekends, and it's all yours."

Quite proud of myself for thinking of a solid plan, I stared at him with a smug grin, waiting for his excitement. A hearty laugh. A celebration. Maybe another round of beer and wine.

All I got was a dull expression that teetered on the line of annoyance and skepticism.

"Why?" he asked.

"Why what?"

"Don't do that," he rumbled. "Don't act like you and Jessica haven't spent years hatching plans to get me to quit playing. You used to tell my wife I needed to quit wasting my time and get a real job."

My back shot straight. "I..." Truthfully, I was unaware he knew about that. Dammit!

He stood up and peered down at me, his dark gaze soulful and sad. "Look, I appreciate what you're trying to do. And if you need help with the kids, I will never tell you no. I love them and would do anything for them. But let's not pretend my music will ever be good enough in your eyes."

I shook my head vehemently. "It was never about you being good enough, Eason. You're amazing, and not just because of the way you sing or play, but the feelings you evoke in a three-minute song blows my mind. And trust me, I've heard them all. Because each time you produced a new demo, Rob had it playing in our house twenty-four-seven. I was worried about *her*."

I knotted my hands in my lap. Grieving two of the most important people in my life at the same time was a constant balancing act. To be honest, Rob had been taking up the majority of my emotional spectrum for the last month. But there were times when I'd just sit and cry, wishing I could pick up the phone and call Jessica one last time. Listen to her laugh.

I swallowed hard, a tear leaking from the corner of my eye. "Jessica had a rough life before you, and incredible talent aside, being a musician's wife was never going to be easy. I wanted the easy for her. If I'd had my way, she'd have married an accountant."

He chuffed. "She would have been bored to tears. Though she would probably still be alive if she had."

It had been bad enough for me to think vile things of him right after the fire, but to hear him verbalize such a deprecating thought made my heart ache for him.

He'd been there for me countless times, most recently that very day. It was my turn to be the friend he needed.

"Maybe?" I deliberately calmed my tone and spoke to him the way I would have spoken to Jessica—the way I spoke to my friend. "But without you, there would be no Luna. She never would have given up that little girl, even knowing how it ended."

His Adam's apple bobbed as he turned away and scrubbed his eyes with his thumb and forefinger.

After slowly rising to my feet, I moved into his space. "If we've learned anything recently, it's that life is short and its impact isn't measured in years. Buy a piano, Eason. Write the songs. Be the star. Flip the entire music industry on its head. But most of all, show Luna that if you work hard and never give up, dreams can become a reality." I quickly wiped away the tears streaming down my cheeks. "And you know what? After this nightmare, I could really stand to see a dream come true."

Emotion sparkled in his light-brown eyes as he turned back to face me. "Are you sure? I mean about me being here all the time and watching the kids. We are two very different people and parents, Bree. This won't be as easy as it sounds."

"Yeah, I know. But we can do it together. Let's just try it without the hating-each-other thing this time."

"I can do that," he vowed with so much hope in his tone that it made my chest squeeze.

"Just promise no more syrup."

Smiling, he wrapped his hand around the back of my neck and stared deep into my eyes. "I swear never to feed your children anything they will actually enjoy again."

I let out a half laugh, half cry, and then, with a gentle pressure at the back of my neck, he pulled me against his chest.

That man—always a hugger.

He rocked us from side to side, more like he was trying to calm a crying baby than slow dance. "We got this, Bree. Me and you. We got this."

And for the first time since our world had exploded, I felt like maybe he was right.

CHAPTER EIGHT

EASON

One year later...

"Rawr!" I yelled, jumping out from behind the couch.

Madison squealed with laughter, racing down the hall with her nightgown brushing her ankles.

Luna stopped dead in her tracks, pinning me with a menacing glare that no nineteen-month-old should be able to produce. "No!" she said, pointing her finger at me. "No, Daddy."

I lifted my hands in surrender. "Okay. Okay. I'll be nice."

She smiled and brought her hand to her nose, but kept the fingertip leveled on me. "No. Scay. Una."

It was crazy how fast the kids grew. Gone was my slobbery baby who'd thought pocket change was an acceptable snack. Stop judging. It happened one time and I'd fished the quarter out of her mouth immediately.

No. I did not tell Bree. All of our lives were safer that way.

With her short, curly, brown hair and a set of teeth so straight they looked like baby dentures, Luna was a big girl now. Or so I told her while trying to convince her to potty train with Madison.

We were still working on both girls, slowly and surely making progress toward a diaper-free paradise.

"Did you find it?" Bree asked, walking into the room.

Luna turned to look at her, and while she was distracted, I pounced. Springing off the floor, I scooped my daughter into my arms.

She fell into a fit of giggles as I tickled her. Squirming and flailing, she extended her arm out to the side. "Bwee, help! Help!"

"Oh, no." Bree caught Luna's hand and brought it to her lips for a kiss. "You are on your own when it comes to the Maxwell tickle monster." She lifted her gaze to mine. "However, if we expect them to be in bed by eight, the tickle monster might want to start singing a lullaby instead."

I glanced at the clock and damn if she wasn't right. We only had twenty minutes to get everyone in bed and—God willing—halfway to sleep. I set my daughter on her feet and accepted the wrath of her toddler glare. She was still smiling, so it didn't pack much heat.

"Okay, Lunes. Go tell Maddie and Ash goodnight."

"Nigh nigh!" she started yelling as she took off down the hall to the playroom.

Grinning like a fool, I watched her go. I loved that little girl so much; it was a fine line between euphoria and pain while watching her grow up.

"Any luck with the phone?" Bree asked.

I sighed and planted my hands on my hips. "Not yet. It must have fallen between the cushions though. The girls had it a little while ago."

"You want me to call it?"

"Please."

She tapped on her phone and a second later a muffled, nearly untraceable buzzing pulsed in the general direction of the sofa.

"How'd your call go?" I once again dropped to my knees and continued my hunt through the cushions.

"About as well as can be expected when your attorney calls you after hours."

"Anything new?"

She let out a sigh. "Not really. Prism's accountants claim everything is in order, but an IRS audit is never going to be completely comfortable for a company."

Bree had been working her ass off since she dove headfirst back into full-time corporate life. She spent long days and longer nights trying to get Prism back to its peak. Rob had taken quite a few risks that hadn't necessarily panned out, leaving Bree to clean up the messes. Luckily, Bree thrived under pressure. Sure, she was tired and stressed most of the time, but overall, she seemed to like being back in action.

Going behind me, she straightened the pillows as I cleared each section. "Why don't we just use my phone?" Bree suggested. "Or sit in the car?"

"Luna's monitor cuts in and out in the car."

She arched a perfectly shaped eyebrow. "Have you been spending a lot of time in your car recently?"

"Only when I'm doing drugs or day drinking."

I paused my search long enough to wait for her scowl. It was a half pucker, half pinch to the side, but it didn't pack nearly the punch it used to. I'd also gotten wise to her eyes changing just a shade or so lighter when she was trying to hide her good humor. God, I loved riling her up.

Never one to disappoint, she leveled me with a squinted gaze.

"I'm kidding. During naptime, the old Tahoe doubles as my home office so I don't wake up the girls."

"Why don't you just use my office upstairs?"

I went back to flipping cushions. "I didn't realize I was allowed in there again after the great Christmas M&M's debacle."

"Eason, you ate all the red ones," she defended. "I allow myself one bag a *year*. Imagine my disappointment when I opened my secret drawer and they were all *green*."

I craned my head back and peered up at her skeptically. "One bag a year? Does this mean we don't count the pastels at Easter or pinks at Valentine's Day or the peanut ones you keep hidden in an empty tub of flaxseed in the pantry year-round?"

Her shoulders squared and her chin lifted haughtily, and then she fought to suppress a grin. "We don't talk about those."

"Okay, good. Because I ate all the reds out of the flaxseed too."

"Eason!"

Bree and I had come a long way over the last year, but it was not a journey without speedbumps—or the occasional sinkhole. As I'd suspected, working for little Miss Perfection had not been an easy adjustment. The first few weeks were awful, and I reconsidered the dueling piano job on a nightly basis. Bree could be very particular. I understood when it came to the kids. She liked them to eat a healthy diet, have limited screen time, and spend the majority of their time outside in the fresh air. It was the good parenting I'd expected and wanted for Luna too.

What I had not expected was to be critiqued on how I folded towels or loaded the dishwasher. Once, she gave me a step-by-step course on how to properly change the toilet paper in Asher's bathroom.

It should be noted that housework was not part of my job description, but she worked hard, so I tried to make sure she didn't come home to a mountain of laundry—or, say, a sock covered in poop because Asher had run out of toilet paper and gotten creative. See the aforementioned class on changing the toilet paper when I'd tried to stash an extra roll on the back of his toilet in case of emergency.

A few weeks in, we sat down for a discussion like grown adults. She presented me with a seventy-nine-page binder of rules and instructions, and I told her I would rather live in a tent under the bridge than read the damn thing. She, in turn, told me where to find Rob's old camping equipment and gave me explicit instructions of where I could shove it before stomping upstairs.

I wasn't really going to move out. Bree knew this. I knew this. Asher, however, called me in hysterics on the walkie-talkie I'd given him for his birthday, begging me not to leave like his dad.

That was the last big argument Bree and I ever had. We all slept in Asher's room that night. The binder was trashed the very next morning, and I started folding towels the way Bree liked— the wrong way, might I add.

Together, we were a team and those kids were our first, top, and only priority.

After that, things got easier. As we developed a mutual respect for each other, trust followed. And then somehow, through the chaos, a genuine friendship was born. I worked a lot of nights, writing music and playing anywhere that would have me. It was exhausting to get home at three a.m. then get back up with the kids at seven, but each time I stepped onto a stage, no matter how small, it felt like I'd found another piece of myself again. On the nights I wasn't working, Bree and I would swap stories about Rob and Jessica. Sometimes we'd laugh, sometimes we'd cry, and on the one-year anniversary of the fire, we sat in silence, unable to even utter their names.

There was no rhyme or reason for the tides of grief. All we could do was hold on and try to keep our heads above the rushing water.

On Luna's birthday, I'd felt like I was drowning, knowing Jessica would never get to see her grow up.

On Christmas, while watching the kids laugh as they tore through presents, I smiled until my face hurt and felt like maybe I'd finally climbed out of the depths of devastation.

On my wedding anniversary, I felt like I was trapped in an undertow, unable to reach the surface no matter how hard I fought.

Over time, Bree hit the same heartbreaking milestones, but day after day, week after week, month after month, we swam the often-turbulent ocean together.

Flat on my stomach, I ran a hand back and forth under the couch, still searching for my illusive phone. "How, in this huge house, do you not have one single radio?"

"Um, because it's not nineteen ninety-nine," she answered. "Here. Just download the app on my phone. I'll meet you out there. I need to start story time."

On a groan, I pushed up off the floor, vowing to never let Luna and Madison play with my cell again. Or so I told myself at least twice a day. Those girls knew I didn't have any follow-through.

Bree and I made fast work of getting the kids in bed, and like a team of trained professionals, we made it to the backyard with time to spare. We spent a lot of nights huddled around that firepit. For obvious reasons, we'd never lit it, but I'd added a strand of white lights inside the burn basin. Partly because it added a nice, relaxing ambiance to our late-night chats. But mostly because I hated the way Bree stared at the fireless pit as though she could see the flames. God knew I still could.

"Here," she said, handing me my phone. "It was in the storage part of the ottoman. Asher knew where it was."

"Awesome. Remind me to share your M&M's with him in the morning."

She settled into her spot in the corner of the wicker sectional, glass of wine in hand. "Forget it. I already re-hid them."

"Inside the box of granola doesn't count as hiding."

"Dammit," she hissed, making me laugh.

While double-checking my connection to the Bluetooth speakers on the patio, I stole a glance at her from the corner of my eye. Just as I'd hoped, she was smiling, and it caused my lips to stretch as well. For whatever reason, keeping her in a good mood kept me in one. Making her smile or chuckle hit different now. Also like, if I could just make her feel better, relax, enjoy a goddamned second of peace—even if it was fleeting—then I could allow myself to do the same.

When she laughed, it made things easy on my heart, and she was pretty easy on my eyes too. Although that was probably more to do with my newfound celibacy than any real attraction. But when you're lonely, it's easy to confuse friendship with something more. Something I didn't even let my mind entertain.

As the radio app on my phone filled the humid evening air with an auto parts commercial, I found my spot on the end, pulling the chair over to use as a footrest as usual. Luna had just started to doze off, so I switched the baby monitor for my beer and took a long pull.

"Are you nervous?" she asked.

I ignored the fact that her expression made her look almost excited by the notion that I was anything but cool as a cucumber. "Why would I be?"

She circled her finger around the mouth of her wine glass.

"Oh, I don't know. Because for the last six months there's been a social media frenzy waiting for Levee Williams's new album and the first single is *your song*."

By all measures, I should have been ecstatic. This was huge. I'd had other songs on the radio before. None performed by artists as big as Levee. "Turning Pages," the duet she'd recorded with Henry Alexander, had already been picked up prerelease to headline the soundtrack of a major motion picture, which from a royalties perspective would no doubt make it my biggest payday yet. But no matter how much I tried to psych myself up about hearing "Turning Pages'" highly anticipated radio debut, I couldn't bring myself to get excited.

It was my song. I knew every lyric and every chord and not simply because I had been the one to put the pen to paper. I'd lived that music, and dammit, I should have been the one performing it.

But my life didn't seem to work that way. The amount I made on gigs was laughable, and after selling the rebuilt house along with the money the insurance had given me for our destroyed contents, I'd stashed away a small nest egg.

Every Friday, Bree had a direct deposit sent to my account.

Every Monday, I had auto pay set to send it right back.

The way I saw it, we swapped childcare. So, unless I paid her for all the nights she kept Luna, I couldn't allow her to pay me to keep her kids. I paid the little she'd allow me to in rent on the pool house every month, but there were still other bills. Private health insurance was a racket, and then there were groceries, diapers, and industry fees to be paid.

Selling songs was the obvious choice; not to mention it was my final commitment to my wife. Assuming you didn't count the utter failure of when I told her I'd be right back.

After the last thirteen months of heartbreak and grief, I should have been basking in my success and clinging to whatever happiness I could find. However, watching your dreams come true for someone else never got easier.

"Not my first rodeo, Bree," I replied before sipping on my beer.

"Maybe not. But I'm proud of you." She wasn't being sarcastic as she carelessly wiggled her sandal off the end of her foot. She was—at least for the moment—content, and it showed in her relaxed appearance. "And I know Rob and Jessica would be too."

With caution, I paired my gaze with hers, a lump forming in my throat. "It was Jessica's favorite song."

Proudly, she beamed. "I know. Rob's too."

I looked back down at my beer.

Right on time, the radio DJ's voice rang through the speakers. "And now, the moment we've all been waiting for: the debut of 'Turning Pages' by none other than nine-time Grammy winning artist, Levee Williams, featuring America's favorite R&B star, Henry Alexander."

I smirked at the ground because it was what I was supposed to do. Songwriters all across the world waited their entire lives to hear their music on the radio, and there I was wallowing in self-pity. God, I needed to get a grip.

As the intro faded in, the DJ kept talking. "Exclusive WQXX piece of trivia for you. A little birdie informed me today that this song was penned by one of Atlanta's very own, Eason Maxwell." My head popped up. "If this one is anything to go by, he might be a name to keep an eye out for."

No sooner than he finished the last syllable did Levee and Henry's sultry harmonies consume the summer air.

They'd nailed the emotion of the song, and if I was being honest, it was a perfect fit for their voices. But that wasn't why my mouth hung open.

I swung my gaze to Bree. "A little birdie?"

She hid her massive grin behind her wine glass. Her long eyelashes batted against her blushing cheeks as she sang, "Chirp. Chirp."

I stared at her for a long minute, thoroughly perplexed as lyrics about forever and stopping time played in the background. I couldn't decide if I was impressed, touched, possibly embarrassed, or some wicked combination of the three.

"What did you do?" I whispered.

"What any good friend would. I took a bottle of Johnnie Walker Blue, a basket containing roughly two bakery's worth of treats, and enough Prism bedding to redecorate an entire house up to the radio station today."

Yep. Totally impressed. "You bribed them?"

"No. I wanted to let my new friends at Q99.3 know that I happened to have insider information on a certain celebrity who currently resides in our great city."

Wait, nope. Definite embarrassment.

I lurched to my feet, dragging a hand through the top of my hair now that it was finally long enough to rely on it for expelling frustration again. "You told them I'm a celebrity?"

She shrugged. "Well, you are. You wrote a song for *the* Levee Williams. *And Henry Alexander*," she said dreamily before quickly cutting herself off. "And this time next year, it will be your voice on the radio. They better start getting used to your name now. I don't want to hear any of that *Easton* crap when you hit it big."

All right, fine. I was touched. I didn't exactly share her positivity about my career. Or her surprising fondness for Henry Alexander.

Was he her type?

Never mind.

Anyway, it was crazy sweet how she'd gone out of her way to make sure I was recognized and more than just in the fine print on the back of the album.

I planted my hands on my hips and gaped at her. I was unsure of what to say and even more unsure if I could say anything at all. So, after clearing my throat, I kept it light for both of our sakes.

"You know, it's moments like these that make me feel really guilty for throwing up on your shoes all those years ago."

Quietly laughing, she stood and strolled over to me. Bree wasn't particularly tall, so I had her by a head and shoulders, but she craned her head back to peer up at me. "I know you were dreading tonight. You always think you can hide it with a clever smile or a joke, but not with me."

Warmth flooded my chest, and I fought the urge to tuck a hair the night breeze had set free behind her ear. So damn much had changed. In all the years before the fire, I'd never really taken the chance to get to know Bree. Obviously, I'd noticed she was beautiful; with her thick, chestnut hair and piercing, green eyes, it was hard not to. But I was learning that beauty was only the tip of the iceberg with this woman.

"I don't hide anything from you."

"Good," she said. "Let's keep it that way."

My throat got thick, and as hypocritical as it was, I hoped the sweat breaking across the back of my neck and the tempo of my racing heart were both hidden. Her proximity suddenly felt suffocating, which was almost as confusing as it was intoxicating.

Together, we stood there, surrounded by white lights and unspoken emotions. There were gratitude and respect, but most of all, there was love. Maybe not the conventional or romantic variety, but it was there all the same.

"I'm *really* proud of you," she whispered.

It was silly. I'd heard those words before. Friends, family, *Rob*. Hell, she'd already told me five minutes ago. Bree seriously wanted me to hear it, and coming from her—easily one of my biggest critics in the past—it meant the world. Pride traveled all the way down to the marrow of my bones, reproducing and spreading throughout my entire being. There was no motivator in the world greater than having someone who truly believed in you.

Shoving my hands into the pockets of my jeans before I had the chance to do something stupid—like drag her into a hug and possibly never let go—I rocked onto my toes. "This time next year, huh?"

Her smile grew. "Yep."

"Okay. Challenge accepted. Twelve months from now and Eas*ton* Maxwell will be a household name."

She barked a laugh. "You gotta nip that in the bud. Don't put it past me to take gift baskets to every radio station in America just so they'll pronounce it right."

"I don't give a shit if they call me Estonian Maxwrong as long as they play my music. Also, I'm really offended you didn't save the Johnnie Walker for me."

"Who says I didn't? We'll crack into it this weekend. Act surprised when you open your fridge, and also bring the basket over for breakfast. There was a blueberry scone I had my eye on."

She'd spoiled her congratulatory gift, but I appreciated it all the same, so I gasped with mock horror. "Dear God. Sugar for breakfast? What are we? Animals?"

Shaking her head, she moved into my side, sliding her arm around my hips, and gave me a long squeeze.

Caught off guard, I froze, head to toe rock solid. Bree and I hugged sometimes. There were usually tears, emotional breakdowns, or panic attacks involved, but we were no strangers to physical touch.

This was different though.

I had no fucking idea why, but as I pulled my hands from my pockets and wrapped her up tight, our bodies sagging as if they'd finally come home, it was *definitely different*.

And I'd be lying if I didn't say I loved every fucking second of it.

The song eventually ended.

So did our embrace.

Within an hour, we were both headed off to our respective beds.

But something changed between us that night. A shift in the atmosphere. A peek of the sun behind the clouds. The turning of the tide.

Or, as I would later learn, the first spark in a wildfire.

CHAPTER NINE

BREE

"Oh, God," I breathed, pitch-black darkness cloaking my vision as I spread my legs wider, his callused fingers sliding over my opening. The ache inside me built as he circled and teased everywhere but where I needed him. "Please," I begged into his mouth, his lips hovering over mine, his panted exhales filling my lungs.

"Not yet," he rumbled, an order and a promise.

Hooking my ankles around his back, I dragged him down, his thick shaft pressing into my thigh, once again missing the mark. "I need you."

"I know." He continued his tender assault with agonizing strokes that did nothing to release me from his breathless torment.

Primal need roared in my ears as I writhed beneath him. Wordlessly, I continued to beg with my body as the game we'd been playing for what felt like an eternity became too much for me to take. "I can't do this. I can't—"

He silenced me with a nip at my bottom lip, the pain traveling all the way down to my clit in a wave of ecstasy that was almost enough.

"Yessss," I hissed, the pressure inside me soaring. So damn

close. One touch and I could have stepped off the edge of climax. One damn touch anywhere on my fevered body and I'd have fallen apart in his arms.

Then everything suddenly stopped.

"Be patient," he ordered. "You're not ready yet."

"I am," I pleaded, my voice breaking with desperation. "I am. I swear."

"Just a little longer," he growled, my body withering without him.

"I'm done waiting," I snapped, frustration overtaking my desires. "Quit playing with me and make me fucking come already. This is cruel."

"Is it?" he asked, his deep voice dripping with challenge.

"Yes!" I yelled, that one syllable scorching my throat as it tore free from my soul.

"Then come get it."

A bright light illuminated the room, my vision returning all at once as Eason appeared in front of me. Dear God, he was the most beautiful man I'd ever seen. And not because muscles lined his torso, a six-pack rippling his stomach. Nor because of his chiseled jaw or his full lips. It wasn't the tantalizing tattoos or messy, blond hair that all but begged for my fingers. It was just him, Eason, and the easy grin pulling at his lips that always managed to warm my chest.

But there was something different written on his face, something desperate and urgent as he stared back at me.

A lump formed in my throat. "Eason," I breathed, reaching out for him, but without moving, he was transported out of my reach.

Panic exploded in my chest, and I lurched from the bed. "Wait. Where are you going?"

"Nowhere." He slanted his head and smiled, but in the next blink, he was even farther away.

I scrambled after him, but my limbs wouldn't cooperate. Instinctively, I knew that if I could just catch him in my arms, everything would be okay.

Another blink and this time he was barely visible in the distance.

"Eason!" I shouted.

"I'm right here," he replied.

But he wasn't, and the pain was paralyzing. "No, no, no. Come back."

Out of nowhere, I landed flat on my back, his heavy weight on top of me, pinning me down. His hands were in my hair. His mouth on my neck. The most chaotic bliss overtaking me as he drove inside me, hard and fast.

"Oh, God!" I cried, my climax once again roaring inside me. If and when I fell over that edge, there would be no turning back.

Then suddenly our roles reversed.

"Wait, wait, wait. It's too soon," I begged, all the while rolling my hips and meeting his every thrust.

"Let go," he growled, his rhythm speeding until it was as blissful as it was punishing. "You're ready." Lifting his head, his smoldering, brown eyes locked on mine. "Hurry up, Bree." He smiled, arrogant and taunting. "Before I'm gone."

Like a rubber band, my body snapped, an orgasm tearing through me, jolting me awake. "Eason!" I gasped, my fingers circling my clit as a shattering orgasm rocked through me. My rational mind broke through the sleep, and the pleasure gradually ebbed into guilt.

"What the fuck," I breathed, my body sagging into the bed.

"Hurry up, Bree. Before I'm gone."

No, seriously, what the actual fuck was wrong with my subconscious. Eason?

Not Shemar Moore or Michael Fassbender or even Henry Alexander?

Of all the men my brain could conjure for a sex dream, it picked Eason?

At just the thought, a vision of him staring down at me as he worked me hard and fast, his cock stretching me in all the right ways, made heat bloom between my thighs again.

Okay, shit. That was not how I was supposed to feel about my husband's best friend. My *dead* husband's best friend. My husband who had only been dead for a freaking year. My best friend's husband. My *dead* best friend's husband.

Jesus, what a double slap in the face.

After rolling out of bed, I wandered to the bathroom and turned the shower on. There was still an hour before my alarm was set to go off, but I didn't trust my brain enough not to cast Eason in a temporal lobe reboot of *Magic Mike*.

Though, if I was being honest, the teenage wet dream of sorts wasn't the only thing I needed to wash off. The fear I'd experienced when Eason had slowly disappeared was the kind that embedded itself in your bones. Now that I was awake, I could process that Eason was only yards away, asleep in the pool house, but the panic and loss still lingered in my veins.

I'd never been one to read into dreams. In high school, I used to have a reoccurring one that my history teacher lived under my bed and kept me awake all hours of the night by pelting me with Pop Rocks and women's shoes. I was sure there was a doctor out there somewhere who could have had a field day with that one. But I couldn't shake the feeling that this one meant something more.

Maybe it was shame, but that morning as I got ready, I saw

Rob everywhere. From his body wash still on the shelf in the shower to his toothbrush on the charger beside his sink. There was a handful of change on his nightstand and a pair of shoes still tucked out of sight under the bed. I'd cleaned and tidied around his things week after week, making sure nothing collected dust, but I'd never quite gotten to the point where I was ready to get rid of them.

But as I stood in the middle of my room, it all felt so sad and suffocating.

"You're ready," Eason repeated in my head with that intense, dominating tone.

Yeah, okay, fine. The dream had been hot, but so was Eason. That was no secret. I was a woman. I had eyes. But a tantalizing game of push-and-pull wasn't who we were. He was Jessica's husband and Rob's best friend. That dream wasn't who we would *ever* be.

But maybe Dream Eason was right. Maybe it was time to finally let go. Rob wouldn't have wanted me to live in limbo forever. Moving on didn't mean erasing him from our lives. He was still Asher and Madison's dad. And my first love. But, at the end of the day, he was never coming home, and while it felt like I'd come to terms with that, I was still holding on to bits and pieces of the life we'd shared.

It was time.

Drawing in a deep breath, I smiled and closed my eyes, trying to conjure a memory of my husband's smile.

Only he wasn't the man on the backs of my lids.

"Hurry up, Bree. Before I'm gone."

Fuck.

"Bree?"

A pair of toffee-brown eyes I couldn't stop thinking about disappeared as my office came back into focus. "Huh?"

"Are you okay?" my secretary Jillian asked as she sat across the desk from me, equal parts concern and bewilderment showing in the wrinkles on her forehead.

Clearing my throat, I straightened in my chair. "Yeah, I'm just a little, um, distracted today. Go ahead and finish what you were saying."

She pointedly lifted her yellow legal pad. "Actually, *you* were saying. I was taking notes."

Shit. "Right. Okay. And…um, what exactly was *I* saying?"

Resting her notepad in her lap, she leaned forward and offered me a tight smile. "How are you doing, honey? I know we hit the one-year mark without your Rob not too long ago. After I lost my Edgar, the anniversaries were hardest."

Yes. The anniversary of the fire had been awful. Eason and I had both been zombies that week, lost in a sea of regret. But that wasn't why a boulder of guilt sat on my chest as the most inconvenient desire of my life sparked between my thighs.

"No, it's not that."

She offered me a warm, motherly grin. "You know I'm always here if you'd like to talk."

Damn, I missed Jessica. Not that, if she were still alive, I could call her up and say, "Oh, hey, I had a sex dream about your husband last night." God, I was an awful person.

Sure, I had Eason. We talked about everything, though I suspected this was going to be a smidge out of his comfort zone. And like twenty-four thousand miles beyond mine.

Jillian stared at me expectantly. "Anything you need, Bree, I'm here, okay?"

I let out a sigh. This was going to feel like talking to my grandmother, but I was just desperate enough not to care. I was sure I could find a way to ask her about it without scandalizing her too much.

"Actually, can I ask you a personal question?"

She inched forward in her chair. "Of course. Anything."

I swallowed hard. "After you, um, lost Edgar, did you ever have a…dream about someone else?"

"Oh," she breathed before stretching her lips in the universal *eek* face. "Wow, you really did mean personal."

Shit. Mayday. Mayday.

Note to self: stick to dictating correspondence to Jillian and not dissecting dreams where your husband's best friend gave you the best orgasm of your entire life.

"You know what, don't answer that. It was completely out of line. I've just had—"

"Now, hold on there, honey. You know I love working here at Prism. Rob made this my home years ago and I would hate to do or say anything inappropriate to ever risk losing that." Using two fingers, she tucked her short, gray bob behind her ear. "But if this is just a little girl talk between two friends, then…" She lifted one shoulder in a half shrug.

"Oh, totally." I waved a hand between us. "This would be off the record. Just two gals chatting during a break. I didn't mean to make you feel otherwise. Your job is always safe, Jillian. Prism wouldn't be the same without you."

"Well, in that case." An ornery smile stretched across her face as she leaned back in her chair, intertwined her fingers, and rested her joined hands on her stomach. "Please God tell me this was an absolutely filthy dream about that fine hunk of man Eason Maxwell."

My mouth fell open at her brazenness—and also her alarmingly accurate guess. "Well…I mean."

"Oh, don't worry, child. I've had so many dreams about that man. We should compare notes."

A laugh bubbled from my throat as I scolded, "Jillian!"

She shrugged. "What? I can't believe it's taken you this long. When you had me call him the day Madison cut her hand, the look on his face when he came flying through the door, white as a sheet and yet still nipple-tingling hot…" She tugged at the front of her white silk blouse comically—but also completely serious—fanning herself. "Lordy, I was hot and bothered for a week. I don't know how you do it, living with him in your guesthouse, seeing him every day. If I were you, I'd wind up either in his bed or in jail for trying."

"Oh my God." I leaned over and buried my face in my arms on the desk.

"Nope. No getting shy on me now. Spill it. I need all the details."

"Are you crazy? I'm not giving you details."

She huffed. "Oh, I see how it is. You get to watch him all sweaty and doing shirtless pushups in the yard, but you won't even share the juicy details of your imagination with a lonely old lady."

My head popped up. "Who said he does sweaty, shirtless pushups in the yard?"

She quirked her eyebrow and shot me a glare. "Oh, please. A man does not have a body like his without pushups. If you aren't watching, invite me over and I will."

Another round of laughter struck me, but I finally sat up and kicked my chair back. "Okay, stop. Seriously. I can't breathe."

For a few seconds, she sat there staring at me with a proud

smile on her plump face. "All right, now that we got the embarrassing stuff out of the way. Tell me why you've been in la-la land all day."

All humor suddenly vanished, my arch nemesis reality clocking in for the day. "Ugh," I groaned. "It is Eason."

"Oh, I know. We covered that."

"No, I mean it's *Eason*. Rob's best friend. Jessica's husband. That's a lifetime's worth of wrong."

"But..." she prompted.

"But...I can't stop thinking about him."

With a loud clap, she sat up straight. "All right. Jillian your best gal pal is gone. Time for some tough love from Mama Jill." Another clap. "Bree, honey. Wake. Up."

"I am awake. Though this being one big nightmare could account for why we just discussed Eason's abs." I pressed my palms to my eyes and then shook my head to rattle away the image of Mama Jill gawking at him beside my pool.

"You aren't awake. You're stuck. And given the way you lost Rob, I don't blame you. But maybe this dream of yours is telling you something. If Eason is off-limits, fine. I respect that. Leave him for the rest of us. But it's okay to want that kind of intimacy with someone else. You two spend a lot of time together. Maybe your brain got some wires crossed. But that doesn't mean you have to feel embarrassed about it. You're a young, vibrant woman with needs. No shame in that."

But shame was exactly the emotion washing over me. "It was more than that though. In my dream, he left. And I was begging him not to go. I was so scared." Tears welled in my eyes and I flicked my gaze out the window in an attempt to fight them off. "It was the abandonment."

"Now that is something different," she whispered. "You've

lost a lot. That kind of hurt sticks with you. It sounds to me like Eason has taken over a lot of roles in your life. You depend on him. Care about him. Trust him. And now, you're starting to feel some things you weren't expecting. But that doesn't make it wrong. Is it possible he might have feelings for you too?"

"No!" I scoffed. "Dear God, no. We're friends. That's it."

"Okay." She slanted her head to one side. "Then why are we freaking out about this?"

"Because I had a sex dream about *Eason*."

"But you didn't *have* sex with him. It was a *dream*. Listen, you're used to being in charge, but you don't get to control those. It's nothing, Bree. This time tomorrow, you'll be telling me about your late-night fantasies with the shorty-shorts UPS guy." She moaned. "Those steel-toed boots do it for me."

Her joke didn't land a chuckle even if she was really on a roll.

I shook my head. This didn't feel like nothing. It felt like a dormant part of me had been awakened for the first time in years. *Years.* Plural. As in more than one, and that was not possible because my husband had only been gone for one.

Maybe I was just desperate.

Maybe I was just hard up and in need of a release.

But why Eason? And why had I been so freaked out when he'd left? And why had my room felt smaller that morning surrounded by all of Rob's stuff?

"I don't know, Jillian. This felt big. Like really big. I snuck out before breakfast so I didn't have to see him this morning."

"Let me tell you a little secret. That brain of yours knows more than you think it does. But none of it matters until your heart gets the memo too. Until then, all you can do is sit back and enjoy the ride. You don't want Eason? Fine. Don't trip and fall face-first into his lap with your mouth open."

My eyes flashed wide. "Jesus, Jillian."

She laughed softly and her shoulders bounced. "Just relax, okay? Let the erotic dust settle and then see how you feel in a few days. I can't speak for Rob or Jessica, but my Edgar loved me with his whole heart. Jealous as a side piece on Valentine's Day and as territorial as a damn grizzly bear. But I like to think that, if I moved on with someone new, he'd be happy for me. Don't underestimate the people who loved you."

I drew in a deep breath, holding it until my lungs burned. Okay. She had a point. There was nothing to get worked up about—yet. Eason didn't know I'd had a dream. No harm done.

Though…relaxing had never been my strong suit.

"You're right. There's no use in getting worked up over nothing."

Her knees creaked as she rose from the chair. "Alrighty, but should you decide you *do* want to get worked up, I have a twenty-dollar-off coupon code for a fantastic vibrator. Ten speeds, waterproof, guaranteed to make you say, 'Eason who?'"

"Okay, that's enough. Back to work. Break time's over."

Chuckling, she walked to the door. "I'll just pop that coupon code over in an email. You know, just in case."

CHAPTER TEN

EASON

"**D**addy!" Luna exclaimed, colliding with my legs as soon as I walked through Bree's back door. Sweaty and shirtless, fresh from a run, I picked her up. "Hey, sweet girl. You miss me?"

She hooked her arms around my neck and rested her head on my shoulder, giving me the only answer I would ever need. And then, in the next heartbeat, she shot up and pinched her nose. "Ew, Daddy tink."

"Oh, holy God…" Bree mumbled, coming to a screeching halt a few feet away.

"What?" I asked.

Using her hand to shield her face, she cut her gaze to the floor. "Where is your shirt?"

I twisted my lips. "Probably in my drawer?"

"Ohhhkay, but why aren't you wearing it?"

I blinked at her for several seconds. I didn't exactly roam around shirtless a lot, but it wasn't unusual if I was working out or hanging out by the pool with the kids.

"Because I just got back from a run? Does it…bother you?"

Her head popped up, but she was still using her hand to block my chest from her vision. "Of course it doesn't bother me. Why would it bother me?"

"Gee, Bree. I don't know," I replied, lifting a hand to mimic her.

Discarding her shield, she rolled her eyes. "Whatever. Now that you're back from doing pushups in the yard, can you watch the kids for a little while? The dealership that bought Rob's Porsche is supposed to pick it up in the morning, so I need to get the rest of his stuff out and wipe down the inside. He'd lose his mind if I let anyone see his baby like that."

I hadn't done any pushups in the yard; therefore, had no damn clue what she was talking about. But there were more pressing parts of her statement that required my attention.

"Whoa, hold up." I set Luna on her feet. "I thought you were going to let me take care of that."

"Yeah, but it's four o'clock."

"And?" I drawled, clearly confused.

It had only been a matter of time before this happened. I just wasn't expecting it that day.

Then again, I'd once read in a book that there is no true timeline for grief. It was always one step forward, two weeks wallowing and cussing the universe back. But, with time, the good days had begun to outweigh the bad.

For over thirteen months after the fire, Rob's belongings had sat untouched. His coat hung on the rack next to the door, his clothes filled the closet, and his precious convertible collected dust in the garage. Bree and I had talked about her packing up his stuff multiple times, but she'd yet to follow through.

I couldn't blame her; I still wore my wedding ring because taking it off felt like betrayal.

However, that week, something had been going on with Bree. She'd been quieter than usual, keeping to herself.

At first, I'd thought I'd done something to piss her off because if I entered a room, she made every excuse to leave. She never missed one of our nightly chats by the firepit though, even if those were weird too. Either she avoided eye contact altogether or I'd catch her staring at me from the corner of my eye.

That's not to mention her reaction when Madison and Asher plotted a sneak tickle attack on her. My job was to pin her arms above her head, just as it had been over a dozen times before. Her face had turned shades of red I didn't know human flesh was capable of that day. She avoided me like the plague for the rest of the afternoon, only forgiving me when I snuck three red M&M's into her napkin at dinner.

However, on Friday when she'd gotten home from work, Bree slipped into a pair of purple pajama pants and a matching tank top and then started sorting Rob's things. Armed with a system of keep, donate, and trash, she refused to let me help other than entertaining the kids and occasionally carrying things down the stairs or up to the attic after they'd been properly boxed for storage.

The helplessness I felt as I paced outside her bedroom door while listening to her broken sobs damn near destroyed me. I'd gotten used to being a team, but that wasn't a goodbye we needed to say together. After the kids went to sleep, I knocked to let her know I was headed back to the pool house. Much to my surprise and staggering relief, she patted the spot of carpet next to her and asked me to stay for a while.

With two video baby monitors humming in the background, we sat on the rug in her room, laughing over Rob's and my old yearbooks for hours. The literal and figurative closet cleaning wasn't limited to just her husband, either. She found pictures of her and Jessica from long before I had known either of them. There were birthday cards in Jessica's handwriting, a few scarves, and even a small pair of gold stud earrings she'd borrowed from my wife and thankfully never returned. No matter how small or inexpensive, they immediately became family treasures I could pass down to our daughter.

It was well past three in the morning before I headed back to my place, carrying a basket full of not only Jessica's stuff but also Rob's favorite T-shirts, the Rolex Bree insisted he would have wanted me to have, and a shoe box of ticket stubs and fliers from my shows that I had no idea he'd collected.

But most of all, by the time we said our goodnights, a weight we had no idea we'd been carrying was suddenly lifted from both of our shoulders. It was almost like we had been too afraid of letting ourselves remember the two people we'd lost out loud sometimes, but that night—after purging memory after memory along with tangible stuff—there was a lot less pain and a lot more peace than I'd ever expected.

As bleak and sad as it probably could have been, after spending that time laughing and basically shooting the shit, carefree into the night, I found myself feeling so lucky I still had Bree. And even luckier that I got to be the one who was there for her.

Saturday was much of the same, though as the house emptied of Rob's belongings, so did the light in Bree's eyes. It had been a silent Saturday night around the firepit, and her one glass of wine gradually turned into a bottle. However, first thing Sunday morning, she was back at it—hungover as hell and full steam ahead.

I tried to convince her to take a break. I even suggested a trip to the park with the kids. But Bree was having none of it. Eventually, she got sick of my hovering and told me to take a hike. I'd gone for a run instead, having found it helped expel this newfound energy I had lately.

"What does four o'clock have to do with anything?" I asked.

"It's getting late, and I need to get the car cleaned up and the kids bathed, and make dinner, and—"

Was it wrong to think she was gorgeous when she was flustered and overwhelmed? Her hair all out of place. Her shirt dirty and wrinkled. The tiny hint of smudged mascara that reached toward her temple beside her left eye.

Was it even more wrong that my first instinct was to wrap my arms around her and tell her I'd deal with what needed to be done and to hell with whatever wasn't finished? The best part for me was just taking something off her plate and watching her exhale for usually the first time all day.

Sometimes the silent, grateful look she gave me stole my breath—*a little.*

"Why don't you just go sit outside for a while and take a breather? I'll leave you alone." I cut my eyes away, not wanting to make her uncomfortable like she'd been around me lately. "I'll take care of the car and the baths, and I'll order a veggie pizza for dinner."

"Pee-za!" Luna yelled, taking off as fast as her little legs would carry her to spread the good news to Asher and Madison.

I grinned, enjoying the fleeting moment where I was taking care of my girls all at the same time. "See, it's a done deal now."

"I can't let you do that. The weekends are supposed to be your free days so you can work." She stretched her neck, again proving the toll the long weekend had taken on her.

"Yeah, well. I'm taking a personal day to help a friend."

Her eyes lit up, but then she quicky frowned, a crinkle forming between her eyes. "You should get new friends. The one you have now is really needy."

The one I have now is sexy as all hell, standing in front of me, dead tired in old Birkenstocks.

"Psh, you should get new friends. The one *you* have now is about to sneak bacon onto the veggie pizza."

She curled her lip. "Isn't bacon after a workout counterproductive?"

"Not if you're only working out so you can eat the bacon."

"Touché." She quietly laughed, her gaze dipping to my chest for a nanosecond. Her whole body startled as her green eyes snapped back to mine. "Ummm, you sure you don't mind? I can handle bath time and even ordering pizza. But I'm emotionally tapped."

"You did good this weekend. Really fucking good." I gave her shoulder a squeeze.

"Yeah. Thanks." She shrugged off my hand.

Jesus, what the hell was her deal? *Okay. Don't read into it.* She had literally just said she was emotionally tapped. The last thing she needed was me reading into shit.

I slapped on my signature grin and fell back on my specialty skill of making a joke. "Now, just to be clear, you did hear the part about bacon on one of those pizzas, right?"

"Extra bacon. I gotcha."

I did not do enough cardio to warrant *extra* bacon, but I sure as hell didn't correct her, either.

After a quick stop for a shower, I made my way out to the garage. I steeled myself before peeling back the tan cover on Rob's ruby-red Porsche 911. Besides the occasional start to keep the battery from dying, no one had touched the car since we'd lost him.

A wave of nostalgia stabbed me in the gut as I opened the door.

There wasn't much to clean. Short of a thin layer of dust on the dashboard, the interior was spotless—an abandoned iPhone charger being the only proof that the car had ever been out of the showroom. I went to work flipping the visors and popping the glove compartment open. Inside, there was all the usual fare: pack of gum, sunglasses, service records, and proof of insurance, but it was a small black cell phone that caught my attention.

Immediately, I picked it up and turned it in my fingers. Rob's cell had been lost in the fire, so I assumed it must have been a work phone or an older model he'd upgraded. Either way, Bree would want it back, so I plugged it into the charger and moved on without thinking much of it.

The small trunk in the hood was empty, and after checking under the seats, wiping down the console, and shaking out the floor mats, I called it a day.

I managed to unwedge my body from the tiny clown car only to remember the cell, so I leaned back in.

And that was when time stopped all over again.

With the battery charged, the phone had turned on and notifications from a local Atlanta number glowed on the screen. There was no name or a photo programmed in for the contact, but based on the text, Rob was more than familiar with the sender.

I can't stop thinking about how deep you got last night.

What.

The.

Fuck.

I sank back down into the driver's seat, leaving the door open. There was no way. No fucking way. Rob and I had been tighter than tight. He'd told me everything. If he had been stepping out on Bree, I would have known about it. At a bare minimum, I would have known he was unhappy.

I scrolled to the next notification.

Same phone number, different jaw-dropping message.

Your lips. Your neck. Your cock. I can't wait much longer to taste them all again.

With my heart in my throat, I glanced up at the door that led to the house. The pizza should have been there soon, and if I was going to figure out what the hell was on the phone before Bree came out there looking for me, I needed to be quick.

With my jaw clenched, I scrolled to the next message. Hell, maybe it wasn't even Rob's phone.

Mr. Winters, promise me you'll make time in your busy schedule to fuck me today.

Shit. There went that theory.

"What the fuck were you doing?" I seethed at my dead best friend. When I ran out of notifications, I typed in what I hoped was the code to unlock his phone.

The little box on the screen shook my rejection.

In rapid succession, I tried Bree's birthday, the code to their alarm system, and the kids' birthdays, and just before getting locked out for sixty seconds, I attempted a combination of all three.

All fucking wrong.

Right. Of course. When having an affair, it was probably best if you didn't use a code your wife would guess. Not that I would fucking know anything about that. The password on my phone was 1-1-1-1.

I drew in a deep breath, but it did nothing to slow the thundering in my ears. There had to be an explanation. My mind spun in a million different directions. The who, what, when, where, and motherfucking why all remained unanswered. Luna had locked me out of my phone enough times to know that if I got my next guess wrong, I'd have to wait five minutes for it to open again. Then fifteen, an hour, and eventually it would disable it altogether.

Unfortunately, Gino's Pizza wasn't that fucking slow. Max, I had two guesses left before Bree came looking for me. And then what?

Did I tell her about the notifications? Could I even get back to them without the passcode? Those texts would have crushed her. Bree was barely surviving the weekend as it was. Did I really want to dump this steaming pile of bullshit at her feet without knowing all the facts?

Had he still been alive, I would have gone straight to Rob. Demanded answers. Best friends or not, the way he lived his life was none of my business. But come on? Cheating on his wife? The mother of his children? Fuck that.

Especially now that said wife was my...well, whatever Bree and I were. An employer of sorts? A friend? Oh, who the hell was I kidding? Bree was family. And this was not shit you kept from your *family*.

Swallowing hard, I racked my brain. Four dots showed on the screen. I needed a four-digit number Bree wouldn't guess but Rob could never forget.

My knee bounced at a marathon pace and my fingers hovered over the screen, restlessly waiting for the countdown to run out, all the while terrified of one wrong stroke.

Maybe I didn't need to know.

Maybe it would be best if I dropped it in the nearest trash can.

Maybe Rob's secrets should have gone to the grave with him.

She didn't need to know.

She didn't—

"Pizza's here," Asher said, appearing mere inches away like a damn ninja in the night.

I bumbled, dropping the phone into my lap. "Jesus, Ash."

He smiled big and toothy, his dark hair sweeping across his forehead. "Ha! Did I scare you?"

"Um, yeah."

Missing nothing—such was the job of a six-year-old—he glanced down. "Did you get a new phone?"

"No," I clipped entirely too roughly. Grabbing the digital equivalent of his father's little black book, I stood up and shoved it into my back pocket.

Asher backed out of my way—nevertheless persistent. "Whose phone is it?"

"Uhh…" I stalled, picking up the small pile of things I'd found in the glovebox and the bucket of cleaning supplies. Great. Now I had to lie too. *Rob, you fucking asshole.* "It's just an old one I use to listen to music. Come on. Let's go eat." Not having one single fuck left to give about that damn car, I used my heel to kick the door shut.

Thankfully, Asher didn't bring the phone up over dinner. We all sat at the table in the dining room, the girls' highchairs pulled up at the ends.

Bree talked.

The kids laughed.

And I stared into space, that damn phone burning like a glowing brick of coal in my back pocket while a matrix of numbers rained through my head.

Not surprisingly, Bree could sense that something was up. Her gaze bored into me with a tangible suspicion that made the hairs on the back of my neck stand on end. This was why people like me didn't have second cell phones or mistresses. I wasn't the cheater, but peeling out of my skin would have been more comfortable than bearing the weight of her scrutinizing gaze for a second longer. Luna was still chewing her last bite of pizza when I picked her up, offered curt goodnights, and then hauled ass out to the pool house.

Unfocused and distracted, I struggled through Luna's bedtime routine. But God bless my daughter; she was half asleep before the end of *Goodnight Moon*.

Leaving me alone.

At last.

With that fucking phone.

"Okay, okay, okay," I chanted to myself as I paced the small living room.

Long before I'd moved in, Bree had decorated the pool house in a beach theme. Tan furniture with teal accents set the mood. Black-and-white photos of starfish and coastal waters graced the walls, and multicolored blue stones on the kitchen backsplash topped off the modern ocean feel. Though, at the moment, as I stared down at Rob's mystery phone on the coffee table, it was a lot like being trapped in shark-infested waters.

I still couldn't believe he'd do that to Bree. That woman was his life, and over the last year of truly getting to know her, I completely understood why. An affair made no sense. My desperate need to understand grew by the minute. However, pacing wasn't going to help me magically figure it out.

"Okay," I said, lowering myself to sit on the couch in front of it. The next lockout was only five minutes. I could do it. I could totally do it.

He'd always been obsessed with cars. They weren't my thing, but I'd listened to him ramble enough to know that a 1969 Shelby was his dream car.

1-9-6-9

Denied.

Fuck.

For the next five minutes, there was a hurricane of pacing, thinking, and cussing.

Maybe it wasn't some code to crack. If he was stupid enough to be having an affair, maybe he was dumb enough to think he didn't even need a code. Sucking in a deep breath, I went with the most generic sequence I could think of.

1-2-3-4

Wrong again.

Shit.

Defeated, I settled in for my fifteen minutes of purgatory.

There had to have been tens of thousands of different combinations, but only one opened the phone and I was running out of guesses. He was my best friend; it shouldn't have been so hard. For fuck's sake, I'd spent three months living in a minivan with him, where we shared ninety-nine-cent cheeseburgers for dinner and took turns standing guard when we had to piss in the middle of the night.

When I said I knew Rob Winters, I meant I fucking *knew* him. I'd titled my life's work after that—

My body turned to stone. It was a summer we'd spent pooling change and trading clean clothes, but no matter how many times we'd doubled over laughing while telling those stories, it always came back to the Aerostar van.

There was a reason my album wasn't *Solstice in the '07*. We'd had a blast playing new bars, meeting women, drinking ourselves sick on whatever shots the bartender would slide our way when no one was looking. But it was the bond we'd forged inside the van that changed our lives.

Rob had told me all about his fears of never measuring up to others' expectations for him. And I'd told him all about growing up with a narcissist who was too consumed with her own life to remember I existed. We confided in each other about shit two twenty-one-year-olds never should have had to experience. And in those captain's chairs, leaned back, staring up at the cloth drooping on the roof, we'd promised to stick together and keep each other accountable.

Nineteen ninety-two. It wasn't a place in time. It was an address where two broken kids had vowed to become men better than the world we'd been born into.

Holding my breath, I typed the numbers 1-9-9-2.

A rush of adrenaline crashed into me like a tsunami when the screen suddenly slid open.

I shot to my feet, victory singing in my veins. For a beat, I was so proud of myself that I'd forgotten about the betrayal and why I'd broken into the phone in the first place.

The home screen was set to default, the standard factory apps neatly stored in folders. The only icon on the dock at the bottom was for Messages and it snapped me back to reality. There was no turning back, but Bree deserved to know.

I could tell her gently. Be there to support her. Remind her that Rob had always loved her no matter what stupid fucking choices he'd made. I'd be the rock on our team this time, give her space and time she'd need to grieve all over again.

But this would be completely different than thirteen months ago. Forget about salt—this would be acid in her wounds. I'd be there for her and, God willing, soften the blow.

Tapping into the messages, I found only one thread—the last text dated the day of the fire. I scrolled up, my stomach churning as I skimmed their conversation. From spur-of-the-moment afternoon dates at a local hotel to weekly Tuesday-night rendezvous wherever the hell "their spot" was. This wasn't something new or an isolated event for Rob. With three a.m. sweet nothings and countless "I miss yous" from both sides, bitterness crawled up my throat as week after week of deception rolled across the screen.

FROM THE EMBERS

In the wake of tragedy, it's strange the things you remember.

I remembered standing inside the guest house—Rob's guest house.

I remembered the sickening weight in my stomach as I tried to figure out how I could destroy a woman who over the last year had come to mean so much to me.

But carved into my soul for all my days to come was the life-altering moment when a naked photo of my wife appeared on the screen.

CHAPTER ELEVEN

BREE

AFTER I'D GOTTEN THE KIDS IN BED, I WENT BACK downstairs to clean the kitchen. For the most part, the bacon pizza was untouched. Only one slice sat half-eaten on Eason's plate, and the guilt of seeing it there swelled inside me. I shouldn't have let him take care of Rob's car. Cleaning out the house that weekend had been emotionally taxing and Eason had been nothing short of amazing.

I didn't know how he did it, but he was always there when I needed him and scarce when I needed time alone. He worried about me, so of course there were moments where he hovered for entirely too long. But that was pure Eason, so I didn't complain—much.

Sometimes, in the shadows of my own grief, I'd forget how close Eason and Rob had been. No wonder he had been so quiet at dinner. Cleaning out Rob's car—the final chapter in his best friend's life—couldn't have been an easy task for him. Yet he'd insisted on doing it anyway.

And after acting like a total maniac and thoroughly ogling his chest, I'd let him.

Nice, Bree. Outstanding way of communicating your gratitude.

Still hungover from my attempt to drown myself in a bottle

of Chardonnay the night before, I grabbed a sparkling water and a beer for Eason, and then I warmed up two pieces of pizza with the hopes of being able to coerce him into eating.

Over the course of the week, my dream with Eason's hands all over me had not faded in the least. There had been approximately five cold showers and one express delivery of Jillian's recommended vibrator that she had lied about because it did not make me forget about Eason at all.

But awkwardness aside, I had long since become addicted to our nightly chats. It didn't matter how hard the day had been. Just the sight of him sitting outside, his messy, blond hair finger-combed to one side, beer in hand with his feet propped up on a chair, quelled the constant storm brewing inside me. I wasn't positive I had the same effect on him, but if he wasn't on his way to a show, he never missed a night.

Judging by the way he'd raced out of the house earlier that evening, he might take his time. Collect himself. Plaster on the fake smile I'd grown to hate.

But he'd be there.

And for Eason, I'd wait.

Sitting on my corner of the couch, I stared up at the night sky with a sense of contentment swirling inside my chest. It had been one hell of a weekend, but I finally felt like I was taking the first steps on the twisted path of moving forward. Every day, I saw Rob in the faces of my children. Because of that, he would always be a part of my life. But I didn't feel stuck in a spiral of sorrow anymore. Cleaning out the closet and donating his things wasn't the same as erasing him from our lives. But living as though he would be home at any second hadn't been doing me or the kids any favors.

I glanced down at my wedding rings, the diamonds sparkling in the lights from the pool. I wasn't ready to tuck them away in the safe yet. And that was okay. It was a process. I'd know when the time was right.

However, as Eason exited the pool house, murder written all over his face, I would soon learn that the time had been right before Rob had even died.

"Did you know?" he snarled from yards away, his voice echoing off the house.

My head snapped back, confusion striking me like a slap. "Did I know what?"

He stopped in front of me, his tall, muscular body vibrating with rage. "That your husband was fucking my wife!"

I scoffed, the mere thought of it so ludicrous that it was almost humorous. "What the hell are you talking about?"

He lifted a phone into my line of sight, revealing a picture of Jessica smiling into a mirror, one arm supporting her naked breasts, her other hand tangled in the top of her hair.

I put my palm out to block the image. "Jesus, Eason. Why are you showing me that?"

"Because she sent it to Rob!" he seethed through clenched teeth. With his finger, he gave the screen a swipe and dozens of blue and gray text bubbles rolled so fast that it was dizzying.

But like a roulette wheel straight out of the Twilight Zone, it stopped on a picture of Rob. Based on the teal-and-white pillowcase, he was in our bed. With his chest bare and a sheet draped over his hips, he had his face turned away from the camera. I could almost hear his rich laughter. However, it was Jessica curled up beside him, her naked breasts pressed into his side, a blinding smile beaming up at the camera, that stole the breath from my lungs.

"Where did you get that?" I hissed, shooting to my feet.

"His car," Eason snapped, his chest heaving as he stared at me with eyes so cold and distant I barely recognized him.

I drew in a ragged breath, and as though oxygen had become poisonous, it burned all the way down.

It wasn't possible.

There was no way the picture was real.

But there was no denying it, either.

"Is this some kind of sick joke? Because I have to be honest, Eason. It's seriously fucked up." A tear escaped the corner of my eye.

As if a light had been switched, his face immediately softened. "I wish," he rumbled, handing me the phone. He started to pace, based on the sounds of his footsteps. I was too focused on the alternate universe in my palm to know for sure.

It wasn't either of their phone numbers on the screen, but there were so many pictures it was easy to figure out who was who.

Jessica: I told Eason I was going to the grocery store. You think you can take an early lunch?

Rob: You're my favorite lunch. Just tell me where.

"I don't understand," I choked out, pain radiating from the knife of betrayal lodged firmly between my shoulder blades.

"What is there to understand?" Eason snapped, planting his hands on his hips. "They were fucking behind our backs."

"No." Shaking my head as if it could erase the images etched in my mind, I stated, "He wouldn't do that to me. *She* wouldn't do that to me."

"Yeah, well, they fucking did it to me, Bree." He reached out and plucked the phone from my hand. "You want to see something fun?"

There was absolutely nothing fun he was going to show me, so I braced for impact as he swiped his finger across the screen, searching for God only knew what.

He sidled up beside me, bringing the phone between us. "Remember when I took her to Savannah for our anniversary?"

He angled the phone so we could both see the photo on the screen. Jessica was making a kissing face at the camera, the strap of a black lacy see-through bra falling off her shoulder. "So this is the bathroom of the hotel from our anniversary trip." He pointed to the bottom corner of the image where it appeared two mirrors reflected off of each other to show the rest of the hotel room. "That's me. Asleep in bed." He moved his finger to her bra. "And that's the lingerie I bought her, but she told me she was too tired for sex, so she never even put it on."

My stomach soured and my mouth dried. Their anniversary? That was months before the fire. "How long was this going on?"

"At least three months, though they'd been talking before that. The first text on there is about him having a new number that was *safe*. They were meeting up for lunch and on afternoons when I'd take Luna out for a walk. That new dance class she'd been taking at night?" He laughed without humor, pain carved in his handsome face. "Yeah, that was just some bullshit so they could meet up at the Four Seasons. Rob had a standing reservation every Tuesday and Thursday."

I blinked several times, trying to make sense of the illogical. I'd always known that Rob and Jessica were friendly. He'd shown me memes she'd texted him about being a workaholic, and they'd get together to plan my birthday or shop for my Christmas presents. But an affair?

"Why? I mean...what the fuck, Eason?"

"I have no idea," he snapped. "I just know, for three months, my best friend gave me advice on my failing marriage—all the while telling my wife he loves her behind my back."

And with that, the dagger in my back plunged right through to my heart. On unsteady legs, I stumbled, my calves hitting the couch and forcing me down to sitting. "H-he *loved* her?"

He let out a loud groan. "I gotta get out of here. I can't be here tonight."

My head snapped up, a wave of anxiety which had nothing to do with my cheating husband crashing over me. "Where are you going?"

"Anywhere." He threw his hands out to his sides. "Being here. His house. His yard. I can't sleep in a bed under his roof, wondering if he ever fucked my wife in it." He leaned forward to grab the phone, but I moved it out of his reach.

"No, I want to see everything."

"You don't need to read that shit, Bree. Take my word for it. You know enough."

But he was wrong.

"No. You can go, take some time for yourself, do whatever you have to. But I need to know every single word of it backwards and forwards, over and over, until something finally makes me understand how they could do this to me—*to us*."

His jaw ticked. "It's not going to make it hurt any less."

"Yeah, well, neither is a vacation and you don't hear me trying to stop you."

He glared at me for a long beat, but eventually, his shoulders fell. "The passcode is nineteen ninety-two."

Oh my God. What the actual fuck, Rob?

Unable to hide it, I blanched.

"Yeah," Eason huffed. "I guess that van wasn't the only thing he and I shared." Dipping his head as he backed away, he added, "I'll let you know where we end up."

I nodded, but my already broken heart shattered as I watched him walk away. It was just like my dream. He was leaving and I had no way to stop him.

There was no sleep to be found that night. The very first thing

I did was strip my bed, cramming the sheets and blankets into a garbage bag and then shoving them out the window. It was a tad dramatic when I could have just carried them out to the trash bins, but banging my fist against his empty side of the bed was only so therapeutic. I considered throwing my wedding and engagement rings in the same bag, but I did have children who might one day want them, so I put them in the safe, hoping I threw them hard enough for them to shatter—just like our vows.

Once I got settled in the guest room, I read every text at least a dozen times. Like a masochist, I zoomed in on every picture, memorized every detail. When I ran out of material, I called the head of Prism IT at five in the morning and requested a record of every text or call Rob had ever made from his work phone. I did the same with our personal cell phone provider as soon as their offices opened, but my search didn't end there.

After we'd lost Rob, I'd used an old backup from the Cloud to download the contents of his personal phone so we wouldn't lose all the pictures he'd taken over the years. I spent many gut-wrenching nights going through his pictures and dreaming of the past. Jessica had never been naked in his photos, but finding her on his cameral roll wasn't unusual. At the time, I hadn't given it much thought. We often made Rob or Eason take pictures when the four of us were together. However, now, with the wool out of my eyes, I had a big day of scrutinizing ahead of me.

It was Monday morning, and as soon as the kids woke up, they asked about Eason and Luna. I didn't have much to tell them. He'd texted me an address somewhere in Tennessee shortly after midnight but offered no specifics on when they were coming back. It stung—a lot. Eason and I were no strangers to emotional up-heaval, but this time, he'd wanted to deal with it alone.

I, on the other hand, wanted him to come walking through

my kitchen door with a smile on his face, Luna on his hip, and tell me everything was going to be okay. Because, somehow, someway, everything was okay when I was with Eason. And yes, I knew exactly how wildly selfish it sounded, but it didn't change the fact that I already missed him like crazy.

I called in to work to let them know I wouldn't be at the office for a few days. With the IRS audit in full swing and Prism gearing up for the new fall line, it wasn't a good time for me to take personal days. Then again, was there ever truly a convenient time to find out your dead husband had been in love with your dead best friend?

Desperate for an escape, I took the kids to the park, then out for frozen yogurt, and eventually to the mall to ride the carousel. I was exhausted beyond reason, but being with my kids was the only thing that eased my splintered soul. The house was blisteringly quiet when we got back. None of Luna's sugary giggles or Eason's rich laughter.

He wasn't there to ask me about my day. Regardless of my answer, his wide smile made it so I knew it was about to get better.

He wasn't there to sit outside and bullshit about nothing, his animated stories making the weight of life seem lighter.

To be honest, he didn't even have to talk. Just knowing that Eason was there, outside in the pool house, working on his music gave me a sense of comfort I'd never expected to find again.

My own pain stung, but my sympathy for Eason was the true slap across the face and it only made me hate Rob and Jessica that much more.

Utterly unable to keep my lids open for any longer, I fell asleep for a while after the kids went to bed, but within hours I was right back up. I covered the bedroom floor with rows upon rows of the text printouts I'd requested. It was a tedious process, matching up timelines, looking back at my old messages to figure out what he'd told me he was doing while he was with her, then doubling back to see if any photos were taken on those days. And what were Jessica and I talking about in our old conversations while they were sneaking around behind my back? I was mentally piecing together a puzzle for which I only had about half the pieces.

The worst part was that I had this visceral need to know why they had done it, but deep down, I knew that none of it mattered. Knowing wouldn't change what had happened. No matter how many lies I uncovered, it wouldn't unbreak my heart.

After the revelations of the last two days, I began to feel like our entire life together and my friendship with a woman, who I'd never thought could betray me, had been nothing more than an illusion. Carefully crafted and expertly carried out, leaving Eason and me fools in their games.

When Rob and Jessica had been lost in that fire, so many secrets perished along with them. Some apparently had only been scattered to the breeze for a while. Regardless, I couldn't shake the feeling that, somehow, we were still smoldering in the ashes of that night, a hotspot yet to be discovered, growing brighter even a year after their deaths.

And as I flipped the page to the next set of their messages, my lids almost as heavy as my heart, the embers of their betrayal suddenly ignited into a conflagration that would consume us all.

CHAPTER TWELVE

EASON

EVEN BEFORE I'D LOST JESSICA, I WAS NO STRANGER TO heartbreak. There weren't many songwriters who were. In my younger days, a woman had cheated on me with a coworker. Another left me for her ex. One just went straight up off the rails and called my mother to tattle about how I hadn't bought her enough flowers. It was all part of the journey, and closure was nothing but part of the process.

However, as it turned out, raging at a ghost was as unfulfilling as breakups came.

There was no one to be mad at.

No tear-filled arguments long into the wee hours of the morning.

There were no lies to sort through. No pleas to stay. There wasn't even the satisfying slam of the door as I stormed out, my head held high, my self-worth in the gutter but knowing I deserved better.

Jessica had been sleeping around behind my back with the man I considered my brother.

I didn't get to drive to Rob's house and bang on his door in the middle of the night, demanding answers to questions no one should have to ask. There were no insults to exchange, no punches to be thrown, and absolutely nothing I could do to soothe the hurricane brewing within me.

So I packed my daughter and my guitar and left in the middle of the night. I hated leaving Bree alone with the fucking phone, but I couldn't stay. The memories the four of us had made in that house before the fire had once been comforting. The afternoons around the pool, laughing and drinking. The impromptu dinners Bree and Jessica would plan where Rob would insist on grilling. The countless times Rob and I watched football, or basketball, or any sport that was in season on the big screen while our wives chatted about everything under the sun.

Now, those memories were poisoned by doubt. Tarnished by deception and lies.

Had he been fantasizing about her as she walked around the pool in a bikini? The very same pool my bedroom overlooked.

Had the dinners all just been a ruse so she could see him and play footsie under the table I currently ate dinner at each night?

While my eyes had been glued to the game, was he plotting a moment to get her alone, maybe pin her against the wall in the hall I walked past every day?

I had to get out of there, even if it meant temporarily getting away from Bree too.

I needed downtime. A place to think and process. No peace would be found, but I'd lived without it for over a year. I could make it awhile longer.

I managed to secure a cabin just north of Gatlinburg with digital twenty-four-hour check-in. It was a small two-bedroom—perfect for me and Luna—with a killer view of the mountains.

I had no idea how long I would stay. I'd booked the place for a week, figuring I'd rather lose money and skip out early than be kicked out before I was ready to go back.

The first day, Luna and I explored the area. It was relatively secluded, save for a few cabins in the distance, but we found a grocery store about thirty minutes away and bought enough Goldfish crackers, crayons, and coloring books to keep Luna busy.

We hiked. We snuggled on the couch. I even managed to turn down the temperature on the hot tub so we could use it like a swimming pool. But when night fell, without the distractions of being a father, my mind assaulted me.

When was the first time? The first kiss? The first touch? Who initiated it? Who wanted it more?

When was the last time? The Thursday before the fire? Did he cop a feel in the kitchen when I was setting up Pictionary? Was she hoping I'd get drunk enough to not hear her fucking him in the bathroom?

How goddamn blind had I been not to have seen it?

Since the day I'd found music, writing had been my outlet. When times got tough and it all became too much, I'd settle behind my piano or drag a guitar into my lap and the chaos would flow from the depths inside me, through my fingers, and out into the world.

When news of the fire had spread through my connections in the music industry, a producer I'd been dying to work with reached out to extend his condolences. He ended the call with, "This kind of heartbreak should make an incredible album for you. Hit me up when you're ready to start recording." I wanted to reach through the phone and snap his fucking neck.

What I'd been through wasn't a run-of-the-mill breakup that inspired heartache-filled ballads. I'd damn near lost everything. I wasn't capitalizing on the death of my wife and friend. And even if I wanted to, writing meant reliving those emotions, dissecting them, tearing them down to a fundamental level, then piecing them back together in a way that was brutal and succinct yet still pleasing to the ear.

There wasn't enough fame or fortune in existence for me to be willing to relive the night of the fire. I leaned on Bree, talked to a therapist, but I never wanted to live in a world where someone somewhere was singing lyrics like "I'll be right back."

Fuck. That.

But this… This wound. This pain. This absolute and utter betrayal. I needed to get it out, shred it, patch it back together, and then move the fuck on with my life.

So, with my guitar in hand, while Luna slept, I got to work.

By the next morning, I was no less pissed off or jaded, but at least I had something to show for the anguish. It wasn't as much a song as a stream of consciousness in C minor, but it was getting there—and eventually so would my heart.

Over the last forty-eight hours, sleep had been an afterthought. I'd doze off, catching a few hours here or there, but reality didn't allow my mind to stay silent for long. Though, when Luna's nap time rolled around and she nodded off in my arms in the middle of her favorite cartoon, I started thinking it might turn into a snoozefest for both of us.

"I not sweepy," she whined, already half asleep on my shoulder, her arms tight around my neck.

"Baby, you were already asleep," I whispered, lowering her into the travel crib. "Daddy loves you. Get some rest."

"Nooooo," she drawled, but that was the last of her objections before she flipped to her stomach, tucked her blanket under her arm, and drifted off again.

I hadn't made it two steps out of her room before there was a gentle rap on the front door.

"Bree?" I said, our eyes locking through the glass.

She lifted her hand in an awkward finger wave, and even with how surprised and physically drained I was, I still couldn't stop the smile as it broke across my face.

I hurried to the door and swung it open. "Hey, what are you doing here? Come in, come in."

She walked inside and I leaned out, searching the driveway. "Where are the kids?"

"They're at home. With Evelyn." She slid her eyes around the cabin, the front door feeding into the large living area with a bedroom on either side and the small kitchen tucked into the back corner. "I was waiting until nap time. Is Luna asleep?"

"Yeah, I just got her down. Perfect timing."

"I hope it's okay that I came. I mean… I know things with us are—"

"Good," I finished for her. With one arm over her shoulder, I dragged her in for a hug. The messy bun on the top of her head tickled my nose, but damn it felt good to see her. "Me and you, we're good, Bree. Rob and Jessica's shit is not ours, okay?"

She tilted her head back, and on any other day, it would have been the cue to let her go. She would have smiled, stepped away, and we'd be nothing more than two friends who had shared an embrace. But now, after all the bullshit and not seeing her for far too long, I just didn't want to.

So I didn't.

And neither did she. Instead, she slipped her arms around my waist and peered up at me with tired eyes. "I know, but you wanted space—"

"Not from you. Just from…all the other shit. I needed to work some things out, and I couldn't do it back at the house."

"How's that going for you?"

Fuck me seven ways to Sunday. I had no idea what was happening or why the constant roar in my ears suddenly fell silent, but I'd been at rock bottom long enough to know not to waste time questioning the good or I could miss it altogether. "Better now."

"Oh, God," she groaned, resting her forehead on my pec, hiding her face.

It wasn't exactly what I had been expecting to hear. Although, I didn't know what I should have anticipated, either, and it sent my brain off like a hamster on a wheel, finally showing up to work. All the gears started spinning in tandem. I'd been so happy to see her that I hadn't truly considered why she'd driven all that way.

"Wait, why didn't you bring the kids?"

She sighed. "Eason, we need to talk."

Four simple words hit me like a brick house. Nothing ever good came from someone saying, "We need to talk." It was never followed by, "Let's go out to dinner," or "We won the lottery." *We need to talk* was universal language for *I'm about to stir shit up*, and if history was any indicator, the universe was going to use a damn blender when stirring my life.

Releasing her, I took a step away, suspicion ricocheting inside me. "Why? What's going on?"

Her green eyes sparkled in the mid-day sun streaming through the floor-to-ceiling glass windows overlooking the mountains. "I found something on Rob's phone that I thought you needed to see."

Relief rained down over me. *Thank God.* I'd already seen the phone. Worst case, she was going to tell me they'd been together on my birthday or something equally as disgusting.

"What is it?"

"It's just, they were together a lot longer than you think."

"Okayyy," I drawled. "I kinda assumed that when I saw the first text about them switching from a different number."

Her lips thinned and a stifling sadness filled the air. "Yeah, but it was…*a lot* longer." Taking my hand, she covered it with both of hers. "Let's go sit down, okay?"

If I could build a time machine, I would go back to that moment. I'd laugh and hug her again. Tell her none of it mattered. Rob and Jessica were the past and they should stay there. I'd offer her a beer, insist we go sit on the balcony, and then get lost in the view—and not that of the mountains.

But I didn't do any of that, and I would regret it for the rest of my life.

Losing my patience, I tugged my hand away. "What the hell is going on? Whatever it is, just say it. You're freaking me out."

Chewing on her bottom lip, she stalled. "Eason…"

"Say it," I ordered.

And then she dealt me the most devastating blow I would ever endure. "I think Luna might be Rob's daughter."

CHAPTER THIRTEEN

BREE

"WHAT THE FUCK ARE YOU TALKING ABOUT?" HE thundered, his voice rattling the windows.

That was not how I wanted to tell him. On the four-hour drive, I'd considered every possible way to break that news, but none of them would have been any less crushing. There was no gentle way to take a sledgehammer to Eason's heart. But he deserved the truth.

When I'd first read the texts, I debated with myself about waiting and telling him when he came home. But if he'd hated Rob and couldn't stand to be in the space he'd once lived after finding out about the affair, he might have never wanted to come back after hearing the truth. And I wouldn't have blamed him one bit. The betrayal burned like lava inside me too.

My husband fathering a child with another woman.

That woman being a wolf in disguise, posing as my best friend.

And once again, I had to share that unique and profound misery with one of the best men I'd ever known.

First thing that morning, unsure of what else to do, I'd called Evelyn to watch my kids and gone to him. He deserved to hear it from someone who cared about him, and I mean *truly* cared about him. Not the bullshit façade Rob and Jessica had crammed down our throats.

I reached for him, needing to touch him, needing him to know I was there, hurting right along with him, but he scrambled away.

"That's not possible," he seethed, the muscles on his neck straining.

God, this was going to hurt.

"I don't know when it started with them. I haven't gotten that far in the messages. But the night after Luna was born, Jessica sent him a text message saying you had just gone home to get her a few things and for him to come meet his daughter."

Eason's eyes flashed wide and rabid, but I kept talking, hoping for the Band-Aid effect.

"Rob told her not to say that, that Luna could still be yours. She called him after the text, so I have no idea what else was said." I dug my phone from my back pocket. "And then I found this picture on his personal phone of him smiling, holding Luna at the hospital." I turned the screen to face him. "I'd seen it a dozen times but never really looked at it. There are tons of pictures of us visiting Jessica in the hospital. The same when you guys came to visit us after Madison was born. But look at the clock." My voice cracked and tears I swore I wouldn't show him welled in the corners of my eyes.

This wasn't about me. I was allowed to be angry. I was allowed to be hurt. But my job, first and foremost, was to make sure he was okay. Because, no matter the situation, he would have done the same for me.

"We came and visited the next morning. I remember because we got there around ten after I'd insisted on stopping to get her breakfast from that brunch place we loved so much. *We* were not at the hospital at six twenty-six that night or any other night, but clearly he was. Either Jessica convinced him or Rob must have thought there was enough of a chance Luna was his that he risked going up there."

"Oh, God," he mumbled, the hope draining from his face right along with the color. "Oh, fuck. Oh, fuck, fuck, fuck." Rubbing the center of his chest, he stumbled to one of the wooden chairs surrounding a rustic dinner table and sank down. "She'd sent me home to get her pillow and a bunch of other random shit she'd said she'd forgotten to pack in her hospital bag. It was a whole damn list, including stopping to get Coke. The kind with crushed ice, not the ones we had at home. It took me for-fucking-ever to find it all. And when I got back, Rob was there." Planting his elbows on the table, he buried his face in his hands. "It didn't seem weird at the time. Why didn't I think that was weird?"

"Because you trusted him. Trusted *her*." I dropped into a squat beside him and rested a hand on his back. "They played us both. This isn't on you."

"But it is on me!" He lurched to his feet and sliced his hand through the air, pointing at a closed door. "That is my daughter. That little girl is my entire fucking reason for living, and you're telling me she might not even be mine? It wasn't bad enough that he was fucking my wife, but the son of a bitch took my baby from me too?" Swiping out his arm, he cleared the decorative candles from the center of the table. They fell to the floor with a loud crash, breaking just like the man in front of me.

Ducking under his arm, I hurried in front of him. "Stop. Eason. Come on. Think about it. It doesn't matter."

"How does this not matter? He took everything from me. My whole fucking life is a lie. Please God, Bree, tell me how to make this feel like it doesn't matter."

I stared at him at an utter loss.

I'd been trying to do just that for days, even before I'd found out about Luna, and I still hadn't figured out how to stop letting a ghost stomp on my heart. There was only one person who ever gave me solace. It was probably wrong given the situation, but as his toffee-brown eyes bored into mine, so much pain carved into his handsome face, I would have done anything to take the agony from him.

Including risking it all.

My heart raced as I lifted my shaking hand. "Because he doesn't matter anymore and you still do."

His eyes flashed dark when I curled my fingers around the back of his neck. One single movement made my intentions clear.

"What are you doing?" he rumbled.

"What I should have done weeks ago."

His eyes flared, but he didn't move.

"Eason," I gasped and he was right there, inches away, swallowing my desire as I pleaded for his.

His mouth hovered over mine while he searched my face. "You're all I have left, Bree. And dammit, you were his too."

As he straightened, I fisted a hand in the front of his shirt. "No, I wasn't. You know it as well as I do. I was a fucking puppet in his show, and I'm done wearing the strings."

I pressed up onto my toes, done with so much more than just Rob Winters.

I was done hurting. Done burning at the stake for a man who had never given a damn about me. But most of all, I was done pretending I didn't want Eason on levels that had not one fucking thing to do with our shared tragedies.

As his mouth came down on mine, his lips parted, and our tongues shared their first dance, Eason made it clear he was done too. Slanting his head, he took it deeper, sealing our mouths together, but even better, he sealed everything else out. He tasted like nothing and everything as we desperately warred, seeking the control neither of us was willing to surrender.

Wrapping my arms around his neck, I tried to get impossibly closer. As if we were sharing the same thoughts, he palmed my ass, lifting me off my feet. My legs circled his hips as he carried us forward, my back hitting the wall with a loud thud.

After all the yelling he'd done, the cussing, the candles shattering—all of it—somehow it was my back against the wall that woke her up.

"Daddy!" Luna cried.

His head popped up, both of us panting, but reality slapped Eason the hardest.

"Oh, God," he breathed, squeezing his eyes shut and lowering me back to my feet.

"It's okay. It's okay," I chanted, framing his face with my hands. "Look at me."

He shook his head but dipped to rest our foreheads together.

"It changes nothing—do you hear me? We don't even know for sure if Rob got Jessica pregnant or not. What we do know, no matter what happened, *you* are her father. She loves you, and biology, one way or the other, will never change that." I tapped my finger over his heart. "Luna is yours in the only way that truly matters, okay?"

"Yeah," he replied, but it was neither convincing nor confident.

Luna let out another cry, and like the good father he was, Eason didn't keep her waiting.

"Shh, baby, I'm right here," he cooed, opening the bedroom door. "Did Daddy wake you up?"

She babbled something I couldn't quite make out, but Eason had no trouble.

"No, nothing to be scared of. Come here. We got a visitor while you were sleeping."

I made quick work of straightening my shirt and smoothing down the top of my hair as he carried her out.

"Look, it's Aunt Bree," he told her.

Taking her hand, I brought it to my lips. "Hey, sweetie."

She leaned into Eason's shoulder and glared at me, less than thrilled to have been woken up by the sounds of me mauling her father. Okay, fine, so she didn't know that part, but she was still sleepy and pissed.

Something in my chest had my eyes darting away from her sweet, chubby face because I didn't want to see it. I hadn't been lying to Eason when I'd sworn that it didn't matter whose DNA ran through her veins. But just like with all those pictures on Rob's phone, with fresh eyes and the whole truth, I could see some very compelling details.

Through the years, Jessica and I had been asked countless times if we were sisters. We had different eyes—hers blue and mine green—but they were both light. We had fair skin, but we both tanned in the summer. And while we each straightened our chestnut-brown hair, we shared similar naturally wild waves.

I'd been further along than she had, but we'd been pregnant with the girls at the same time. We used to joke that they would probably come out looking like twins. Jessica was obviously working with slightly more information than I was, but there was no denying Luna and Madison looked alike.

Whether it was because of their mothers' similarities or the fact that they shared a father, I had no idea. However, it was up to Eason if we would ever find out.

"Do you need to get back to the kids?" he asked, snapping my attention back to his.

I cleared my throat, praying he couldn't read my mind. "I can if you want time alone."

"And if I don't?"

I smiled, a whole swarm of butterflies taking flight in my stomach. "Then I'm here for whatever you need."

He dipped his head with gratitude, plastered on a grin that never made it to his eyes, and lifted his daughter into the air above his head. "All right, cranky pants. Short nap means early bedtime, but we have the whole afternoon ahead of us. What are we doing today, ladies?"

CHAPTER FOURTEEN

BREE

T HE DAY WAS SOMBER, BOTH IN MOOD AND IN VIEW. An afternoon fog rolled in, grounding us to the cabin—not that Eason was up for doing much more than sitting on the couch and staring at his daughter.

They colored.

He let her brush his hair.

They even played a lively game of "Luna, where are you?" in which she sat in front of him and he pretended he couldn't see her.

I tried to stay out of their way by tidying up the cabin and eventually preparing soup and grilled cheese for dinner. But every so often, I'd feel Eason's gaze slide my way. I didn't have to look at him for my cheeks to heat or my stomach to flip.

Holy shit. Had I really kissed him? And oh, holy shit one further… Had he really kissed me back?

Honestly, what God-awful timing. He'd just found out that his daughter might not be his. Obviously, that's an appropriate time to put the moves on a man. But it didn't feel wrong, either. Emotions were high, the shards of our broken hearts crunching on the floor beneath our feet, but just as it had always been, even while we'd been shattered and gasping for breath, it was just Eason and me, surviving in the only way we knew how: together.

We ate and I was impressed he actually had an appetite.

I drew Luna a bath, and he sat on the floor next to her, splashing his hand in the water, the most beautiful love I'd ever seen blazing from his eyes.

While he got her ready for bed, I swept already clean floors, wiped down crumbless counters, and reorganized the clutter-free fridge. Unfortunately, I'd had enough practice in being there for Eason in the midst of catastrophic upheaval, but the kiss had me reeling. There were lines and boundaries now that had never been there before. Only a day earlier, a hug had been just a show of support or an offering of comfort.

It also was entirely possible I was reading too much into our kiss. Maybe it was just a moment of weakness, the desperate desire to replace his anguish with pleasure.

Was it different now that I knew how he tasted?

Was a touch more than a touch now that I knew how it felt to have his strong hands gripping my ass?

Had it been a one-time thing?

Should I apologize?

Kiss him again?

Launch myself into his arms?

Grab my keys and…

"You okay?" he asked, suddenly appearing outside Luna's room, quietly pulling the door shut behind him.

"Oh, um…yeah. Sorry, I was zoning out." I put the dish I was redrying back in the cabinet and discarded the towel next to the sink. "How'd it go in there? Is she asleep?"

He blew out a hard exhale and gripped the back of his neck,

his tattooed forearm giving a spectacular show. "She's exhausted, so she fought it for a while, but I think she's finally out."

"That's good."

"Mmm," he hummed, the long top of his blond hair falling into his face when he looked down at his feet.

My stomach knotted as an awkward silence blanketed the room. I hadn't been with anyone other than Rob in almost a decade, so I had no idea what the proper protocol was after you put the moves on your closest friend on what was possibly the hardest day of his life. And besides looking purely mouthwatering standing there, Eason was giving me no clues to work with, either.

Though it might have been the most telling part of all. That awkwardness. The uncomfortable silence. Insecurities. That wasn't us.

Us was something I knew how to do.

After padding barefoot around the counter, I stopped in front of him. "How ya holding up?"

His head tipped back and his weary eyes flashed open. "I'm tired. I need to hit the bed before I pass out standing up."

"Yeah. Of course. I could sleep for a night or twelve too."

He nodded and gave my hip a squeeze before walking past me to the bedroom on the other side of the living area.

Right. Okay, so maybe I was overthinking things for nothing—again. This wasn't eighth grade. Adults could kiss and it not be a big deal. Tomorrow morning, we'd probably laugh about it. I might even make a joke about how absolutely perfect his lips were...

Shit.

But it was a conversation for another day. He was exhausted. That was fine. REM provided a plethora of mental and emotional benefits. I would never deny him that—not even for my own selfish sanity.

I crossed my arms over my chest and glanced around the living room. The couch looked about as comfortable as a pile of rocks, but the cushions pulled off the back, so I hoped I'd get lucky and find a sofa bed.

Eason stopped at the doorway, his chin meeting his shoulder as he looked back at me. "You coming?"

"I'm sorry, what?"

"To bed. You coming?"

I blinked and my stomach dipped, that damn schoolgirl inside me already sprinting his way. The wiser, more rational Bree who was freaking the fuck out stood like a statue staring at him.

What did that even mean? He was expecting me to sleep in the same bed with him? Like actual sleeping? Or was he expressing the more suggestive use of the term *sleeping together?*

I mean, honestly, it didn't change my answer. Though clarification would give me a heads-up on which DEFCON I needed to alert.

"Um, yes?"

With his confusion matching my own, he turned all the way around. "Okay? Then what's the holdup? Did you bring something to sleep in, or do you need a tee?"

I glanced at my bag, which he had insisted on retrieving from the car earlier, and tried to remember what I'd packed. Unsure where the day would take me, I'd thrown a few things into a duffel, though none of them were the proper attire to share a bed with a man for the first time. Especially not with that man being *Eason Maxwell.*

I had pajamas. Flannel pants and a matching top that were almost as attractive as a burlap sack. And that's not even scratching the surface on the sensible underwear and full-coverage bra. *Outstanding. Every man's fantasy.*

I blinked again, smiling through the horror. "A T-shirt would be great."

"You got it." He disappeared into the room, and I took a moment to practice a little breathing exercise I liked to call hyperventilating.

Jesus, what the hell was wrong with me? It was Eason. The last man on Earth I should have been nervous around. But this wasn't one of our nights around the firepit. Or at least it wasn't for me. For all I knew, he was in there thinking this was nothing more than a casual sleepover between two friends.

Damn. The thought of our kiss meaning nothing to him shouldn't have hurt as bad as it did.

This caused more hyperventilating, which in turn caused me to continue standing in the living room and avoiding the inevitable.

"Bree." He stuck his head around the doorjamb. "Hustle up. You got the bathroom first."

Awesome. We were sharing a shower too. "On my way."

We were quiet for the most part as we got ready for bed. His hand found my hip more than once as we slid past each other in the small room, most of the space occupied by a king-sized bed and two rustic end tables. His touch never lingered, leaving me more confused on what "coming to bed" entailed in Eason's mind. But I was never one to go into a situation unprepared.

I spent an obscene amount of time in the bathroom, shaving and plucking, brushing my teeth, and styling my hair into something that I hoped would be attractive without the use of the blow dryer I had not brought. I put on makeup and then took it off, not wanting to look too eager. Seriously, who puts makeup on before bed? Besides, Eason had seen me at my worst, so I wasn't sure my efforts were even worth it. They made me feel better though.

All of my trouble fell to the wayside as I walked out of the bathroom and found him sound asleep on top of the duvet, shirtless in a pair of sweats, lights still on, his phone on his chest, his legs crossed at the ankles.

I was almost as relieved as I was disappointed.

He didn't budge as I covered him with a blanket and stealthily moved his phone to the nightstand. His charging cord was lying there, so I plugged it in and then turned the lamp off.

Light from the moon illuminated the space. However, the face of Eason's cell glowed brighter. I couldn't remember the last time I'd looked at his phone. He let the kids play on it even after I'd warned him not to. He thought it was hilarious that, at not even two years old, Madison and Luna would take ridiculous and usually accidental selfies. Asher got in on the action too and would swipe Eason's phone to make videos of the new moves he'd learned in karate. Eason had told me once that his favorite part of the day was opening his camera roll to see what surprises the kids had left him.

He must have had a million hilarious and heartwarming images he could have used instead, but right then, his home screen was a picture of me sitting on the floor, Luna in my lap, Madison at my side. My mouth was open with laughter as Asher clung to my neck from behind. It had only been a week or so ago, and I remembered the day well. I'd just beaten Ash in a highly competitive game of Memory, and he had declared a dog pile on me for cheating. I had no idea Eason had taken the photo, much less programmed it to his home screen.

I stared at it until the light dimmed and then extinguished.

Overwhelmed by emotion, I brought a hand up to cover my mouth. It was something so simple. But after everything we'd been through, that one picture meant more to me than he could ever have known. I'd spent the last two days pouring over old phone records and pictures, clawing my way down the rabbit hole of a man who had claimed to love me for better or worse but destroyed our family with his every lying, cheating breath. Meanwhile, Eason had spent the last year taking care of a family that wasn't his own—at least not by blood—to the point that he kept a picture of us front and center on his phone—and I had a sneaking suspicion in his heart as well.

How was he so incredible? And how had I not seen it all those years?

Oh, right, because we weren't Rob and Jessica, looking for something new and exciting when we already had it all. What a joke.

I didn't know what the thing between Eason and me was or what it might grow into, but I never wanted to look back and wonder if we were only trying to get back at them for the way they had broken us.

I wanted Eason, despite it all.

That afternoon, while I'd been safe in his arms, his mouth moving over mine, feeling more alive than ever had solidified that for me. But risking him, risking us, for a moment of passion wasn't something I could do in good conscience. Our lives were so intertwined that the slightest misstep could be earth-shattering for everyone—including the kids.

Smiling down at him, I rested my palm on the side of his face. Poor guy was so tired he didn't even stir. "We'll get there," I whispered. "*Together.*"

CHAPTER FIFTEEN

EASON

The house was silent as I roused from a desperately needed deep sleep. For several beats, I had no idea where I was or even what month it was. But as the exhaustion cleared from my brain, everything came flooding back.

The phone.

The affair.

Luna. *God, Luna.*

And as I stretched my arm out to the side, silky skin met my fingertips.

Bree.

A smile pulled at my lips as I glanced over at her. Sound asleep on her side, facing me, her chestnut hair cascading on the pillow around her. It was still dark out, so I couldn't see much, but I didn't need a light to know she was too fucking far away from me. After that kiss, she could have been on top of me and it still wouldn't have been close enough.

Fuck me. *That kiss.*

Bree had always been sexy; that was not something I'd missed just because she was my friend. I'd noticed her ass every time she'd come back from a run in those skintight shorts. There had been too many nights when a chill had caught her by the firepit, her tank top doing nothing to hide the peaks of her nipples. And let's not even get me started on those fucking skirts and heels she wore to work. I hated every man at Prism on a daily basis because they got to stare at her all day. All I got was to see her in the moments before work and, if I was really lucky, as she walked up the stairs to change when she got home.

But it wasn't all about physical desire with Bree. I was drawn to her in ways I'd never experienced before. *With anyone.* She was fierce and confident and poised to the point that she could run the entire world if she wanted. She certainly had a way of keeping me in line. Although it had to be said that I took much pleasure in getting under her gorgeous skin every now and then.

She was thoughtful when no one was watching, and she'd deny everything if she got caught.

Her green eyes were beautiful, but never more so than when she looked at her children. Two of the luckiest kids I'd ever meet.

Naturally nurturing, she took care of everyone and never expected a damn thing in return.

But at the end of the day, I'd never allowed myself to go there with Bree because she hadn't belonged to me. She'd been Rob's, and him being gone hadn't changed that.

But you know what did change it? Rob's being a piece-of-shit bastard who'd crossed every line that had ever been drawn in the sand.

All bets were off.

Guy code or whatever the fuck you wanted to call it. It was done now.

Bree was no longer off-limits, and earlier, when she'd pushed up onto her toes, her lips aimed at my mouth, declaring she had never been his, denying myself a woman I could never have evaporated into nothingness.

Fuck them. Bree was mine. My friend, my family, and if I had my way about it, my everything.

I inched over, hooking her around the waist and dragging her to meet me in the center of the bed.

"Eason?" she murmured, sounding so soft and sultry it made my cock stir. Or maybe it had more to do with finally having her in bed with me.

"Yeah. It's just me." I brought her flush against my front and found her lips for an all too brief kiss. "I didn't mean to fall asleep. I was really hoping to catch a glimpse of you in my shirt." I grinned against her mouth, sliding my hand up her side, the cotton bunching in the dip of her hip. "But I'm thinking the view of you without it might be better."

She sucked in a sharp breath. "Eason, wait. We need to talk."

And there they were again, my four least-favorite words in the English language.

"I'm done talking," I growled.

She caught my hand at her hip and gave my wrist a squeeze. "Okay, but I don't want to be like Rob and Jessica."

My whole body went solid and my chest got tight, feeling more of an impending implosion than a grief-stricken ache. "What the fuck, Bree?" I rolled to my back, but she followed me over, draping her leg over my hips to keep me close.

She pushed up onto an elbow, resting her chin on my chest, and ran a finger back and forth across my collarbone. "Stop. I don't mean it like that."

"Then how about you find a way of saying shit without bringing *them* into this bed with *us*."

"But don't you see? They're already here. Because of the kids, they'll always be here."

I arched an incredulous eyebrow. "You got Ash and Mads hidden over there?"

She lifted her head to look at me. "What?"

"I said do you have Asher and Madison tucked in the covers over there, because I don't have Luna, which means in this bed, right this second, there are no kids. And there sure as shit isn't Rob and fucking Jessica."

She opened her mouth to argue, but I didn't give her time to muddle shit up.

"We are nothing like them. Do you hear me? This thing between us—whatever it is—it does not involve them. I'm not married. Neither are you. We aren't sneaking behind people's backs and destroying their lives. They do not get to be in this bed with us."

She was quiet for a long second. The moon lit one side of her face, but the shadows made her expression unreadable. "I saw the picture on your phone."

"What picture?"

Despite my defensiveness, her voice was even and measured. "The one of me with the kids you have as your home screen."

"Yeah, and?" That picture was worth more to me than gold and the humans in it were priceless.

"And it made me realize how much we have to lose."

I twisted my lips and stared back at her, thoroughly perplexed. "If that's what you took from that photo, then we're in bigger trouble than I thought." Slapping my hand out, I patted around the nightstand until I found my phone. With a tap on the screen, the light flashed on, Bree's beautiful smile shining front and center. "I found this picture right after I got here. I'd had one of Jessica and Luna on there since the day I got this phone, but I couldn't stomach looking at her after reading her texts with Rob. I was searching for the one of Luna in the pool a few weeks back, but this one stopped me dead in my tracks. We've been through hell the last year. And that's not including the dumpster fire I found out about today. There were so many nights when everything hurt and I wasn't sure I'd ever be able to breathe again. But there you were. With me every step of the way." I tapped the screen again when it started to dim. "This picture, Bree. It's not what we have to lose. It's what I've already gained."

"Oh, Eason," she whispered, her hand coming up to rest on the side of my face.

I turned into it, kissing her palm before twining our fingers and bringing it back down to my chest.

"Look, I know this is going to complicate the hell out of things. But being with you is the only thing that feels right in my life. I'm gonna be real honest: I'm mad at them. I'm hurt. I'm embarrassed. And I can't even begin to imagine the agony that's going to follow over the next few weeks as we sort this shit out with Luna. But there are two things I know for sure: I want you, Bree, and I'm not waiting one fucking second longer to make my move."

In one swift motion, I rolled over and tucked her beneath me. Smoothing the wisps of hair out of her face, I added, "I can't wait any longer to kiss you from head to toe, to make you feel good and know for sure it was because of me."

Her breath caught as I stroked her lip with the pad of my thumb, and her thick lashes fluttered.

"I need to hear you say it first though." I pressed my lips to her temple, her cheekbone, her jaw.

"Eason, just tell me what you want to hear." She paused and the sexiest hum vibrated through her to my mouth. "I'll say anything."

"That's not how this works, Sug."

Her brow pinched, and momentarily, her focus returned and her beautiful, green eyes searched mine. "Excuse me. Sug?"

It had been spontaneous, but now, I was convinced that the name fit her even more. "Short for Sugar."

A life-changing bellow of laughter erupted from deep in her chest. "That's rich, Eason. Why Sugar? You'll never find a person on Earth who'd describe me as sweet."

"Good," I easily replied. "Then you can save all that sweet for me."

Her face relaxed and her chin tipped higher as she reached out to me. Slipping my hand behind her head, I paired her mouth with mine.

If I'd thought working her up and pushing her buttons to get a rise out of her around the house had been fun, I'd been sorely undershooting the enjoyment I could have with her in other ways. Ways that had her quickly sitting up and ripping the borrowed tee off, revealing no bra and modest cotton panties.

When she caught me appraising her as I tugged and kicked my sweats off, she glanced down at her underwear and apologized. "I'm sorry. I didn't think that... I'll just take them—"

I swatted her hand away. "Don't you dare." And because I couldn't resist, I cupped one of her breasts and captured the other with my mouth. "Let me work for it," I said against her soft skin. "Besides, no matter how badly I want to just..." I couldn't find the words and hissed through my teeth as she arched into my touch. "God, I want to work your gorgeous body over so fucking hard— soon." I kissed the space between her breasts, across her collarbone, and up her neck to her ear before finally resting my forehead against hers. "But I've waited too long not to take my time."

Chin to chin. Eye to eye. She said the words I'd wanted to

hear at the beginning of all this. The words I'd needed to hear straight from her mouth. Not only because I respected her, which I wholeheartedly did. But I desperately needed to know what I was feeling was mutual.

"Eason, I want you. Please."

The magic words.

Boy, had I talked a good game about going slow. But in practice, it was monumentally more challenging.

I kissed and sucked my way up and down her body. My cock ached to find its way inside her.

But not yet.

Not until I had tasted every fucking inch.

After unwrapping her like a candy and sampling the sweetness between her legs, her hands balling the sheets beside my shoulders, I nearly lost my mind.

Just before I tipped the scales out of my favor, she annihilated them altogether by rolling on top of me. "In my dreams, you said I wasn't ready. But I'm ready, Eason. I'm so damn ready for you."

She'd had dreams.

About me.

Fucking fuck, I could have come from that thought alone. "I don't… have a condom or anything."

"I trust you. I've always trusted you. We're good. I'm on birth control."

I wrapped my arms around her as she sank down on my cock with a sigh against my ear. For a beat, she remained completely still and then looked directly into my soul.

"There you are," she said breathlessly.

It had been a long time, but it had never—ever—felt like that.

"I'm right here," I replied, my head spinning. An intoxicating cocktail of pleasure and desire and need and purpose and sensation and belonging all at once hit my bloodstream. Lacing my hand through her dark hair, I gripped a handful and steered her lips to mine on a whispered, "You're perfect. You know that? So fucking perfect."

Slowly, Bree rose and fell. Taking me deeper with every swell and grind of her hips. She nipped at my neck and held on to me so tight that I suspected she'd left marks in places. Evidence I'd wear like a badge of honor.

And when she'd worked us both into a fevered knot of moans and flesh, panting against one another, I failed to resist the urge to take her.

Not that I hadn't been right there with her the whole time.

It was that I needed to be the one to give it to her.

With an arm around her waist, I rose onto my knees and lowered her back to the bed underneath me, never breaking our connection. With her legs spread wide, I buried myself inside her and then shut out the world.

"Yes," she praised. "*Yes.*"

Needing to feel her climax around me, I slipped my thumb between us and gently applied pressure to her swollen clit. The moment her body rolled into it, guiding me to what she wanted, I kept a rhythm with her until her back arched, her thighs trembled at my sides, and the words, "God, Eason. I'm coming," filled my ears.

A fuse ignited, my spine became rigid, and as I spent myself inside her, I dove into the ocean of Bree, praying I'd never return.

We were left panting in a tangled mess of sated sweat.

There'd been a damn good chance that things after what had just happened would be different. For the better or the worse, I wasn't sure. But catching my breath, naked, and sharing a now wrinkled sheet with the woman beside me, I had a sense that no matter what was to come, there were no two people on this great big Earth who could handle it more than we could.

We were battletested. We'd experienced a baptism by fire—quite literally. To be honest, there was no one I trusted more or had more confidence in than Bree. Though I was terrified she couldn't say the same.

Settling on my side, I stretched my arm out under the pillow, bringing us nose to nose again. But if there were words left in the English language, my brain couldn't find them.

"What are you thinking about?" she asked, her usually satiny voice now gravelly and hoarse.

How nothing in my life had ever felt so right.

I kept that to myself and went for the humor that came so easily when I was with her. "Those naughty cotton panties. You have found my weakness."

With a playful smack, she caught me right across the chest.

"Ow," I mumbled, laughing at her murderous glare.

"Give a girl a break, it's not like I planned to come up here and seduce you."

"Oh, but you did. Tell me more about these dreams you had about me. Was I always naked? Or just in the really good ones?"

Under the sheet, she kicked at my leg. "Eason!"

This was the Bree I was falling for. The fighter. The fierce and scrappy hothead. A gorgeous pain in my ass.

"What? It's a valid question."

Her weak attempted assault on me halted. "The only valid question is where we go from here."

Sliding my hand down to her ass, I pulled her against my front. "What do you want me to say? I think it's a little late for 'Bree, will you go out with me?'"

Her brow shot up.

I was tiptoeing out onto the thinner ice and I knew it. And I was so fucking happy I just didn't care. "Okay, okay," I said. "At home, we just act natural. It's not like I'd bend you over in front of the kids at the dinner table."

"Oh my God. I know. But you don't think we should say anything?"

I pulled her closer and stroked her arm. "I don't. At least not for right now. Neither of us are going anywhere. There's no rush to define anything or confuse them. They've seen us together. Honestly, they're the happiest when it's all five of us anyway." I pressed a kiss to the top of her head. "Besides, we all know about your policy with sugar in the house."

She pinched my nipple. "I'm serious here," she said, her voice not just becoming serious, but revealing her vulnerability. "What if we don't, you know...work?"

"All right. Relax. It's good. We're good. We're two grown adults who have been through far worse than any breakup could throw at us. I really want to explore this thing between us. So far, we've made a stellar team, and clearly getting naked together was not an exception. But on the off chance we don't work, nothing changes. I'll write a tragic breakup song about you, make a million dollars, and you'll have to listen to it on the radio every day for the rest of your life. But besides that, we'll be fine."

Her soft laughter made my heart ricochet off my ribs, but it was her words that made it feel like they were breaking. "I'm scared, Eason. I can't lose you."

"Hey," I soothed, drawing her into a hug. "I'm not going anywhere."

She tucked her face into my neck and clung to my back, her nails biting my back in desperation. "For the first time in a long time, I'm happy. With you, I'm happy."

"Then, babe, you have nothing to worry about. I promise I'll always be honest with you, and if this isn't working out for me, I'll let you know. With you, *I'm* happy too. The rest will fall into place, okay?"

She didn't voice her agreement. She didn't actually speak again at all. But for the rest of the night, she never let go. That was good enough for me.

In what should have been the worst of days, with the road ahead bound to be rockier than ever, I couldn't help but feel like with this woman by my side, together, we'd get through it all.

CHAPTER SIXTEEN

BREE

ALMOST EVERYTHING HAD CHANGED IN THE LAST twenty-four hours. I still had no idea where Eason's head was about Luna. When it came to dealing with personal disasters, I had two speeds: obsession or turbo obsession. There wasn't a lot in between.

Eason, however, took a much slower path when processing his emotions. He'd get quiet, sit on it for a few days, and work out all the different scenarios in his head, and only when he'd looked at it from every possible angle would he come to a conclusion.

Yes, I was curious if he'd consider a DNA test to confirm or disprove what we both feared, but it wasn't my place to even suggest such a thing. When Eason was ready to talk about it, he knew where to find me. And after last night, that somewhere would not be on the other end of the couch around the firepit.

He kissed me good morning, slow and reverent.

He stroked my thigh under the breakfast table where Luna couldn't see.

And when I told him I needed to get home to Asher and Madison, Eason—being even more incredible than I already knew him to be—gave me a hug and told me to give him a few minutes to pack his stuff because he was coming too.

Unfortunately, some things were still the same, mainly the house we had to go home to and the memories that would forever live inside it. As much as I would have loved to move and get a fresh start somewhere new, it was important for me to maintain stability for the kids. Rob was still their dad regardless of how he'd broken me. It was my job to keep his memory alive for them, and if it meant pictures hanging on the wall in the house he'd called a home, then that was a sacrifice I would have to make.

Given the situation, it sucked knowing Eason had to make that sacrifice too.

However, not all change was bad.

While he packed up Luna's stuff and prepared the cabin for us to leave, I made a phone call to Jillian. As I explained our situation, I was met with outrage on what Rob and Jessica had done, curses banishing them to hell, and, finally, pleas for all the details on what Eason was really like in bed. But by the end, she promised she would take care of a few things for me at home. With it only being a four-hour trip back, I didn't have high expectations for how much she could accomplish.

Though, as we pulled up to find two furniture delivery trucks and three others marked Hud Construction filling the brick horseshoe driveway, I couldn't help but laugh. Clearly, Jillian's skillset was far greater than answering the phones and providing vibrator coupon codes.

Damn, that woman needed a raise.

Smirking, I parked on the street. Eason pulled up behind me to do the same.

"What's all this?" he asked, folding out of his black Tahoe.

"I'm not entirely sure."

Confusion crinkled his forehead. "Does that mean you know what's going on and were expecting one truck instead of six or that you have no clue and I should probably stretch out in preparation for hand-to-hand combat with whoever the hell is robbing us right now?"

I chuffed and walked over to him, fighting the urge to kiss his handsome face off. "Chill out, Chuck Norris. I asked Jillian to do me a favor, and clearly she was up for the challenge."

"What kind of favor?"

"You'll see."

He narrowed his eyes but didn't delay in getting Luna out of her car seat. Together, the three of us meandered up to the house.

"No," Jillian said as she walked out the front door, jogging down the steps, a clipboard held against her chest. "You two aren't supposed to be back yet. What happened to bathroom breaks or quickies in the back seat?"

"Excuse me?" Eason's eyes flashed wide.

I bit my bottom lip. "Yeah, so I may have told Jillian about… um, *us*. She's kinda my only friend."

"Only and best," Jillian corrected, her gray bangs bouncing as she gave a proud nod.

"Right," Eason clipped, but with the way the side of his mouth tipped up, he wasn't fooling anyone. He liked the idea of there being an us and that I was already comfortable with it enough to spread the word.

Jillian bent down and offered Luna a high five. "Well, hello there, beautiful. Auntie Jillie Bean has quite the surprise for you."

Leaning into her father, Luna hid her face against his leg and tried to disappear. Eason had heard her loud and clear though.

"You have a surprise? For Luna?"

Jillian's face damn near glowed. "Yes. And several for you too, handsome." She winked and rose to her full height, turning her attention on me. "Soooo, I may have gone a teensy, tiny bit overboard."

I pointedly glanced around at the trucks. "Ya think?"

She lifted her chin. "I don't feel bad about it, but if you don't like it, you can always…suck it up and be grateful. I had to strike a deal with the devil himself to get this done in the time frame you gave me." She swept her hair away from her face. "I've always known that I looked like an angel, but I never realized until today that I am also a miracle worker." Turning on a toe, she called over her shoulder. "Come on, you two, the kiddos are in the pool, so let's start out there."

I too might have gone a teensy, tiny bit overboard when I'd told Jillian there was no budget for this particular project. Lesson learned. Acknowledging that to Eason could wait until he wasn't boring holes in the side of my face with a questioning glare.

"You heard her. Come on," I said, power walking around to the back of the house.

I hadn't gotten one step through the fence surrounding the pool before Asher was out of the water, sprinting my way.

"Mom!" he yelled, colliding with my legs. He was getting so big, in both age and size, that it wouldn't be long until I couldn't hold him at all.

Water be damned, I'd take the chances while I still had them. Lifting him up, I planted him on my hip. "Hey, buddy."

Madison was in the pool in a pair of floaties, giggling and kicking her heart out as Evelyn guided her to the side. "Yook! Mommy, yook! I do it. I sweemin'!"

"I see you," I laughed. "Good job, pretty girl. Did you guys have fun with Evelyn while I was gone?"

"Totally!" Asher declared, but his smile grew exponentially as his gaze flicked over my shoulder. "Eason, Eason, guess what?

We got you a new bed! And Luna too! And a new couch and table things. You too, Mom! We even got to paint the walls." His shoulders fell. "Evelyn said there were fumes, so we had to leave and let the *professionals* do it. I didn't even know football players knew how to paint, but I guess maybe if they don't have a game or something."

"Uhhhhh," Eason drawled. "You did what?"

Asher continued, "We got new stuff! I didn't get a new bed, but Jillian got me a cool tent for my room. And Madison and Luna got princess castles. It's so cool! You gotta see it."

When I'd devised that plan and called Jillian to implement it, I seriously thought it was the best idea I'd ever had. The anxious energy rolling off Eason had me second-guessing a few things. Like, say, all of them.

"Bree, can I get a word? In private?" he asked.

"Yeah, sure. Just let me say hey to Madison first."

I took my time hugging my sopping-wet daughter. She had a ton to say—about two-thirds of which I understood. In that time, I noticed Jillian in heaven, sidled up next to Eason, talking his ear off too. He probably understood less than two-thirds of what she said because his stoic gaze was locked on me.

When Luna had bored of her father, she sprinted over for a reunion with my kids, stealing their attention and my ability to stall any longer.

"We'll be right back," Eason told Evelyn as she corralled the kids around the firepit for a snack. Using my elbow to pull me out of the pool area, he strategically closed the gate in time to shut Jillian inside.

"Oh. Okay, then. I'll be right here when you're ready for a tour!" she called after us.

Silently, he guided me all the way back around to the front of

ALY MARTINEZ

the house, and had it not been for a *wet paint* sign hanging on the front door, he probably would have dragged me inside too.

"Would you stop," I finally said, batting his hand away.

He did not stop. Like not at all. Actually, after a quick glance around to see if anyone was watching us, he grabbed my hips and dragged me against his chest. His palm glided up between my shoulders and higher, to my nape. And then, with a gentle tug, he forced my head back. Not a heartbeat later, his hot, predatory mouth came down on mine.

The surprise rocked me back a step, but I fisted the sides of his shirt for balance. His tongue swept mine as he explored my mouth in a scorching kiss. In a way, I was just another instrument Eason instinctively knew how to play and would never be tired of it.

When air became necessary and not a second sooner, he moved his attention to my neck. "A new bed?"

"Um," I breathed, tilting my head to allow him more room to roam. "About that."

"And for Luna too?"

I moaned as his teeth raked my sensitive flesh, just on the right side of pain. "I mentioned upgrading the girls from their cribs. Though the princess castles are news to me."

"Jesus, Bree. Why did you do all this?"

"I didn't want you to come home to those memories."

He stopped and lifted his head to catch my eye. "I came home with *you*. I could have changed the sheets and been fine. You didn't need to do this."

Swaying into him, I wrapped my arms around his waist. "I don't want to grow this thing between us in their shadows. We can't move, at least not right now, but we deserve a space that isn't tainted by them."

"Oh, you sweet woman," he whispered, bringing his hands up

154

to frame my face. He kissed me deep and lingering before allowing me to continue.

"I don't know when or where they were together in the past, but I think we can both assume, given the circumstances, that they didn't have much tact or respect for anyone—especially not us. You told me at the cabin that, inside that bed, they didn't matter. Well, I want it to be true every night. We deserve more than to spend one more night in their bed of lies."

Tender emotion flooded his eyes as they roved over my face. His fingers curled into the back of my hair, his thumb feathering my cheekbone. "What you and me have is brighter than any shadow they could ever cast, but I'm not gonna lie. I will sleep a hell of a lot easier knowing *you* aren't in the bed you shared with *him*."

"I can sleep easier knowing that too."

His lips pulled into a playful smirk. "You know I'm paying you back for all this shit, right?"

"Okay, but we better go check it out and make sure you like it first."

His lips thinned and his brows drew together. "I gotta be honest here. I'm slightly afraid of Jillian."

I patted his chest. "Good. You should be. Insider information: She has a bum knee, so if you're ever trapped in a room alone with her, run."

Chuckling, he released me. "Come on. Let's get this over with. Asher owes me a cannonball competition."

I smiled huge. God, I loved that he loved my kids. "He's going to beat you again, ya know?"

"Don't be so sure. I have it on good authority the judge has warmed to me since the last time." He winked and lifted my hand to his mouth for a kiss.

Eason's place looked amazing. Well, technically, it still looked like a madhouse covered in drop cloths and filled with half a dozen workers, but I could see Jillian's vision as she gave us the penny tour. My beach décor had been replaced with a pallet of dark blues and the occasional pop of red. He had a new leather sectional, a café table for two tucked into the small kitchen, and a giant platform king-sized bed covered in rich navy Prism bedding in the bedroom. A team of men in Hud Construction polo shirts were touching up the paint, while others drilled hooks into the wall that would later hold Eason's guitars.

Based on the massive grin on Eason's face—and the hug he gave Jillian as we exited to allow the men space to finish up—he adored every single bit of it.

And he wasn't alone in that. My bedroom had been transformed into a sanctuary. The new regal high-backed bed with matching ornate dressers and end tables was a stark comparison to the modern aesthetic Rob and I had chosen together. I adored how different it made the room feel, in both ambiance and aura. In contrast to the dark furniture, a kaleidoscope of pinks and teals were woven together so skillfully that I feared Jillian's talents were being wasted behind a desk at Prism. She'd joked about being my best friend, but there was no way anyone else could have put together such a perfect room for me.

My favorite part though? Eason's pure satisfaction as he stood in the doorway, his shoulder propped against the doorjamb, sexy as all sin without the enormity of Rob's ghost weighing him down.

The kids dragged us around the rest of the house, showing us what else Jillian had done. Like moving all of Rob's pictures, including a few from our wedding, to the long hallway leading to the kids' bedrooms. Every night, they got to see him and the façade of a family we'd once had. But I no longer had to stare back at him while relaxing on the couch or preparing dinner in the kitchen.

Eason became overwhelmed with emotion when she told him she'd planned to do a similar setup in Luna's room with pictures of Jessica as soon as the lavender paint on the walls dried. This earned her another hug from my guy. And it earned my guy a breathy moan from my girl. I laughed at both.

Nothing had been solved. There wasn't enough furniture or paint in the world to cure the pain Rob and Jessica had carved into our souls. But there was something to be said about having space to breathe. Something promising in the fresh start of it all. Something that simply moving Rob's things out hadn't done.

We were making it ours, and despite how scary it was to let go and have faith again, with Eason and our small family happy, I was happy too.

And for the rest of the day, Eason and I breathed real easy while he lost three cannonball contests in a row.

CHAPTER SEVENTEEN

EASON

SINCE THE DAY I'D MOVED IN WITH BREE, I HAD MADE an entire hobby out of sneaking junk food behind the kids' backs. I was a damn black belt at deceptive cuisine. Cookies snuck in a bag of baby carrots, chocolate wrapped in the plastic of a protein bar. Hell, I'd once eaten an entire burger and fries disguised as a salad while sitting directly across from them.

Sleight of hand, distraction, and redirection were my weapons of choice.

However, for two weeks, I hadn't been able to sneak more than thirty minutes alone with Madison and Asher's mother. It wasn't completely their fault. My real beef was with a rare summer bout of Influenza type A.

Luna might have technically lived in a different house, but she spent every waking hour with Asher and Madison. So, when Madison came down with a fever the same night we got back from the cabin, the three of them went down like a set of dominos. But worst of all was that, by the end of the week, Bree and I went down even harder.

We still tried to meet by the firepit at first, but body aches and a hacking cough didn't make for good company. As we started to mend, Bree worked from home while I juggled the kids and called in favors from every musician I knew in Atlanta to fill in for me so I didn't have to outright cancel more shows. Booking managers tended to get rather testy when you left them hanging three weekends in a row.

By the time Friday, my last night off for the foreseeable future, rolled around, I was back to feeling like myself and desperate for some alone time with Bree.

"Eason?" she called, walking down the stairs at exactly five o'clock.

"In here!" I shouted from the kitchen. Rising from the barstool, I smoothed down my white V-neck and buttoned my blazer. I wasn't a suit guy if I could possibly avoid it, so I'd paired them with dark jeans and a pair of dress boots so she'd at least recognize me.

She was holding her empty coffee mug from that morning when she rounded the corner. Hair straightened, makeup flawless, cream silk blouse hanging over a pair of pajama pants. Work-from-home chic if I'd ever seen it.

She froze the minute she saw me, a slow grin brightening her face. "Wow, you look good."

"You too, Sug. Well, at least from the waist up."

"Sweet lord, please stop calling me that." She laughed. "Why are you all dressed up? Do you have a show tonight?" She frowned and damn if it didn't make my chest get tight.

"No. I have a date."

"Oh, you do?" Understanding dawned on her as she curiously scanned the room. "Where are the kids?"

"Playing with Evelyn in Luna's room."

Her eyebrows shot up. "Evelyn's here?"

"Please refer back to the aforementioned part about me having a date."

She bit her bottom lip and shuffled her slippers over to me. After setting her mug on the bar, she looped an arm around my neck. "Who's the lucky lady? Anyone I might know?"

Encircling her hips, I drew her in closer. "Oh, I don't know. Sexy brunette, tight little body, sneezes like a tornado siren."

"Hey!" she objected. "The flu does not take it easy in the name of beauty. Need I remind you that I caught you with a tissue hanging out of your nostril?"

"I have no idea what you're talking about."

She scoffed. "Well, unfortunately, I do. My therapy bill has increased substantially since then."

It was my turn to laugh. The therapy was no joke. We'd both mutually agreed to go back as soon as we were feeling better. Our relationship had been on a bit of a pause after getting sick, but we'd still swapped nightly texts, and I'd even managed to steal a chaste kiss or two. But the lingering anguish of Jessica and Rob's betrayal threatened us at every turn.

I was still trying to organize my emotions about Luna's possible paternity.

Some days, I told myself I didn't want to know. She was my daughter, end of story.

Other days, I'd catch a glimpse of Rob in her features and it would damn near annihilate me.

And depending on which day you caught me on, I needed to know the truth more than my next breath or I never needed to know the truth even with my final breath.

So, yeah, I clearly had shit to work through.

And the heartache and confusion weren't limited to me. Bree had to deal with the fact that the little girl she loved and considered her second daughter was now potentially her husband's love child with her best friend. Those were not emotions that would just disappear because we'd decided to explore the sparks between us. It actually terrified me that, if not dealt with properly, they had the power to extinguish them altogether.

However, those were problems for Monday when our respective doctors opened their offices again.

It was Friday, and I had a long-overdue date with a gorgeous woman I couldn't stop thinking about.

I tickled her side. "All right, smartass. Let's get back to that date."

"You have my attention."

From my back pocket, I retrieved three envelopes I'd spent all day preparing. Fanning them out like poker cards, I brought them up between us. "Would you do me the honor of spending your evening doing whatever the hell you would like as long as it's with me?"

She twisted her lips. "That is quite the proposition. Is there cash in those envelopes? Now is probably the time to break the news that I'm not a hooker."

She squirmed against me as I tickled her again.

"I know that you tend to..." I sucked in through my teeth. "How should I put this... *Make* the plans, not necessarily go with the flow."

She slanted her head in a bored glare. "Just say it. You think I'm boring and allergic to spontaneity."

"No. I did *not* say that at all. You are a strong, independent, sexy woman who knows what she likes, and somehow that *what* is me, so I am not in any way, shape, or form going to complain about it. But knowing you aren't fond of surprises and wanting to make you happy the way I do, I have come tonight bearing options."

Her smile returned. "What kind of options?"

I kissed the tip of her nose. "I'm so glad you asked. In these three envelopes"—I waved them out to the side like a magic fan—"are three different variations of our first date. Each one includes every detail of our evening from transportation, restaurant, wine, after-dinner activity, right down to the flowers I may or may not be bringing you when I pick you up."

Her smile didn't just spread, it lit her entire face. "You planned *three* dates?"

"Yep. We have Sophisticated and Classy, Fun and Adventurous, and just in case you still aren't in the mood to go out, we have Netflix and Chill. Now, milady, I will turn these over to you and allow you a few minutes to peruse each one while I eagerly await your decision." Quite proud of myself, I offered her my handiwork with a dramatic Oscar-worthy bow.

Only she didn't take them from my hand. She just stood there. For an absurdly long time.

Finally, I glanced up to see what was causing the delay only to find the most beautiful adoration staring back at me.

"I don't need to see those," she said quietly. "You could take me anywhere in the world right now and I'd go just as long as you were there too."

Fuck, why did that feel so good? I'd spent all day planning because I'd wanted the night to be perfect—for her.

And in one sentence, she'd made it perfect—for me.

I narrowed my eyes. "Anywhere? You may have just bitten off more than you can chew. There are filthy bat-infested caves I would love to explore somewhere in the world."

Pressing up onto her toes, she wrapped her arms around my neck. "I trust you. You pick. I want the true Eason Maxwell experience tonight, surprises and all."

I brushed my nose with hers, denying her the kiss she was so clearly asking to receive. "You sure?"

"I'm positive," she replied breathily.

"Okay, then." I slid my hand down her back, slipping it into her pajama bottoms to grab her ass. "You might want to put on a pair of jeans, Bree. It's not nearly as much fun for me to take them off at the end of the night if you aren't wearing any to begin with." And with that, I removed my hand, tucked the envelopes into my back pocket, and turned on a toe, headed for the back door, calling over my shoulder. "Pick you up in thirty."

∽

All my hard work of putting together three dates worthy of Bree was wasted. Though it easily became the best date of my entire life. That had less to do with what we actually did and more to do with the company.

Using a combination of all three of the flowers from my planned dates, I showed up at the front door with a giant bouquet of lilies, daisies, and silk panties in the shape of rosebuds. What? After two weeks of chaste kisses, I had big plans on the off chance she'd picked the Netflix and Chill envelope.

Standing there in jeans that could stop traffic and a bold red off-the-shoulder number, she laughed—as I'd hoped. And then, after putting them in water and saying goodnight to the kids, I guided her out to an UberBlack. If she wanted the true Eason Maxwell experience the way she'd claimed, it did not include the private driver I had on standby or the Harley I'd borrowed from a buddy and tucked away in the garage. Honestly, the Eason Maxwell experience didn't even include the UberBlack, but it was a first date, so I sprang for the upgrade.

Grinning like two fools, we held hands all the way to a small sushi joint downtown. Yelp called it "trendy and authentic," and given how we were like eighty-five-year-olds eating before the sun had gone down, we were able to slip in before the dinner rush.

The reviews of *Sushi Run* had not been wrong. It was an incredible restaurant, and while I had never personally been to Japan, the raw squirming octopus tentacles on the sushi conveyor belt felt pretty damn authentic. I thought Bree was going to crawl under the bar each time they passed us. I laughed harder at that dinner, shielding her eyes every three minutes, than I had in years.

And the night was just getting started.

We hit a martini bar Bree seemed to love, and two cocktails later, we meandered to a brewery down the street. We talked. We laughed. We kissed anytime we wanted. My hand never left her thigh, and if I wasn't touching her, she was touching me.

Like two thirty-something parents who hadn't been out of the house for anything other than work in roughly a million years, we were total lightweights. By the time nine p.m. rolled around, we were already tipsy and utterly love drunk. Which was exactly how we ended up at a karaoke bar—and not a good one at that.

It was an interesting crowd. The long, wooden bar filled with middle-aged men sipping on Scotch and swapping literal and figurative war stories were a sharp contrast to the tables surrounding a makeshift stage filled with college kids playing "retro" board games like Connect Four and Battleship.

In her red-bottom heels, Bree marched right over to an empty high-top and claimed it while I grabbed drinks from the bar. Then, together, we endured the most horrific karaoke MC I'd ever been unfortunate enough to witness. The poor guy couldn't get a singer on stage to save his life. He sang *horribly*. Seriously, he was like a-long-tailed-cat-in-a-room-of-rocking-chairs bad. The dude played—and I use that term loosely—a keyboard that I swear had to be missing a few keys. His jokes were even more horrible than his voice. To the point that I just felt bad for the guy. So I did what any professional musician would do in that situation...

"All right, all right. We finally have our first performer of the evening," MC Kerry O'Key announced, damn near giddy to finally be let off the hook. "Ladies and gentlemen, put your hands together and give it up for Bree Winters!"

I had never in my life been leveled with a glare harder or faster. And never in my life had I enjoyed it more.

"Right here!" I called out, waving my hand in the air.

"Eason," she hissed. "Are you crazy? I'm not singing."

"Come on. You wanted the Eason Maxwell experience. Well, this is it. Show me your chops."

"I have no chops. I can't even carry a tune enough to sing 'Happy Birthday' to the kids. That is literally the only reason I keep you around."

I laughed at her pink cheeks. "You don't have to be good. It's just supposed to be fun."

"What gave you the idea that I'm fun?"

"You're the best kind of fun. Because you're *my* kind of fun." I leaned in for a kiss, smiling against her mouth. "Come on. We'll do it together."

She let out a sigh and begrudgingly followed after me as I towed her to the stage. After flipping through the world's oldest song book, nothing newer than 2005, I finally just asked if I could use the keyboard. MC Kerry probably would have let me borrow his soul as long as it meant he got a break.

Luckily, I'd been wrong and all the keys were intact, so I played a soft intro to nothing as I asked Bree, "So, what do you have in mind, beautiful?"

With trembling hands, she stood beside me, shifting her

weight from side to side, nervous as all hell. "What's the shortest song you know?"

Chuckling, I played all seven notes of "Shave and a Haircut" and peered up at her, ready for more heat from that gorgeous glower. She did not disappoint, but while I was thoroughly enjoying riling up my best friend, I remembered I was supposed to be impressing my date.

Lifting my arm in the air, I continued to play with my other hand and tipped my chin to my lap. "Just have a seat right here and hold the mic for me." I almost felt guilty at her relief when she sank down across my thighs.

I did not, however, feel guilty when her cheeks turned red as I belted the opening note of Marvin Gaye's "Let's Get It On."

I think people stopped talking when I started singing. They might have even looked up from their games or swiveled on their stools to get a better view. But on that stage, it was just the two of us.

I struggled to reach all the keys with her sitting sideways across my lap. But I didn't care if it sounded like a third-grade piano recital. There was no fucking way I was going to let her leave. After the final note, I wasn't quite done, so I played straight into Boyz II Men's "I'll Make Love to You" before shifting gears to a little Color Me Badd's, "I Wanna Sex You Up."

I nearly swallowed my tongue when Bree loosened up enough to get in on the action, singing the background ooo's. And with her coming out of her shell, I couldn't stop there. By the time I reached the first chorus of "Sex on Fire," Bree was right there with me, laughing and dominating the mic.

There was a definite theme for my impromptu set that night, and as Bree stared back at me, a smile on her face and a fire in her eyes, I was hoping that energy would follow us home.

"Let's get out of here," I all but shouted into her ear as the final note faded into the chaos of the bar erupting into loud cheers.

She nodded enthusiastically. "You close our tab and I'll order the Uber."

"Deal."

It seemed Bree and I were just the grease O'Key needed to get the ball rolling. As I stood at the bar waiting to get my credit card back from the bartender, a woman took over the stage singing a classic Whitney Houston tune.

An older, round bellied man sidled up beside me, saying something I couldn't quite make out.

I cupped my hand to my ear. "Come again?"

He leaned in closer. "I said: What's your name? You were great up there."

"Ah, Eason Maxwell." I grinned. "And thanks. Appreciate it."

"You ever considered making music a career?"

I barked a loud laugh. "Once or twice." Almost instinctually, I found Bree as she exited the hallway from the bathroom, her sexy hips swaying as she weaved through the maze of tables.

As it did so often, my body began to hum the closer she got. After everything we'd been through, everything we were *still* going through, how was it possible to be that damn happy? And most importantly, how the hell did I hold on to it? I didn't have the best track record with the universe. But then again, it was Bree I'd carried out of the fire that night. Even knowing what I knew now, I still harbored an enormous amount of guilt for not being able to save Jessica and Rob. But one look at Bree and I felt like maybe someone had been looking out for me after all.

The older man interrupted my thoughts. "Listen, a friend of mine works at a studio. I'd love to get you two in contact."

"Oh yeah?" I said, regrettably tearing my eyes off Bree.

Everybody had a friend, aunt, uncle, or cousin six times removed in the music industry. The majority of them were small-timers who had studios in their guest room or dabbled in sound production or lighting. But I was in no position to turn down an opportunity.

The bartender slid my credit card in front of me and I signed the slip before retrieving my wallet. Trading my Visa for a business card, I handed it to the gentleman. "My agent's info is on the back. Good to meet you. Now, if you'll excuse me, my—" I stopped and slanted my head. Girlfriend? Lady? Woman? What the hell did I call her? She was so fucking much more than all of that, but I didn't feel like having a three-month-long conversation with the man to make him understand. "*Date* is waiting for me."

He lifted the card between his fingers. "Really fine job tonight."

I tipped my head and slid past him, locating Bree beside the front door.

"What was that all about?" she asked.

I gave the door a hard shove and then threw my arm around her shoulders as we walked out onto the sidewalk and into the steamy Georgian air. "Just weeding through all the offers to sign the incredible Bree Winters to a recording contract. Of course, I told him I'd have to discuss it with you, but I warned that if they couldn't come up to a billion-dollar advance, it wasn't even worth our time."

She elbowed me in the side. "*Hilarious.*"

I dipped low and found her mouth for an all-too-brief kiss. "You were pretty incredible up there tonight."

"I didn't think karaoke would be my thing, but I had a

really good time. Thanks for forcing me out of my comfort zone. I can see how you'd fall in love with being p on a stage like that."

At the moment, it wasn't the stage I was falling in love with. Though I wasn't sure falling was the correct terminology. Looking back, I'd been in love with Bree before we'd even shared our first kiss.

Curling into my chest, she put her chin on my pec and peered up at me. "Thank you for tonight, Eason. This was hands down the best date of my life."

I grinned, wholly and completely sharing the sentiment. "It's not over yet."

CHAPTER EIGHTEEN

BREE

WITH MY HAND THREADED THROUGH THE LONG, tousled hair on Eason's head, which was between my legs, a second orgasm wrung me out. I wondered if he knew my body better than I did. As I found my release and sagged into the plush new linens, Eason gave me one last languid lick up my center.

"Mmmm," he murmured. "So sweet. All mine."

Although arguing was my first language, there was no question he owned me.

And when I thought I couldn't take any more affection or euphoria, he crawled up the bed and sank into me with devastating control. Having already been over the edge twice that night myself, I found even more pleasure from experiencing how this gorgeous man found his.

Every day, Eason was easygoing and laid-back, but in bed, he was a completely different animal. He was powerful and strong, almost unyielding in the way he ravaged my body with his. He was bold and sure, confident in knowing everything I needed even before I could anticipate it myself. He was demanding and gentle, but above all else, he didn't hold back.

Eason gave. I took.

He went harder, faster. I begged for more.

"Yes," I panted.

"I swear to God, Bree, your fucking body was made for me." His hips twisted as he pushed deeper. "I can't do much lo—"

I silenced him with my mouth on his. "Shh. Then don't. Give it to me. Give me everything."

Breaking the kiss, he went up onto his arm, looked down at where our bodies were crashing into each other, and then pressed his forehead against my shoulder as the most erotic moan rumbled through his chest. "*Fuck.*"

His heavy weight collapsed on top of me as he pumped and twitched his release. For as ugly and tainted as the world could be, the sight of Eason losing himself in an orgasm would forever be one of the purest and most beautiful things I could experience.

Dizzy and spent, he shifted to the side where he lay panting for several seconds, his lips finding my shoulder more than once.

"Did all three of my date options end like that?"

He smiled against my shoulder. "Netflix and Chill started that way."

I laughed, and he held his palm out in the air to me.

"What?"

"Don't leave me hanging, Sug." He panted, air heaving as he fought to catch his breath. "That was some of my best work."

I started to slap his hand, anything to make him stop, but I paused. "On one condition. No more Sug."

"Oh, come on. It'll grow on you."

"No."

"I don't know what glucose did to you in a past life, but you should talk to your doctor about it." Swiftly, he leaned over and pressed a kiss t my neck, his hand still dangling in the air. "What should I call yo then?"

I smiled, fding younger than I had in years. It was these silly, quiet momets that had pulled me out of the destruction of the past year, and was so thankful that, with everything that had changed, Eason ard I were still the same. Okay, maybe not exactly the same. Maybe btter.

"What about jst your girlfriend?" I half teased.

He slapped my hand so fast that it stung. After rolling onto my chest, he peered lown at me with the most charming grin I'd ever seen. "That's a fcking deal right there, Sug."

"Hey. You just agreed not to call me that anymore."

"Sorry. I'm trying to quit, but it's not gonna be easy." He playfully acted like he was going to bite my nose and instead pressed a small kiss to the tip when I flinched. "All that sweet of yours, you give me dia-bree-tus, but I'll work on the girlfriend thing."

I gasped. "You did not just say *dia-bree-tus*."

"What?" He laughed. "It's a serious condition, Bree."

I wanted to give him hell, but as insane as he could be sometimes, he always managed to make me laugh. "Oh, you have a serious condition, all right—in that ridiculous head of yours. And to think, people pay you to write songs."

"I'm a true wordsmith. What can I say?"

It didn't matter what he said. He honestly didn't have to say anything at all. Eason was crazy in the absolute best way possible.

There had been a part of me that worried how things were going to change between me and Eason as we took our relationship to the next level. I was scared of losing the man who had become not only my best friend, but a fixture in my life that I prayed on a near daily basis would be permanent.

But nothing was different.

He was still attentive and kind.

Thoughtful and selfless.

The world's sexiest goofball.

And I was his.

What more could I ask for?

∽

I sat straight up at the sound of my bedroom door opening. Normally, that wasn't a reason for alarm. Asher's favorite pastime was waking me up before the sun rose. However, that morning, as the soft squeak of my door roused me to consciousness, there was a half-naked man curled around me.

Shit. What the hell had happened to our alarm? I glanced at the clock to see it was only five—thirty minutes before it was set to wake us up.

"Mom?"

"Hey, buddy. You're up early." Very aware that I was in the bare minimum of clothes—panties and a silk camisole—I hurried to the end of the mattress, shrugged my robe on, and threw the comforter back as I lurched out of bed, hoping to disguise Eason as a lump in the covers.

No such luck when the lump bolted upright and flipped the lamp on. "What's wrong? What's going on? You okay, Ash?"

Asher stopped, a little green sketchpad held against his chest, his sleepiness transforming to surprise as he flicked his gaze back and forth between me and Eason. He didn't say anything immediately, but I swore I could almost see the gears turning in his head.

Okay, so I guessed that it was time to tell the kids. I was kind of hoping to get a little further down the road in our relationship than *one* date, but Eason and I had made things official, and I trusted both o_1s to make the kids a priority if things didn't work out between us There could have been worse times. Though catching us in bed together definitely changed the dynamic of said talk.

I flashed Eason an expression that read *busted* and he had the good sense to look sheepish.

"Did you have a nightmare?" I asked my son, trying to distract him.

"What's Eason doing here?"

Obviously, I'd failed. "Well," I started, ready to spill all things about men, women, and dating.

Asher shrugged. "Actually, this is probably better." Without another word, he climbed up onto the bed and crawled on all fours to the spot in the middle. "Scoot," he ordered Eason.

Eason obeyed, but his wide eyes flicked to me. "Maybe I should go make coffee?" He lifted the blanket and got a bird's-eye view of nothing but a pair of black boxer briefs and then reclined back against the headboard. "Or not."

"Stay. I need to talk to both of you anyway," Asher said, opening his sketchpad. He flipped through the pages until he found what he was looking for and shot me an impatient glare. "Come on. You can't see from over there."

Ohhh-kay. So we were piling into the bed. Together. At five a.m. With the man who he had considered an uncle for the majority of his life who was now my boyfriend.

Sure. Why not.

Shoot me.

I perched on the edge of the bed, but he was having none of it. He tugged at my arm. "Come on, Mom."

"Ash, baby. Maybe we should go downstairs and talk."

"Why?" He curled his lip. "We're all here. The girls are still asleep, right?"

"Yeah, but—"

"Mom, Eason's not even wearing pants. How's he supposed to go downstairs?"

My mouth fell open as I stared at my son. It was way too early for this conversation—actually, any conversation, but especially this one.

Eason let out a cough to cover his laughter. "Maybe we should hear the boy out, Bree."

Out of arguments—or at least the caffeinated brain power to process more—I got back into bed. "Right. Okay. What's up, bud?"

Dramatically, Asher cleared his throat. "So the girls and I had a talk last night." He flipped the page in his notebook to reveal a crayon rendering of three *sad* kids—both of the girls crying. Everything was dark, the sky gray and the grass brown.

Eason leaned in close and threw his arm around Asher's shoulders, the tips of his fingers grazing my arm. "What's happening here?" he asked, the same concern filling my chest thick in his voice.

"Well…" Asher blew out a hard breath. "This is a picture of me, Madison, and Luna now." He turned the page. "And this is me, Madison, and Luna *with a cat.*"

All three of them were smiling. The green grass mixed with pink and purple flowers, and the yellow sun hung high in the sky, surrounded by blue clouds. But it was the orange cat, approximately the size of a small airplane if he'd drawn to scale, that was the center of the picture.

Eason and I exchanged a knowing glance, a smile growing on both of our mouths.

I ruffled Asher's hair as he turned the page.

"This is us with a black cat." Another bright and cheery picture. He flipped the page again. "And this is us with a brown cat." This time, he had added text bubbles from Madison and Luna's mouths with *ahaha!* and hearts inside. He flipped again to another bright piure of them with a white cat, this one with a stick figure standing n the clouds. "And this is Dad in heaven, a long, long, long way away from our house. So he's not al-ger-ic to our cat." He paused ad twisted his lips, looking over at Eason. "You're not al-ger-ic to cas, are you?"

Eason chuckd. "Allergic and nope. I love cats."

Asher's eyes l as he swung a damn near giddy gaze my way. "Please, Mom. Pleae. Can we have a cat? Madison and Luna said they would help m walk it and feed it so you don't have to do anything."

"Cats don't go n walks. Plus, the girls aren't even allowed outside without an adult. I'm not sure that should be your selling point. Let's talk abou who's cleaning the litter box."

"Please. Please. Please. I'll take care of it. I promise. *I swear,* Mom."

Laughing, I shook my head, his desperation and excitement explaining his Christmas morning-esque five a.m. appearance. "Ash, I haven't even had coffee yet. Can we please save the cat talk until after breakfast?"

"No," he whined. "Because at breakfast you're going to make us talk about you and Eason getting married."

I clamped my mouth shut.

But Eason let out a long, "Whoooooa!"

"Wait, if Eason's my new dad, that means he can get us a cat." He turned to Eason. "Please. Please. *Please.* Eason. Just one little kitten. I don't even care what color it is. I just want a cute one."

"Slow down, kid. One thing at a time. Your mom and I…" He lifted his gaze to mine in a silent request for permission and I nodded, trusting him implicitly.

Okay, fine—and a little curious as to how e was going to handle this too.

"Your mom and I are dating, Ash. We're no getting married. At least not yet. And maybe never." His lips crled into a warm smile as his eyes locked with mine. "But I have ny hopes."

My chest got warm as I stared back at hin After losing Rob, I never thought I'd even entertain the idea of geting married again. But I couldn't deny that being with Eason gve me a few hopes of my own.

"For now though," Eason continued, "shs my girlfriend. This means we're getting to know each other ard spending time together. But, Ash, if and when your mom and I ever do decide to get married, and even if we don't, I'm herefor you in every way you could possibly need me. But I'm never going to replace your dad, okay? You already have a pretty amazing dad. Him being in heaven doesn't change that."

And that was the exact moment I fell all-the-way, head-over-heels, unapologetically in love with Eason Maxwell.

I hated Rob Winters. I had few positive memories I clung to, most of which revolved around the kids, but after seeing the selfish and disgusting things he and Jessica had done without thought or regard for us, I'd come to terms with the fact that I'd been married to a stranger.

And Eason—God, poor Eason. He still didn't even know if his former best friend, who had been sleeping with his wife, had fathered his daughter or not. I couldn't imagine he held anything other than disdain for Rob.

But there he was, his arm wrapped around Asher's shoulders, preserving Rob's place in his life all because it was the right thing to do for my little boy.

I looked away and swallowed hard, hoping to keep the emotion at bay.

"Does this mean you guys kiss now?" Asher asked.

"Yep," Eason replied.

"And sleep without pants?"

"It would appear so. Though not all the time. We're going to take this slow and make sure you guys are comfortable with it. Man to man, I should have come to talk to you about things first. And I apologize for that. It'd mean a lot to me if you gave me your permission to date your mom."

Okay, seriously. How sweet could this man get? Maybe he was the real sugar in this relationship.

"I care about her a lot, Ash. I won't do anything to hurt her."

Okay, so Eason was damn near perfect. Cue. All. The tears. I continued to stare at the far wall so they couldn't see my face.

Asher hummed for a minute. "If I say yes, does it mean I get a cat?"

"Nope. But it does mean you get chocolate chip pancakes while we discuss it over breakfast."

"Yessssss!" he hissed.

Eason laughed, and still unable to look at them, I heard the telltale slapping of their high-five handshake and fist-bumping routine.

"All right, kiddo. Get out of here and give me a few minutes to get dressed and talk to your mom. I'll be down to cook in a few. Do *not* wake up the girls. Yeah?"

"Okay." With two bounces on the bed and a loud thud on the floor when he landed, he was off.

"Shut the door," Eason called.

In the next second, I heard the click of the doorknob.

And in the second after that, Eason's strong arms wrapped

around me, dragging me to the center of the bed. He rolled to his back and jostled me like a rag doll into a position with my head on his shoulder and my leg draped over his hips, and only then did he let out a long exhale. "All right. Talk to me. How'd that go for you?"

There was literally only one answer. Drying my cheeks, I tipped my head back to look up at him. "You're incredible."

"I don't know about all that. I just committed us to not sleeping without pants all the time. I have regrets already."

"I'm serious, Eason. The way you handled that… It can't be easy for you to talk about Rob after everything that's happened, but what you just gave Asher… I can't say thank you enough."

He pressed a soft kiss to my forehead. "Not one good thing will ever come from him knowing how much I hate his father. Right now, he trusts me, so he talks to me. If he knew, he'd feel like he had to choose sides. I'm not putting that shit on him. Rob and I *were* best friends. None of the kids need to know why that ended after he died."

And what if Luna was Rob's daughter?

What if we had to tell them that their father had an affair with Jessica?

What then?

I said none of that though. Those were problems for a different day when Eason was finally ready to learn the truth. He'd get there, and it wasn't my place to rush him.

"Like I said, you're incredible."

He inched down the bed, bringing us eye to eye, a playful smile tipping his lips. "Good. Keep that in mind, because you know I'm totally getting them a cat, right?"

I let out a sigh, but it was strictly for show. A cat wasn't high on my to-do list, but it wasn't too low, either. "I feared as much."

CHAPTER NINETEEN

BREE

EXHAUSTED WASN'T A STRONG ENOUGH WORD FOR THE week I'd had. Being that it was past nine p.m. on a Sunday and I was just getting home from the office should have said it all.

However, the ringing of my cell phone from a number at Prism was the icing on the cake.

With a sigh, I pressed the answer button on the screen on my dash. "I am turning into my driveway now. You have thirty seconds before I lapse into a coma for the next hundred years."

"They arrested him." Paul, the *new* head of Prism's accounting department, said through the speakers of my car.

This was good news, but it didn't exactly solve my problems. "Did he happen to have a briefcase with one-point-seven million dollars with him?"

"That would be a no."

"Of course not."

The thing about the IRS is they are quite possibly the most hated entity in the US, and after experiencing the audit process, I thought that hatred was more than fair. But when it came to dis-covering that your former head of finance had been embezzling company funds for over three years, they were surprisingly helpful. The tax bill they'd slapped me with? Not so fun.

Between hiring an outside company to do an internal audit, finding someone to replace Doug, the State's newest inmate, and then spending the entire weekend with the police while they gathered evidence to build a case against him, I was *beat*.

Unfortunately, my working overtime meant Eason was working overtime, which meant Evelyn had to be brought in so he could go to his gigs and work some more. It was a vicious circle of overtime for all of us. This also meant that, since our date a week ago, I had not seen him for more than a few minutes each morning.

Damn, it was hard to be a working single mom trying to find time to have sex with a working single dad while all three children were in the house twenty-four-seven. And we lived on the same property, so I couldn't imagine how hard it would have been if he'd lived across town like a normal relationship.

Something had to give.

We'd told the girls about our new relationship status—not that they understood. But Eason and I weren't shy about holding hands or the occasional peck on the lips. Anything more and we'd sneak into the pantry while the kids were preoccupied. I lived for those stolen moments when I got to lose myself in his arms. I'd almost mastered the ability to tune out "Baby Shark" playing on the other side of the door too.

I pulled into the garage and put the car into park. "Do you have anything else for me?"

"No. With Doug gone and the audit officially closed, it should be smooth sailings from here on out."

"Don't say that. You'll jinx us."

He chuckled. "Okay, fine. We're in a holding pattern until the next disaster. Is that better?"

181

"Much. Now I need to go. Keep me in the loop if you hear anything else."

"Sure thing."

"Bye." I hung up and cut the engine. After collecting my brief-case and three travel mugs that had been riding back and forth with me to work all weekend, I headed inside. "Sorry, I'm late," I called out to Evelyn as I walked into the kitchen.

"Shhh," someone said in the distance, but it wasn't Evelyn, so a huge smile broke across my face.

I hurried to the kitchen to drop my stuff on the counter and kick off my heels. Then I set out to find him.

A quick pass through the empty living room led me down the hall to the playroom. A light flickered inside, but the room was si-lent. Tiptoeing in, I found Eason standing like a sentry in front of the muted TV, all three of the kids sound asleep in a pile of tangled legs and arms on the couch. His gaze found me over his shoulder, but I was nowhere near ready for the devastation that struck me.

"What happened?" I whispered, rushing over to him.

"Nothing. Everything's fine," he mumbled, tossing an arm around my shoulders and curling me against his chest for a long Eason Maxwell specialty hug.

My whole body sagged in his arms. "Jesus, you scared me. What are you doing here? I thought you had a show tonight?"

"Bar lost their liquor license. Canceled everything and shut down for a few days until they can get it fixed."

"Oh. So, you're *off* tonight?" It was spoken as a whisper but there was no hiding my excitement.

His chest shook with humor. "Yeah, Sug. I'm off."

I leveled him with a pointed glare, but I was too excited to care too much and let it slide. "This is a good thing? Right? Why are you standing here looking like the kids ate all your cookies again?"

His chest expanded with a deep inhale, and his lips found the top of my head. It wasn't a kiss. Not exactly. He just pressed them against my head as he breathed into my hair.

"Eason," I prompted when my elation faded into concern.

"Look at 'em," he rasped as though he'd barely been able to force the words from his throat.

Following his gaze, I looked at our children. Asher was on the left, leaning against the arm of the couch, his mouth hanging wide open. Luna had her head in his lap, a stuffed dog hugged to her chest, and Madison was flat out on her stomach, her legs intertwined with Luna's while her arm hung off the side of the couch. It was rare for them to crash out at the same time like that, but not unheard of.

"Was there some kind of sorcery involved in getting them to sleep tonight?"

He gave me a squeeze. "Close. We ate popcorn and watched *The Wizard of Oz*."

My stomach sank, disappointed that I'd missed it. "That sounds like fun."

"It was. The girls oohed and ahhed when they saw the good witch, and Ash laughed so hard he almost peed his pants when I told him he looked like a member of the Lollipop Guild."

I brought a hand to my mouth to muffle my giggle.

"They don't know a life without each other," Eason rushed out like the confession burned his lips.

My eyebrows drew together, and I craned my head back to get a better view of his face. "And they won't ever have to. It doesn't matter what happens between us, Eason. We'll always be a family, remember? We do this together."

He shook his head. "No, I don't mean that. If she's their sister, they'll want to know."

I sucked in a sharp breath. Suddenly, his somber demeanor made a lot more sense. Eason hadn't said much about Luna's paternity since we'd left the cabin. I was trying to give him time and space to work it through in his head and his heart, but I'd be lying if I didn't admit I'd thought about it a fair amount over the last few weeks. But that was a decision he needed to make for himself; my curiosity on the matter wasn't a factor.

Shifting in front of him, I wrapped my arms around his neck. "You think you want to do a DNA test?"

"No," he breathed, a storm brewing in his eyes. "I'd honestly convinced myself that I didn't need to know. It wouldn't change anything. Not how much I love her. Or how she will forever be sewn into the fiber of my being. But *they* deserve to know. There have been enough secrets and lies without us keeping more. If she truly is Rob's, I have no idea how we will ever make them understand, but I don't want there to be a day when she feels the rusty knife of betrayal, wondering why I didn't tell her." His voice cracked and he brought a hand up, scrubbing his eyes with his thumb and his forefinger. "God, why is everything so fucking hard?"

"Because you're a good dad." Using his wrist, I pried his hand away from his face. "And you know how you handle this now will have an impact on her life. You are making the hard decisions and carrying that weight so she never has to. DNA be damned—that's how I know you will always be her *real* father. It's not my place to have an opinion, but I think you're making the right decision."

"What do you mean it's not your place to have an opinion? Jesus, Bree. She might be your husband's *daughter*. Are *you* ever going to be able to look at her and not see Rob and Jessica together?"

Oh, my sweet Eason. His whole world was upside down, on the verge of falling off axis, and he was worried about me.

Pushing up onto my toes, I pressed a deep and promising kiss against his mouth. When I released him, I kept our faces close, needing him to feel my words as much as he heard them.

"I see you in her, Eason. The way she giggles when she steals one of my M&M's when she thinks I'm not looking. The way she loves with her whole damn heart and smiles with her whole body. The sparkle in her eyes when she sees you sit behind the piano, ready to dance wild and carefree. All the things I love about that little girl have not one thing to do with how she was made, but rather they're because of who you made her to be."

"Oh, God," he rumbled, full of emotion as he wrapped me up in a hug so tight I wasn't sure I could breathe.

But while I was safe in the warmth of Eason's arms, oxygen was an afterthought.

I smoothed a hand up and down his back. "We're going to do this. We're going to do it together and we're going to make it okay for them. That's what we do, and no matter how this plays out, that is what we will continue to do, okay? I'm here, Eason. I'm right here."

His embrace drew me even closer. "God, Bree. I love you so fucking much."

My heart stopped and I fisted the back of his shirt. I had no idea if that was a romantic *I love you* or genuine appreciation for being there in his time of need, but no matter what form it came in, it didn't change the truth. "I love you, too."

His arms cinched around me.

We stood there in the middle of a messy playroom, holding each other, supporting each other, and loving each other through everything life had thrown at us. But in those seconds, with our entire world sleeping on the couch, it felt like maybe there had been a purpose to the hell we'd had to endure to find each other.

"Will you stay with me tonight?" I whispered. "Luna can sleep in Madison's room. We'll sleep in pants and set an alarm so you can get up before Asher? I just really need to be with you tonight."

His head popped up, his brown eyes finding mine with a blistering intensity. "There's not a force in the world that could keep me away."

My cheeks got hot, and I bit my lip to hide my smile. "Then we better hurry up and get these three in bed before the universe takes that as a challenge."

Eason didn't as much disagree as he sprang into action.

CHAPTER TWENTY

EASON

"WHAT ARE YOU DOING?" Asher asked as I exited the pantry.

"Ummm…" My back shot straight and I quickly shut the door, leaning against it as I panicked under his scrutinizing eyes. "I, um, was just…looking for a snack."

"What kind of snack?"

"What is this, a pop quiz?"

He canted his head to the side. "Maybe. Were you kissing Mom in there again?"

"Maybe."

It wasn't my fault. Bree had come downstairs in a pair of sexy-as-fuck jeans and a tank top that hugged all her curves just the way I liked. We were heading out as soon as Evelyn arrived, but there had been less than a zero percent chance of me keeping my hands off her for that long.

He stared at me for a long second, and it did not matter one bit that he was a kid and weighed less than fifty pounds, he could be terrifying—just like his mother. Finally, he gave me a curt nod like he was the freaking Godfather. "Can I have candy after lunch?"

"Sure." Anything to stop the interrogation.

He grinned. "Is it okay if we use the cushions off the other couch for our fort?"

I shrugged. "Works for me."

"Cool." He sprinted away.

I waited until he'd disappeared before cracking open the door to the pantry. "The coast is clear."

On the other side of the door, Bree unscrewed the top of a container of protein powder. "I'm not sure giving him a mouthful of cavities is the best way to handle your guilt for feeling up his mother." She pulled out a bag of M&M's and dumped a few in my hand.

"I panicked, okay? He's a nice kid. But he can be seriously scary sometimes now that he knows about us."

She laughed and put her secret candy stash back on the top shelf. "He's working you, ya know? Stop being weird when he catches us. I get not wanting to shove it in his face, but candy isn't going to change the fact that he's eventually going to have to get used to us touching each other."

"Bree, he gags when we kiss."

"Yeah. That's what kids do when their parents kiss. Trust me. He's happy for us. The kitten you promised to get them this weekend doesn't hurt, either."

"Okay, fine. I was just trying to avoid the awkwardness. We have enough emotional upheaval for the day without adding to the circus."

Her face got soft. "How ya holding up?"

I lifted a shoulder in a half shrug. "I just want it to be over. One way or another."

"Daddy!" Luna yelled, her feet pounding the wood floor as she raced down the hall.

Madison giggled and then shouted, "Eee-sin!"

I dropped Bree's hand like a hot potato and slapped on a smile, turning just in time to see them round the counter.

"I want candy," Luna said, patting her chest.

Madison bounced beside her. "Me too. Me too!"

I closed my hand around the M&M's and tucked it behind my back. "What? Who said I have candy?"

"Asher." Madison pouted her lip, and Luna glanced at her before mimicking it.

We'd done the DNA test, a simple home version where I swabbed both my mouth and Luna's while she slept and then mailed them in. Bree had done the same with Madison. It wasn't enough just to know if she was mine or not. We needed to know if she was Rob's. For all I knew, Rob could have been one of many. My trust in Jessica was officially nonexistent.

Though, while I stared at them right then, their bottom lips pushed out, the same dark curls and button nose, there was no denying that they looked like sisters. I'd resigned myself that it wasn't an *if* Rob was her father situation anymore. Everything came down to how we handled it.

The results had arrived in an email earlier that morning, but I'd yet to open it. There was something I needed to take care of first.

"Everybody has to eat all their lunch. Then you can have candy."

"Yay!" they cheered, dancing and hugging.

They were so damn adorable, and Bree and I both laughed.

Three grilled cheeses, a head of broccoli, and a small orchard of fresh apple juice later, Evelyn had arrived and Bree and I were gone for the afternoon. It wasn't a grand date night, and originally, I'd planned to go alone, but Bree had insisted on coming with me. We grabbed a quick bite to eat at a little Italian place I'd overheard her and Jillian talking about on the phone one night. The food was good, but the mood was all wrong. As many pep talks as I'd given myself over the last week, from knowing that tonight was the night, I was anxious, and sitting still that long made me crazy.

As soon as we arrived at the tattoo studio, my anxiety ebbed as the high of new ink sank in. Bree was cute, roaming around, inspecting all the art on the walls. I didn't suppose little Mrs. Prim and Proper had ever been inside a studio before. And, if I was being honest, it was a turn-on to pop that cherry for her.

Standing shirtless in front of the mirror, I turned from side to side. "What do you think?"

She slanted her head. "It's bigger than I was expecting."

I was too pumped to even make a joke about that one. "That's kinda what I was going for. I don't want there to be any question in her mind when she sees this that she is and will always be mine." I met Bree's green eyes in the mirror.

"Then I think it's amazing."

"Yeah?"

"I don't think you needed it for her to know any of that, but judging by that look on your face, it makes you happy. Therefore, it's *perfect*."

While I stared down at the purple stencil on my chest, my body thrummed with pride. It felt perfect too. After days spent working with an artist at my favorite studio, we'd finalized a three-dimensional rendering of a half-moon as seen through a telescope from Earth. The outline traced the curve of my pec, and hours of shading would bring the dips and craters on the moon's surface to life. The top and the bottom curled into the signature crescent shape, but the center faded into Luna's name in block letters running horizontal across my heart.

Until then, my ink had been isolated to a colorful sleeve I'd gotten in my twenties, but this one covered almost the entirety of my pectoral. And I fucking loved the idea of having my baby girl there, so close to my heart the way she always would be.

I wanted to get it before we read the results of the DNA test. To mark my body the same way she had marked my soul the day she'd been born. I wanted her to know, genetics aside, I would always be her daddy and no fucking test could ever tell me any different.

"All right. Let's do it."

"Umm." Bree raked her teeth over her bottom lip. "Ya know, I think I'm just going to hang in the lobby."

"What happened to being here for me?"

"Well, I am. But maybe I can cheer for you from outside." She crinkled her nose adorably. "Needles aren't really my thing."

I'd have given her shit, but even being there was out of Bree's comfort zone. Chuckling, I dragged her into a hug, careful not to smear the stencil on my chest. "You know this is going to take hours, right?"

"Yep. And I'm here for every minute of it. You need coffee or a riveting chat from outside the door, I'm your girl."

"I'll keep that in mind."

She tipped her head back and puckered her lips, asking for a kiss I would never be able to deny.

"I love you, babe."

Her mouth split into a beaming smile that could light even the darkest corners of any room. "Love you too, Eason."

I spent four hours in the chair, and by the time we were done, we had to schedule a second session to finish up the shading. But the only part I truly cared about was seeing my daughter's name on my chest.

As I drove us home, dread once again filled my gut. We'd agreed to read the results by the firepit after the kids had gone to bed. It was the logical choice; it was where Bree and I did our best emotional damage control. Almost like neutral ground. Though the minute we pulled into the driveway, from knowing we had to go inside and act like it was just another day and the clock wasn't a ticking timebomb counting down to my worst nightmare, bedtime seemed too painfully far away.

After parking in my spot in front of the pool house, I cut the engine but made no move to get out.

As always, Bree knew exactly what I needed and quietly sat beside me, her hand locked with mine, while I organized my thoughts.

I scrubbed my free palm on the thigh of my jeans. "I think I just want to rip off the Band-Aid. They deserve more than for me to spend one more night faking smiles with my stomach in knots. I'm just ready for this to be over. All of it. It's been one punch to the gut after another for too long now. I'm done. I want our problems to be which kitten to bring home and whether Asher makes the pee-wee soccer team this year. Fuck, Bree. I'm terrified that, if we keep screaming into the past, the future is going to become nothing but an echo."

"I know," she said, releasing my hand but only long enough to wrap hers around the back of my neck. Leaning over the center console, she brought her forehead to mine. "This is it. After this, they have no more control over us. We read these results and then it's just me and you and those kids making a life together from here on out." Suddenly releasing me, she sat back in her seat, lifted the corner of her shirt, and inched the waistband of her jeans down to reveal a piece of clear plastic taped on all four corners.

It was small, but never in my entire life had anything felt bigger.

In black typewriter font was a tattoo of three simple letters divided by two tiny hearts.

A M L

Asher. Madison.

And Luna.

"Bree," I rasped, raw emotion filling my throat. I reached out to trace the corners, careful not to touch her angry, red flesh. "You got a tattoo?"

"We're a family, Eason. Regardless of what the email says. Your tattoo is important to you because Luna will always know you love her. Mine is important to me because *you* will never have to question how I truly feel. Those kids are my life. All *three* of them."

My chest got painfully tight as I dragged her into a hug. She'd said that it didn't matter if Luna was Rob's multiple times, and I'd believed her.

But this was more.

This was different.

This was indelible proof on her body for all the days to come.

And this meant more to me than she ever could have imagined. "I love you so much."

"It's you and me, Eason. Let's rip off the Band-Aid, go in there, play with *our* kids, give them the absolute best life possible, and never look back." She leaned away, righting herself in her seat, and extended her hand in my direction. "Give me your phone."

With my heart in my throat, I held her gaze and passed it over.

This was going to hurt.

This was going to absolutely slay me.

But with Bree and her hand in mine, I didn't feel like I was suffocating under the weight of those results.

"You ready?" she asked, using her free hand to navigate to my email on my phone.

"As I'll ever be."

With an odd sense of calm washing over me, I dipped my

head, staring at my lap, my girl's face smiling on the backs of my lids. She was happy. She was healthy. She was just inside that house, waiting for her *daddy* to come home. Nothing else mattered.

"Eason!" Bree gasped.

I gave her hand a squeeze.

Here it comes. Just hold on, Eason. It's almost over.

For a long second, she was eerily quiet. I couldn't even be sure she was breathing. The only sound in that SUV was my heart pounding in my chest.

Deep breath in. *It doesn't matter. It changes nothing.* Jagged exhale out.

"Oh my God!" she all but yelled, her voice echoing off the windows. And then Bree said the two words that somehow healed every wound I had and would ever experience. "She's yours."

My head snapped up so fast it was a wonder I didn't break my neck. "What?"

She let out a loud laugh, the most beautiful tears of joy filling her eyes. "She's yours. Luna's yours. Look." She shoved the phone in my face, and sure as hell, to a 99.999997 percent probability, I was Luna's father.

In utter disbelief, I snatched the phone away and scrolled down, searching for her results in comparison to Madison. Maybe there had been a mistake. If I dropped my guard and let myself believe this even for a minute and it was wrong, I wouldn't survive that crash back to reality.

The probability of Luna and Madison sharing parents was a heart-stopping, euphoric, big, fat, fucking gorgeous *zero percent.*

"Oh, fuck," I rumbled, the relief so staggering my whole body trembled. "She's my baby. She's mine. It's over and she's mine."

I flicked my gaze to Bree. She had a hand over her mouth,

tears streaming from her eyes, but I didn't need to see her lips to know her smile was epic.

And sure, I knew, whether or not she'd ever admit it, Bree had a lot of emotional turbulence riding on those results as well. But the all-consuming happiness radiating from her stunning face was for me, and if I hadn't already been head-over-heels lost in that woman, that would have been the moment I knew there was no turning back.

Bree and I sat outside in the car for a while.

Laughing. Hugging. Kissing.

Just generally basking in an unfamiliar feeling of good news.

And when we were finally done, we got out and gave Rob and Jessica the biggest fuck-you we had to offer.

We walked inside to *our* family.

CHAPTER TWENTY-ONE

BREE

FOR THE NEXT SIX WEEKS, LIFE WAS GOOD. No. STRIKE that. Life was *incredibly* good.

With the IRS Audit in the rearview mirror, things slowed down at Prism. I hired a new support team to allow me more flexibility and blissfully went back to working nine-to-five as often as I could. Eason was still gigging a lot, but with summer coming to an end, his shows were almost completely limited to the weekends.

We'd finally taken the kids to the shelter to get a cat. Picking one out was easy. There was a little black-and-white kitten who adopted us the minute we walked through the door. He played with Asher, chasing him around like a dog, and then hung like a rag doll as Luna and Madison carted him around the shelter visiting room. And yeah, okay, fine, I didn't necessarily want a cat, but as Eason filled out the paperwork, the kitten we'd not-so-cleverly named Oreo curled into my lap for a nap. It was love at first purr.

The following weekend, he'd disappeared to the tattoo studio. When he didn't come home for five hours, I had a sneaking suspicion he was getting more done than just a touch-up on Luna's moon. Sure enough, that night as we got ready for bed, he revealed a brightly colored orb covering his right pec. Asher and Madison's names curled from the rays of the sun in brilliant red and orange hues. I may have cried. Laughing, but still crying. I couldn't help myself, it was gorgeous—just like the man himself.

Being surrounded by so much happiness was a nice change of pace for us. Eason and I went back to family dinners, tag-teaming bedtime routines, and then quiet nights around the firepit. Though, this time, Eason wasn't on the opposite end of the couch. Or if he was, my head was usually in his lap, his fingers tangled in my hair as he smiled down at me.

Being in love with Eason Maxwell was the easiest thing I'd ever done. I'd spent so many years trying to build the perfect life with the perfect husband, the perfect kids, and the perfect company. But mastering the perception of perfect isn't the same as finding genuine happiness.

I'd thought I was happy with Rob. I'd thought I'd found my person, my soul mate, the one. What I'd found was a con man, a manipulator, and a liar. But even if you took all of that out of the equation, knowing what I now knew about how it felt to have a man truly support me—a man who always kept his family at the center of his thoughts and intentions, his dreams so big that they inspired everyone who met him—I'd still choose Eason. Every day of the week.

As cliché as it sounded, Eason made me a better person. At the core, I was still Bree—stubborn and reserved with a spontaneity level of negative four thousand. Eason got me though. He was my total opposite—fun, lighthearted, and laid-back. But he didn't judge me or try to change me. He accepted me for who I was, no matter how difficult that might have been at times. He laughed when I got uptight. Held me when I became overwhelmed. Made love to me like I'd been made just for him.

And as the weeks passed, a glorious calm settled over our lives and I began to believe maybe Eason had been made for me too.

"Mmm," he hummed, wiping a drip of ketchup off the corner of his mouth. "That's...*delicious*," he lied, nodding his head at each of the kids.

Luna and Madison just sat there staring at him, their lips curled, completely unconvinced.

"It is good!" Asher agreed, food spilling from his mouth. Our boy must have been growing. He'd already plowed through half of his burger.

When the girls began to pick at their sweet potato fries, Eason leaned into my side and whispered, "Okay, what the hell is this?"

"It's a veggie burger."

"I got that. But I've grown to enjoy your veggie burgers and this is not that." He lifted his top bun and pulled out a stalk of green, pointedly dropping it on the corner of my plate. "What did I do to you? Asparagus? In a burger? That is some seriously unnecessary violence, babe."

I barked a laugh. "I didn't have enough black beans. I had to get creative. Look, Asher likes it."

"Yes, but I've had concerns over his taste buds for years." Eason took another bite, adding another hum of approval for good measure.

He was right. They were terrible, and there weren't enough mmm's in the world that would get the girls to eat it. But running to the store had meant missing hide-and-seek with the kids, and quite honestly, I was sick of missing the good stuff.

For years, I'd been a stay-at-home mom, spending twenty-four-seven with my kids. It wasn't glamorous, and I used to have to beg, barter, and steal to get even a single minute to myself. But I loved it. I loved my kids. I loved watching them grow. I loved being the one to teach them their 123s and ABCs. It was the hardest job I'd ever had and that included building a multimillion-dollar company from the ground up. Every blowout, tantrum, or meltdown fell on my shoulders. But so did the sweet snuggles when they got tired and the giggles when I pushed them high on the swings at the playground.

I missed those days. Asher was in first grade now, and Madison and Luna cared more about pretty dresses and hairbows than rattles and blankies. As much as I would have liked them to stay babies forever, it was all part of growing up. I just hated that it was racing right past me.

So, that night, we were having disgusting black bean-and-asparagus veggie burgers because I'd refused to miss anything else. And I felt not one ounce of guilt about it.

I took a bite of my burger, cringing and then grinning as I chewed.

Eason's phone started ringing and he glanced down at the screen, his eyebrows drawing together. "It's an LA number. I should probably take it. Can you hold down the fort?"

"Yep. And there will be three clean plates by the time you get back." They would be clean because I dumped them in the trash and made peanut butter sandwiches, but he didn't need to know that.

Bending over, he kissed the top of my head and then excused himself to the other room while answering, "Hello... This is he."

Asher not only finished his burger, but he polished off the rest of mine too. Eason was right, I needed to schedule him an appointment with the doctor about his clear lack of taste. When the girls finished their sandwiches and Eason still wasn't back, I treated them to pirate dessert. This was just three bowls of water filled with fruit, and I gave them little plastic drink swords to use as skewers. It was a smaller, not slobber-infested version of bobbing for apples and they adored it.

While they giggled trying to catch their dessert, I set out to find my man.

I tracked his voice down to the formal sitting room at the front of the house. "Mhm. Yeah, of course." His eyes found mine as soon as I rounded the corner. His hair a mess as though he'd been running his fingers through it, but it was the white pallor of his face that made my heart stop.

"What's wrong?" I mouthed to him.

Shaking his head, he lifted a finger for me to wait. "No, that's not a problem at all." His Adam's apple bobbed as he swallowed. "Yeah. No, I appreciate it. This is…" He laughed, and while it sounded genuine, it was packed with more emotion than just humor. "Thank you." He finally smiled, huge and white. "I'm looking forward to it. Right. See you then. Goodnight." With a tap on the screen, he hung up. Or at least I think he did. He lifted it back to his ear, saying "Hello. Hello. Anyone there?"

"What are you doing?" I asked. "Who was that?"

"Just a second." With his head down, he kept pressing buttons on his phone and only then did I notice the small shake of his hands. "Jesus, how do you turn this thing off?"

I took several long strides toward him. "Eason, honey. What's going on?"

"Just a second. Just a second. Just a second." He marched over to the couch and peeled back one of the cushions, stashing his phone beneath it. Still not happy yet, he grabbed the other two cushions and stacked them on top of it too.

"Okay," he said, finally turning back to face me.

"Why are you burying your phone?"

"Because I was really trying to play it cool and don't want

Levee Williams to hear me scream—" He sucked in a deep breath and then yelled at the top of his lungs. "I'm playing at the fucking Grammys!" Rushing forward, he tackled me in a bear hug.

"Holy shit! Are you serious?" I laughed as he spun us in a circle.

"She was supposed to do 'Turning Pages' as a duet with Henry Alexander for a special performance, but he's sick and she needs someone who knows the song and can fill in for him on short notice. My name came up in conversation, and as someone who started as a songwriter herself, she thought it would be perfect. She wants me to perform with her. On the Grammys. In front of everyone who is anyone in the music industry. In two days!"

"Wait. Two days? Like two days, two days?"

"Yep. This Sunday. They're booking flights for first thing in the morning." His chest heaved by the time he finished, but he never set me on my feet.

He did, however, kiss me—stealing my breath.

"What are you guys yelling about?" Asher asked, rushing into the room, two miniature-sword-wielding girls hot on his heels.

I had no idea where to even start explaining to them about how huge this was for Eason.

I'd sat outside with him the night the song debuted on the radio. His solemn face as they'd announced Levee's name. The spark in his eye when he'd found out I'd gone to the radio station and asked them to credit him as the songwriter.

This was his shot after over a decade of dreams. The highest of highs when he'd been signed to a record deal. The crashing low when he'd been dropped. Shamefully, I hadn't been supportive of Eason during those days, so even though we'd talked about it all at great lengths, I could only assume the heartbreak he'd experienced during that time in his life.

But what I knew firsthand was how hard he worked. How many hours he spent, night after night, at his piano or with a guitar in his hand. Coming home exhausted after a show and waking up only a few hours later so he could be there for me and the kids. The backhanded slap of people slamming doors in his face in his attempts to become an artist, all while those same people asking if he'd written anything new.

It was love and demanding work.

Trials and tribulations.

Hitting rock bottom and still getting back up.

But there was no way I could make the kids understand any of that.

So I went with something they would definitely get. "Eason's going to be on TV!"

They all started screaming and jumping around with us. Eason lowered me back to my feet, but only so he could scoop all three of the kids up in one giant hug, their little legs swaying as he swung them from side to side.

They say when it rains, it pours. For going on two years, that had been exactly the case for us. Drama and tragedy, one after another. First with Luna, and now with this—it was good to see that joy also came in storms.

And even with as absolutely elated as I was for him, Planner Bree came out in full force. "Oh my God, Eason, what are you going to wear? Come on. You have to start packing. I'll help."

He set the kids down and prowled my way. "What do you mean *I* have to start packing? *We* have to start packing."

My back shot straight, and he gathered me in his arms, aiming that sexy smirk down at me.

"You have lost your damn mind if you think I'm going to Los Angeles for the biggest day of my career without you."

I stared up at him in horror.

This man. This wonderful, gorgeous, talented man—he clearly did not know me at all.

I couldn't plan a trip to the freaking Grammys by morning.

We had no sitter for the kids. I had no dress. No shoes. My nails were a mess, and my hair was in desperate need of a trim. I had work on Monday. Meetings on my calendar. Asher had school. And honestly, it was worth mentioning again: I had no dress.

But on the other hand, the same wonderful, gorgeous, and talented man I loved with my whole heart and entire being had just been handed the biggest opportunity of his entire life.

And he wanted me there with him.

Therefore, even if I had to go in a pair of jeans and with my hair in a ponytail, carrying all three kids on my back like a pack mule, I was getting on that plane first thing the next morning. Because if Eason wanted me there, dammit, then that's where I'd be.

"Okay," I breathed. "In that case, you get the luggage from the attic and I'll call Evelyn to see if she can keep the kids."

His smile was so wide I swear I thought it was going to swallow his face. "That's it? No freaking out about it being short notice?"

"Oh, there is plenty of that going on in my head right now. But I love you and I am so damn proud of you I'd be honored to go." I blew out a dreamy sigh. "And let's be real: A sexy rock star asking me to be his date to the Grammys isn't exactly a hardship."

The kids made gagging noises as we kissed, our smiles never faltering even as our lips locked together.

Yeah…the saying was right. When it rains, it definitely pours, and I was all too happy to drown in Eason Maxwell.

CHAPTER TWENTY-TWO

EASON

I N THEORY, TWO DAYS DIDN'T SEEM LIKE A LOT OF TIME TO prepare for music's biggest stage.

In reality, it was even less time than I'd imagined.

As always, Evelyn was amazing. As soon as Bree told her about my opportunity, she dropped everything to be there for our kids while we were gone.

First thing the next morning, with suitcases so full we had to pay the airlines a small mortgage payment in extra weight fees, Bree and I were off to California. It was an absolute whirlwind from the second we stepped off the plane.

Cars were waiting for us when we arrived—two of them. Bree was swept off to the hotel, and God bless Levee Williams, she'd arranged for her stylist to take Bree out for hair and nails and shopping. I hated letting her go. I didn't give a damn if I had to spend the day holding her purse while she tried on every dress in Los Angeles. I should have been there with her. But with thirty-six hours until showtime, I didn't have much of a choice.

After she'd climbed into the back of a black Escalade, I leaned in for a kiss. "I'll see you tonight, okay?"

"I'll be the woman in your hotel room. With any luck, you won't recognize me."

I chuckled and kissed her again. "Then be naked. I've memorized every curve of that body, Sug."

She wrapped her hand around the side of my neck and teasingly acted like she was going to choke me for using the pet name she hated. But she didn't say a word about it. "You're going to be incredible. Try not to be so amazing you make Levee look bad, okay?"

I laughed, but so much love swelled in my chest it was a wonder I was able to breathe. "I'll try."

She brushed her nose with mine. "I love you, Eason."

There wasn't a word strong enough for the way I felt for Bree, so I made do with what I had. "Love you too."

The rest of my day was crazy. I spent four hours rehearsing with a woman named Jo while at least eight skeptical men and women huddled in the corner. Levee owned Downside Up Records, so I assumed she got the final say, but I had a sneaking suspicion that Levee's asking me—Eason Nobody—to replace superstar Henry Alexander hadn't been a thrilling idea for everyone on her team. However, if they wanted "Turning Pages," a song of love, loss, and moving on—a song I'd written long before I'd known the true depths of any of those emotions—there wasn't a person on Earth who could make it more authentic than I could.

I played to a room full of mumbled conversations. And I didn't give the first damn what they were saying. I followed my heart and let the music speak for itself. When I finally finished, I had everyone on board with swapping the arrangement so I could play piano instead of filling in Henry's shoes on the guitar. I could play both instruments, but if I wanted the world to remember my name, my best bet was behind the ivory keys.

After everyone had appeared satisfied that I wasn't a royal

fuck-up, I was driven to The Staples Center, sent through wardrobe, met with hair and makeup, and then weaved my way down a press corridor. They had exactly no idea who I was and most didn't try to pretend they did. Pretty much every question revolved around how I knew Levee. And the truth was I didn't.

She'd been MIA all day, but as they dropped me off at the hotel that night, I had a dozen texts from equally as many people outlining my packed schedule for the next day that started well before the sun would be up.

It was surreal.

Stressful.

Intimidating as fuck.

And I loved every damn minute of it.

Bree was asleep by the time I got back to our room. I was so tired that I didn't even have the energy to take advantage of her in a hotel bed two thousand miles away from the kids.

"Mmm," she hummed as I crawled into the sheets behind her. "How'd it go?"

"Crazy. Incredible. Exhausting." I kissed her shoulder. "And perfect now."

"Mine too," she murmured, rolling over, resting her head on my chest, falling right back to sleep.

I didn't know how she did it.

I'd been in relationships before. Hell, I'd been married.

But it was different with Bree. After a day spent experiencing high after high, living the life I'd dreamed about for the majority of my existence on Earth, coming home to her was still my favorite part.

"Eason! Eason, over here."

I squeezed Bree's hand, lifting my other to wave at the line of paparazzi camped out outside Levee's afterparty. Not one single person had known who I was when I'd woken up that morning, but after a standing ovation from the biggest stars in the world, my name was making the rounds.

And much to Bree's relief, none of them had called me Easton yet.

The performance had been a huge success and a damn near religious experience for me. When the lights came on, revealing Levee in a floor-length ballgown made to look like pages from a book, the massive train taking up half the stage, and me in designer black jeans and a gray fitted vest, the sleeves of my white button-up rolled up to my elbows, I came alive behind an onyx grand piano.

There was a reason the world called Levee the Princess of Pop. She carried herself with the grace of royalty, poised with power and experience. But behind the scenes, she was down to Earth and so damn kind. For the first twenty minutes after we'd met, she'd asked a dozen questions about my family and then sidled up beside me to scroll through pictures of the kids on my phone.

On stage, our voices blended flawlessly, her personal brand of sultry harmonizing with my style of edgy soul. With "Turning Pages" as popular as it had become, I'd worried about living up to the standards set by Henry Alexander, but if I'd failed in any way, no one was letting on.

"This is wild," Bree said as a hulking security guard pulled the door open for us, no questions asked.

I folded my hand over hers and shot her a smile. "I know. Out past midnight and we haven't turned into pumpkins yet. Who knew?"

She laughed as we navigated our way through a virtual who's who of the music industry.

Bree suddenly froze, pulling me up short. "Oh my God, is that Shawn Hill? Ohhhh, sweet lord it is."

Chuckling, I leaned into her. "Yes, and after letting your boyfriend hear that moan, we will be staying on this side of the party for the rest of the evening."

"I'm not suggesting we invite him back to our hotel room for a threesome. But maybe just a picture I can send Jillian. She gave me a list of people I'm required to slip her phone number to this weekend."

I curled my lip. "And twenty-two-year-old Shawn Hill was on there?"

Bree shrugged. "What can I say? She likes younger men. And now that you're off the market, she's on the prowl again."

"Then we should definitely go over there and warn him." Draping my arm around her hips, I put my lips to her ear. "Did I happen to mention that you look incredible tonight?"

She beamed up at me. "Maybe a time or seventy-five."

Bree was always gorgeous; it didn't matter what she was wearing: sweaty workout clothes, power suits, or just jeans and a tank top. Though a red backless dress with a high slit up one of her legs definitely never hurt. And neither did the low-cut little black dress she'd changed into for the afterparty.

"Well, let's make it seventy-six." I smirked. "You look—"

"Eason, you made it," Levee said, stopping beside us, her hand linked with a man who had thick tattoos running up both of his arms.

"Hey, congrats on Album of the Year."

She tucked a rogue brown ringlet behind her ear. "Thanks. I still have no idea how 'Turning Pages' didn't get you a nod. Though, after that performance tonight, I'm sure next year's nominations are going to look a lot different. My phone has been blowing up, everyone trying to figure out who you are and where I've been hiding you."

"If it was a record executive on any continent, including Antarctica, tell them to check their pile of demos over the last hundred years. I'm sure I'm in there somewhere."

She giggled melodically. "I get it. Trust me. I spent my fair share of time in the trenches too." Slanting her head at the man beside her, she said, "This is my husband, Sam. Sam, this is Eason Maxwell."

I extended my hand.

He met me with a firm shake. "Nice to meet you. You killed it out there tonight."

"That was all your wife." Releasing his hand, I pulled Bree against my side again. "This my girlfriend, Bree. Bree, Levee and Sam."

Levee aimed her smile down at Bree. "I heard a lot about you today. I think your guy might like you a little bit."

Bree tilted her head back and smiled up at me. "Well, the feeling is very mutual. I kinda sorta maybe like him too."

"Oh, please. She loves me. Really, it's more of an obsession. Though I think she might be holding out for Shawn Hill over there?" I winked and Bree pinched my side.

"Well, I have a feeling the rest of the world is holding out for Eason Maxwell now." Levee laughed. "Hey, I'm glad I ran into you. We were actually on our way out."

"What? Why? Isn't this *your* party?"

"Yeahhhh," she drawled, glancing around the room. "It's good for the label, but this isn't really my scene anymore." She slid under her husband's arm and nuzzled into his chest. "I'm more of a bathrobe, glass-of-wine, room-service-while-going-through-the-swag-bag type of girl these days."

Bree put her hand to her ear. "I'm sorry. Did you say swag bag?"

Levee snapped her finger and pointed at Bree. "I see you're my type of girl too. Don't worry. It will be in your room when you get back. But listen, while I have you here, I have no doubt the offers are going to start rolling in for you tomorrow. But Henry and I would absolutely adore to have you join the Downside Up team."

My whole body turned to stone and the oxygen that had been freely circulating in the room suddenly disappeared. "Like…as a songwriter?"

She grinned. "Sure, if you have words to spare. But I was thinking more along the lines of a solo artist."

Bree grabbed my hand and gave it a hard squeeze, which I was only vaguely aware of through the surge of adrenaline roaring in my veins.

"I…um—"

She waved me off. "Don't answer now. There are agents and managers and lawyers who need to talk first. But I was really impressed with you tonight, Eason. No commitments or strings attached. I've got a few weeks off. Maybe, instead of going home tomorrow, you could take a detour through San Francisco for a few weeks. I'd love to pick your brain on a couple songs I've been working on. We could even collaborate and see about getting a single out for you while the world is still aflutter with all things Eason Maxwell."

"Oh wow. That sounds amazing, but I don't know if I can do San Francisco. I have kids. Bree has to get back to work and—"

"He'll be there," Bree interjected, the tip of her high heel landing painfully on my toe. "Just let us know where and he'll be there."

Levee grinned. "You've got a smart lady there. Listen to her.

210

It was nice meeting both of you. Good luck treasure hunting in the swag bag tonight."

"Thanks," Bree replied. "For everything. This has been an amazing experience for both of us."

"You're very welcome, but I'd be lying if I acted like I did do you a favor. You're gonna be big-time, Eason. I'm just trying to get in on the ground floor. We'll talk soon." She looked at her husband. "You ready?"

Sam gave us both a chin jerk then threw his arm around his wife's shoulders, and together, they sauntered to the door.

I stood like a statue, trying to process everything that had just happened. A potential record deal with Downside Up. An invitation to collaborate with Levee. Hell, even the prospect of her "picking my brain" could score me a cowrite credit on her next album. None of these were bad problems to have. Though I had no idea how I could get away for a few *weeks* to make it happen. A long weekend, sure. Bree would step in, and we could always count on Evelyn to pick up the slack. But *weeks*? As in plural. Logistics aside, I didn't know how I felt about leaving Luna for that long.

The back of Bree's hand slapping my chest snapped me out of my thoughts.

"Have you lost your damn mind? When Levee Williams asks you to come work with her, you don't say"—she lowered her voice into a deep tone that sounded nothing like me, or at least I hoped it sounded nothing like me because I sounded seriously dumb—"'Oh gee, I don't know. Bree has to work. Who would ever babysit the kids.'" She slapped me again. "Are you insane?"

I laughed and lifted my hands in surrender. "It's the truth."

"No, it is not. Eason, when we made this agreement about you keeping the kids, it was so you could have the time at night to pursue music. The opportunity that was just laid out in front of you was literally *the goal*. All bets are off now."

"I still have responsibilities. I have a daughter who—"

She stabbed a finger toward the covered tattoo on her hip. "*We* have a daughter, Eason. And I am fully capable of handling the responsibilities while you are gone. But you have to go. Taking care of our family means taking care of yourself. After all these years, this is your time. Don't you dare ignore it in the name of responsibility. We're a team, remember? You do your part in San Francisco and I'll do my part at home, okay?"

My chest got tight as I stared at her in the middle of an A-list afterparty, feeling every bit of the imposter I was but still knowing I was the luckiest man in the room.

Circling my arms around her hips, I pulled her flush against my chest. "Okay, but what am I going to do without you for two weeks?"

She smiled and ran her hands up my arms to my neck. "Now *that* I'm not sure about. But just think of how much fun we can have when you get home. All that—"

A man's tenor interrupted our conversation. "I'm sorry. Are you Bree?"

My head jerked up and she spun in my arms. And sure as shit, Shawn Hill was standing in front of us, his bare chest only covered by a leather jacket. Long, flowing, blond hair and the bluest eyes I had ever seen, and not looking at all like the geeky college kid I had at his age, but like a grown-ass male model who had never heard the word no from a woman in his life.

"Uhhhh," my *girlfriend* who was not at all drooling mumbled.

He smiled down at her, so hypnotizing that for a second I feared she was planning to throw her bra at him.

"Hi, I'm Shawn. Levee sent me a text saying I should come talk to you."

I wanted to be jealous. After Jessica and Rob, my ability to trust should have been nada. But it was Bree and she was hilariously star struck. Yet I still knew that Shawn could have dropped to his knees right then and there and it wouldn't have mattered one bit.

Bree was mine.

The way it always should have been.

We spent the rest of the night making the rounds. Meeting people. Making friends. Taking pictures and sending them to Jillian. We left around four in the morning and thankfully Bree bypassed the gift bag in lieu of making love until the sun came up.

She flew home the next morning, exhausted, sated, and alone, while I made my way to San Francisco, my dreams at my fingertips and my entire heart in Atlanta.

CHAPTER TWENTY-THREE

BREE

"Ewwww!" Luna laughed, pushing the slime into a small plastic cup to make a loud *flllarp* noise. "Mom, mom, mom. Listen to mine!" Asher exclaimed.

They all giggled hysterically. Seriously, it didn't matter how old kids were, apparently fart sounds were always funny.

Never one to be left behind, Madison frantically started shoving hers into the container, yelling, "My turn!"

"Okay, hang on, Mads. Everybody get together so we can send a picture to Eason. Come on, Luna. Daddy needs to see your beautiful smile." Leaning on the counter with my elbows to steady my arms, I aimed the camera on my phone at them covered in school glue and food coloring. Their shirts were ruined and I had a feeling I was going to be wiping down the counters for days, but they were happy.

And because they were happy, I was happy too.

In the almost two weeks since Eason had been gone, we'd been busy. We'd made slime, painted suncatchers, and used potatoes as stamps. We'd spent almost every afternoon at the park and our nights teaching Oreo to fetch a little felt mouse. I bought a trampoline for the backyard and we'd gone through more sidewalk chalk than I'd known was possible.

And I loved every single minute of it.

The day after I'd gotten home from LA, I'd loaded up Madison and Luna and gone to the office while Asher was at school. I spent a few hours tying up loose ends while Jillian entertained the girls. Once that was done, I emailed the entire company to let them know I was taking a vacation for a few weeks—effective immediately. I must have gotten fifty responses in the first two minutes: emails, phone calls, the heads of departments stopping by my office with a laundry list of questions. I answered exactly none of them. Instead, I closed my computer, gathered my girls, and went to get Ash from school, and the four of us went out for smoothies without a single regret.

I could have called a nanny agency and gotten a temporary sitter. I could have worked from home, burning the candle at both ends. But none of that felt right in my heart.

I'd given Eason a talk about how taking care of the family meant taking care of yourself. And there I was, the hypocrite, in a job I'd come to despise when all I truly wanted was to be at home with my kids. Depending on who you asked, people had very strong opinions on the age-old working-mom-versus-stay-at-home-mom debate. But in my experience, there was no right answer. Or wrong answer for that matter. It all came down to what worked best for the individual family.

And over the last few months, watching my kids grow up in the one-to-two-hour window I got with them every night just wasn't working for me anymore.

"Cheese!" the kids shouted, but I didn't get to take a picture before the phone lit up with an incoming FaceTime.

A massive smile spread across my cheeks. I hit the answer

button and then held my breath as his handsome face filled the screen. "Hey!" I said, turning the phone so the kids could see him too.

"Daddy!"

"Eason!"

"Eeeee-sin!"

The house hadn't been the same without him. Too boring. Too quiet. Too healthy. Who would have thought there would be a day when I missed him smuggling cookies in?

He'd called as much as he could, but with the time difference on the West Coast, it got challenging. But not a day had passed where he hadn't made time to at least check in.

"Daddy, where are you?" Luna asked, standing up on her stool as if it would bring her closer to him.

"I'm still in San Francisco." He spun in a circle, showing off the soundboard in an empty studio. "Everyone just broke for lunch. What are you guys doing?" He leaned in close, the top of his blond hair falling into his tired eyes. "Is that slime?"

Asher launched himself forward and took the phone from my hand. "Listen, listen." Precariously balancing the phone, he started shoving his finger into the container, and in the next beat, Luna and Madison joined him for a symphony of fart sounds.

"Wow!" Eason exclaimed. "I bet your mom is just loving that."

"Totally," Asher replied.

And if I was being honest, he wasn't wrong.

After that, the kids took turns carrying the phone around the house, talking Eason's ear off, and showing him everything from the same pictures they'd shown him yesterday to a lone sock Luna had found Oreo carrying around the house. About a half hour later, Madison brought me back my phone and then disappeared into the playroom with Luna.

I settled into the corner of the couch, lifted the screen up into my line of sight, and asked, "You got any time left for me?"

He leaned back on a couch and waggled his eyebrows. "For you, I've got forever."

"Smooth. You should work that into a song."

He quirked an eyebrow. "Who says I haven't?"

I sighed. "So, how's it going out there? Tell me, Mr. Famous. Have you bought a mansion and decided to abandon us for celebrity life yet?"

Levee had not been wrong about the world taking notice of Eason Maxwell. For days after the Grammys, his name had been plastered all over social media. Women were going nuts over him. Stills of him smirking at Levee on stage had gotten the gossip mill running. Paparazzi images of them out to dinner and leaving Downside Up studios together only fueled the media frenzy. It had gotten so bad that, by the end of his first week in San Francisco, Levee's husband, Sam, called me to see how I was holding up. He was a really nice guy who assured me that nothing was amiss and this was just how things went in the industry. Especially with someone as new and captivating as Eason.

Truthfully, Eason's newfound fame had been a little hard to swallow. Photos of us on the red carpet were circulating, and while I'd printed and framed a few, I'd strategically cut out all the headlines of our "scandalous affair."

While digging into his past, trash media outlets had found out about the fire. Oh, what a juicy day it must have been for them as they'd flashed a photo of me, Rob, Eason, and Jessica at a charity fundraiser Prism held once a year beside an arial image of Eason and Jessica's demolished house. They harped on the fact that Rob had been Eason's best friend and even managed to find a cell phone video of me holding Luna and forcing a smile outside of Jessica's funeral as "proof" of our betrayal.

They didn't know about Rob and Jessica's affair.

Nor did they know that Eason and I had barely been friends before the fire.

They didn't understand that our love had been slow like the seasons, built on a foundation of honesty and trust.

Nobody understood, yet within days, Eason and I were labeled *backstabbing* and *taboo*.

It was a whole big thing and Eason had lost his mind, but I'd put my foot down when he'd tried to come home early. People would forever talk and make assumptions, but at the end of the day, the only things that mattered were that Eason and I knew who we were, how we had fallen in love, and where the future was leading us.

What hurt him the most was that one day the kids were going to read that bullshit, but if we did our jobs right, by the time that day rolled around, they would never have to question the truth.

"No, I'm ready to abandon the celebrity life to come home to you," Eason rumbled. "God, I wish you were here, Bree. And the kids. It's only been a few weeks, but I swear Luna looks like she's going to be asking to borrow the car soon."

"I think it's Asher you need to worry about. He's got this girl in his class and he keeps telling me she's so pretty it makes his stomach hurt."

He barked a laugh. "Oh man, that's serious. Though I'm slightly injured he hasn't said anything to me about her."

"I'm sure he's just waiting for you to get home. Speaking of… Any clue when that will be?"

He let out a low growl. "All right, what do you want first? Good news or bad news?"

My stomach sank. The only good news I wanted was for him to come walking through that door, and I assumed that, whatever the bad news was, it wasn't going to be conducive to me getting that. "Let's get the bad news out of the way."

"Since I signed with Downside Up, Levee hooked me up with her producer. He's incredible. Completely gets my vision. We worked on one hook today that I'd been stuck on and he had it knocked out in less than two minutes."

I twisted my lips. "And how is that a bad thing?"

"He wants me back in the studio to rework parts of what Levee and I had done. And he's right. It had too much of her fingerprints and not enough of mine. It's gonna be another two weeks at least. Maybe closer to a month if I can get the studio time. I've been writing like crazy and have more than enough material for a full-length album. I just need a little help getting the tracks down."

Yes, a month sounded like an eternity with the way I missed him. But he was also missing me and the kids something fierce, so he didn't need me piling guilt on top of it. "Eason, it's not bad news. You have a record deal with a major label who is spending time and money to put you with one of the best producers. We knew the distance was going to be hard, but these are not bad problems to have."

He shifted the phone from one hand to another, raking his free hand through the top of his hair. "I know. I know. I just feel bad leaving you there with the kids. You'll have to go back to work eventually. Maybe we should talk about hiring a nanny. I can pay for someone full time. I know me being here is putting you in a bind and I'm sorry you're having to pick up all the slack."

"Would you stop already? I'm not in a bind. I'm doing what needs to be done for our family. The same way you did when I was working eighty hours a week during the IRS audit. Stop feeling guilty for being successful. If you want the truth, I've kinda been thinking about *not* going back to work."

His eyebrows drew together, and he sat forward. "Wait, wait, wait. What? Is this because of me?"

I dropped my head back. "No, it's because of me. I've been doing some thinking. I hate missing the kids grow up. We only have so many years with them, and pretty soon they'll all be in school and too cool to hang out with their old mom. I could maybe go back to work then. My heart just isn't in it anymore. I worked my ass off to build that company. Maybe it's time I turned over the reins to someone else and followed my own dreams."

His face got soft, and he leaned into the camera. "Bree, I'm not actually there right now. But I'm here for you. If this is what you want, don't ever go back to Prism. I can take over the bills. I kinda failed Jessica on that front, but it's different this time. I'm not going to get dropped. I can take care of us now. All of us. I swear I can."

Oh, my sweet Eason. After everything, he still felt like he didn't do enough.

"First of all, you did not fail Jessica. Jessica failed Jessica. Despite what she led us all to believe, she was not some helpless dandelion blowing in the wind. She could have gotten a job, but she chose to spend her free time with Rob instead of taking care of her family. You don't get to carry her failures as your own."

"Babe," he whispered, emotion thick in his throat.

"Secondly," I continued, "you *have* been taking care of us. Since day one. And that has not one damn thing to do with who was paying the mortgage. The kids and I would not be here, so damn happy and loved, without you. You have the biggest heart of any man I've ever met, and given how many times that thing has been ripped from your chest, that's saying a lot. I don't need you to take care of us. I'll still have Prism. I just won't be the one running it. But if that's something you need to do for yourself to finally see all your hard work paying off, I'll transfer all the bills to your name tonight. I don't need money, Eason. I need you. That's all I'll ever need."

"Dammit, Bree. How do you always know exactly what to say?"

"It's a little skill I picked up from you. Now, if that was the bad news, tell me the good."

The side of his mouth hiked, so much love blazing in his eyes I could feel the tangible heat through the screen of the phone. "I'll be home tomorrow."

My heart leapt into my throat. "Seriously?"

He chuckled. "Yeah. I've got a week before they have time for me in the studio. So I am coming home to my woman and my kids. I swear I've never been so excited in my life."

"The kids are going to flip. Let's make it a surprise."

"And what about you? You excited?"

I teasingly slanted my head. "Why, superstar Eason Maxwell, are you fishing for a compliment?"

"I don't need a compliment. I need my kids, and then after they go to bed, I need you in some seriously scandalous lingerie. If I'm going to be gone for a month, we need to spend the entire week filling my head with enough naked memories to get me through."

I nodded, biting my bottom lip. "I can do that."

And oh my God, I could soooooo do that.

"Good." He winked. "I'll send you my flight details. Now, I have to go before everybody comes back and I'm sitting here hard as a fucking rock. Love you, babe."

"Love you too, Eason."

CHAPTER TWENTY-FOUR

EASON

I HAD AN UBER DROP ME OFF AT THE POOL HOUSE, AND I stashed my bags just inside the door. Armed with a huge stuffed unicorn, a stuffed cat, a plastic Minecraft pickaxe, and a jar containing every red M&M I could find in San Francisco, I snuck around the back of the house. As planned, Bree had the kids outside, drawing on the patio with sidewalk chalk. Just the sight of their three little heads all huddled together caused a wave of contentment to crash over me.

Bree stood up as I walked through the back gate, her hair blowing in the breeze. As if it were the first time I'd ever seen her and not closer to the millionth, my stomach knotted. Two weeks didn't seem like a long time, but after living together and spending every day with one another for going on two years, holy shit, I had missed that woman. FaceTime was not cutting it.

"Hi," she mouthed, the pure joy on her gorgeous face transferring to my chest.

I put my finger to my lips in a silent *Shh*!

Retrieving her phone from her back pocket, she called, "Hey, kiddos, look at me. Let's send Eason a picture of our chalk drawings."

"Mine's the best!" Asher exclaimed. "Take a picture of mine."

The girls giggled, sword fighting with the chalk, but with the hundreds of pictures Bree had sent me while I'd been gone, they were trained circus animals and lined up for a photo.

"Say cheese," Bree directed.

"Cheese," they all sang.

After dropping all the toys and carefully setting Bree's M&M's aside so nothing got ruined, I snuck in close, squatted low, and said, "Cheese."

After that, it was a chorus of the most beautiful shrieks of my life. Asher's face was priceless as he spun around, his mouth wide open, his eyes the size of saucers.

Madison crashed into my arms first, screaming, "Eeeeee-sin!"

My sweet baby Luna just stood there clapping and cackling, "Daddy home. Daddy home."

I was a man. Like the consummate example of pure, unfettered masculinity. Or at least that's what I told myself when I looked in the mirror. But in truth, I teared up like an onion factory had moved in next door when they all tackled me. Falling back on my ass, I became the happiest guy to ever find himself at the bottom of a dog pile.

For several minutes, it was chaos, everyone talking at once, a million questions and stories sailing through their lips faster than my ears could process. As much as I loved my kids, I had a certain someone I needed to get my hands on next. Luckily, there was one failproof method of escaping a dog pile, and I had planned ahead.

"Who wants a surprise?" I asked.

They were off me in the next heartbeat, hopping and chanting, "Me!"

After climbing to my feet, I walked over to my pile of goodies. "All right, girls. These might look like normal stuffed animals, but they are so much more. They have babies inside them." The gasps made those damn creepy toys worth every penny. "And don't ask me if I peeked because I didn't. But also don't ask me how a unicorn became pregnant with a rabbit. Here, Luna, Rainbow Sparkle Twinkle Toes is yours." I handed her the unicorn, which was roughly the same size as her.

"Tanks, Daddy!"

I kissed her on the top of the head, my heart so full that I had no idea how it still fit in my chest. "And, Mads, that means Bootsy Glitter McWhiskers is all yours." I passed her the cat and I swear her eyes were so wide she looked like I'd handed her the world. She tucked Bootsy under her arm and gave my legs a long hug, expressing her gratitude without words.

But it was Asher's exuberant "Yesss!" that made me laugh the hardest. "That means the pickaxe is mine," he said, hopping around on one foot, pumping his fists. "That's what I wanted. I wanted the pickaxe."

Laughing, I shook my head and bowed, presenting it to him on both hands. "Happy mining, Ash."

"Thank you!" He snatched it and took off at a dead sprint to the trees in the side yard, and the girls plopped down at my feet, pulling out unicorn and cat rabbits, oohing and ahhing over each one.

I had about five minutes before the novelty wore off, so I grabbed the jar of M&M's and went to properly say hello to my woman.

She held her hand up to block the sun as I made my way over to her, a grin twitching the side of her mouth. "Is that—"

I did not let her finish the statement before hooking her around the hips, pulling her against my chest, and planting a long-overdue kiss on her sexy mouth.

"Mmmmm," she hummed, circling her arms around my neck.

"That sounds like you missed me, Sug."

She frowned, but it was exactly what I'd been going for, so it'd worked.

"I haven't missed you calling me Sug. But maybe I missed you…*a little bit*. Are those for me?" She dipped her chin at the gallon-size jar with the black metal lid.

"What, these? Nah, they're mine. I saved you a Ziploc bag of all the other colors though."

She pinched my side.

"Okay, okay. You can have them. No need to resort to violence."

My heart stopped as she took it from my hands. I shouldn't have been nervous. There was no way Bree would be eating M&M's before dinner. Not on a good day anyway. But seeing her hold that jar caused a high I never thought I'd feel again.

"Shit, this thing is heavy," she said. "Did you really sort through this many M&M's?" She lifted it to the sun and turned it in her hand. "There must be a thousand in here."

I shrugged. "Three thousand nine hundred and ninety-nine to be exact. I ate the last one to give it an authentic feel."

She laughed and pushed up onto her toes for another kiss. One I did not deny her.

"Is this to replace all of mine that you stole?"

I swayed my head from side to side. "More like a down payment. But we'll get there."

Giggling, she face-planted against my pec, and for several minutes, we just stood there, our chests rising and falling in synchronized breaths. We didn't have to say anything. There were no expectations or pressure. Just having her in my arms was enough for me.

God, it felt good to be home again.

"Mom!" Asher yelled. "What's for dinner?"

Luna shot to her feet. "I want dinner."

"Meeeee toooo," Madison called.

And just like that, our quiet little moment was over. But the chaos was just as sweet.

"All right." I released Bree and clapped my hands. "We're going out to dinner and then maybe to an arcade and then the bounce park and anywhere else we can find along the way."

The kids cheered like we'd been holding them captive, never letting them see the light of day.

Bree snapped her fingers. "Everyone needs to clean up the chalk first and put your new toys in your rooms."

They leapt into action, swirling around, arguing over who'd had what color chalk first, and I threw my arm around Bree's shoulders and smiled, enjoying every second.

She tilted her head back to stare at me, still holding the ridiculous jar of M&M's and filling my soul with new life. "Eason, you just got home. Are you sure you want to go out? I was going to cook something simple so you could relax. You have to be exhausted from traveling all day."

I absolutely was, but I had big plans with Bree that night. "So, here's what I'm thinking. If we stay here, have a lazy and quiet family night, those three are going to be jazzed by the time bedtime rolls around. We'll end up spending hours answering questions, giving goodnight kisses, and refilling water cups. Luna isn't going to want to let me go, so I'll have to lie down with her. We know from experience, once I get into a horizontal position, there is no coming back for me. I'll be asleep and the night will be over before it ever got started."

I slanted my head the other direction. "Orrrr we go out for hibachi, where the chef cooks in front of us, making them think grilled chicken and broccoli are cool. Then we go to the arcade, let them run themselves ragged while we enter into a *not-so-friendly* Skee-Ball tournament where the loser owes the winner wicked things with their mouth later on. Then we take the kids to the bounce park, let them jump until their legs give out, and then come home with three exhausted kids who will pass out before we even get them in bed. Leaving us completely alone, for you to make good on the loss you suffered earlier in the evening." I smirked.

"Wow. Someone gave this some thought."

I lifted one shoulder in a half shrug. "What can I say? I had a lot of spare time while separating four thousand red M&M's." It was a lie. I'd ordered them online, but that was one secret she didn't need to know about.

She let out a loud laugh and shook her head. "Yeah, fine. I missed you more than a little bit."

She didn't have to tell me. I saw it in her eyes every day that I was gone. I heard it in her voice every time she whispered, "I love you." And I felt it in the way she was still holding me tight, her lithe body sagging in my arms.

Bree and I tag-teamed getting the kids ready to go. Luna and Madison hung from my legs as we walked up the stairs. Then, while Asher got dressed, he insisted I stand outside the door so he could fill me in on all things *Abigail*, the girl who made his stomach hurt.

I loved being in LA and San Francisco. The sun, the energy—there was just something about knowing I was walking the same streets, visiting the same restaurants, and on more than one occasion, running from the same paparazzi as all the legends who had come before me.

But there was magic in watching the kids clap when the chef made an onion volcano and hearing Bree laugh as I purposely lost Skee-Ball, throwing each ball in the ten-point chute because I had every intention of ending my night with my mouth between her legs. I'd dreamed of a life in the spotlight, but there was immeasurable happiness to be found in cranking up the radio and singing at the top of my lungs in order to keep the kids awake on the drive home.

My plan to exhaust everyone had worked a little too well, because when I came back into the bedroom after reading the girls a story and locking up the house, Bree had pulled an Eason Maxwell and was sound asleep on her side, the barest hint of black lace showing on her shoulders.

After the day we'd had, and with finally being home, I couldn't even be disappointed. I'd let her sleep for a while. Middle-of-the-night sex definitely had its merits.

As I stood there staring at her, I chuckled at the jar of untouched red M&M's on her nightstand. I only knew they were untouched because she still hadn't found the engagement ring inside. She'd get there though.

Maybe one afternoon while I was in the shower, she'd go for a handful and scream.

Maybe she'd sneak a few first thing in the morning and I'd wake up to find her staring at me with tears in her eyes.

Maybe she'd find it next week when I was back in California. A long-distance proposal wasn't ideal, but the element of surprise she so fiercely hated would definitely be worth the payoff.

Was it too soon? By most people's standards, probably. But not for me. I'd found her. The one. There were no nerves or fears. No second-guessing or cold feet. I knew down to the marrow of my bones that Bree had been born to be mine. Our bond might have been forged through tragedy, but our love flourished through patience, genuine respect, and understanding.

Life was never easy, and ours had been harder than most.

However ugly it might have been at times, there was beauty to be found when looking back at all the pain and heartache and devastation, knowing we'd come out the other end better off and more in love than I had ever known possible.

So, as I fell asleep in bed with her that night, a smile on my face, love in my chest, contentment coursing through my veins, I had no idea our greatest trials were yet to come.

"Mom!" Asher screamed, his terror palpable as he came racing into the bedroom.

I jolted upright, and so did Bree, just as fast, beside me. Throwing the covers back, I jumped out of bed; three long strides carried me to him.

He launched himself into my arms the second I got close enough. His whole body was shaking head to toe.

"What's wrong?" On instinct, I set him on the bed and frantically began patting him down, searching for injury. It was the only explanation my sleep-fogged brain could come up with.

Bree flipped the light on then sidled up beside us, giving him a once-over, both of us coming up empty for anything physical that could explain his hysterics. Palming either side of his ghostly white face, Bree squatted in front of him. "Breathe, buddy. It's okay. Mommy's right here. Everything's okay. Did you have a nightmare?"

He shook his head, fat tears continuously flowing from his terrified eyes.

In the distance, I heard Madison start crying, the chaos clearly waking her up too. My heart already started to slow, my brain coming to terms that there was no immediate danger my adrenal system needed to handle.

Drawing in a deep breath, I looked at Bree. "You deal with this. I'll take care of the girls."

"You can't!" Asher yelled. "He took her! He took her!"

"Who?" Bree asked.

In his next breath, my whole world stopped.

"Luna! Daddy took her!"

"Asher, baby," Bree soothed. "That's not possible. Luna's daddy's right here."

In the middle of tragedy, it's strange the things that become engrained into your memories.

I remembered when it struck me that only Madison was crying in the background.

I remembered busting into the room to find Luna's bed empty.

I remembered the frantic search as I yelled for Bree, my heart still clinging to hope that Luna had just gotten out of bed and gone downstairs.

But carved into my soul for the rest of my days would be the earth-shattering sound of Asher shouting, "Not her daddy! *My* daddy!"

CHAPTER TWENTY-FIVE

BREE

"FIND HER!" EASON ROARED AT GRAY-HAIRED Detective Hoffman while at least a half dozen police officers roamed our house.

"Mr. Maxwell, I assure you we have a team of officers on this. If she's out there—"

"Don't say if," he snapped. "Don't you dare fucking say *if*. This is my daughter we're talking about. We know she's out there. Now, do your goddamn job and bring her home."

It was only ten in the morning, but it had already been the hardest day of my life.

An endless symphony played in our heads.

Where was she?

Was she safe?

Was she scared?

Or my biggest fear: Was it already too late?

For over six hours, Eason and I had been in a constant state of panic. Time passed, seconds felt like hours. Much like the stages of grief, the emotional process of finding out someone had kidnapped your child while she'd slept soundly under your roof just yards away from your bedroom door started with denial.

It felt impossible to believe someone had taken her—Asher's claims of it being Rob who'd done it were even wilder.

Regardless, Eason had taken off out the unlocked back door, sprinted around the house, and searched the surrounding areas while I'd called the police. As we waited for them to arrive, Eason had been rabid, racing around, calling her name. With both Asher and Madison crying, I towed them around with me for fear of letting them out of my sight. The pool had been my first stop. As terrified as I was to find our sweet baby in the water, the fear amplified by not finding her at all.

While outside, I noticed that the door to the pool house was cracked. The relief made my head spin as I sprinted over, hoping she'd just woken up disoriented and gone looking for her dad. Eason met me out there, his brain following the same path as mine.

There were so many factors we hadn't even considered in those first few minutes of looking for her.

How could she have gotten through the baby gate at the top of the stairs?

How could she have unlocked the back door?

Why hadn't the alarm gone off?

But desperation didn't allow for logical problem solving.

Luna hadn't been in the pool house.

Not in her room.

Not in Eason's.

Not anywhere.

And every second that passed sent my anxiety skyrocketing.

But just as we started back outside, hearing sirens blaring in the distance, Eason noticed a folded paper sitting on his piano bench.

Two lines typed in black ink. Nothing special yet completely earth-shattering.

$5 million to buy her back

Followed by a twenty-six-digit number of some sort.

That was it.

No instructions or explanation.

Just one demand and five lives that would never be the same.

I'd seen Eason broken and shattered.

I'd seen him bleeding and blanketed by fire.

I'd seen him hollow and emotionally demolished.

But as he fell to his knees, his hands shaking, the unimaginable setting in, the man I loved was obliterated.

She was gone.

When the police arrived, they separated me and Eason for questioning almost immediately. Anger was Eason's next response. For over two hours, I listened to him raging in the kitchen. The absolute agony in his voice matched the pain inside my chest.

They asked me questions, but I only had so many answers.

We'd been asleep. The house had been locked up tight. Yet someone had walked right in and taken our little girl.

Security footage from the camera on the front of the house showed nothing. No car pulling in or out of the driveway. No shadowy figures approaching under the shade of darkness. There was nothing on the side cameras, either. The only lead we had came from the back of the house, which showed a three-second clip of a person dressed in black, wearing a ski mask and gloves. We couldn't even make out if it was a man or a woman before the wires were cut, disabling the camera altogether.

Then there was Asher, who swore up and down, unwaveringly, that he'd woken up to see his dead father carrying Luna down the hall.

After several hours of questioning us separately, we were no closer to finding Luna. Eason was a mess, completely inconsolable, and I felt like I'd done a backslide into the past where everything hurt and nothing made sense. Finally, they brought us back together in the living room. A female officer sat with the kids in the playroom, and as much as it destroyed me to hear Asher's muffled cries, this wasn't something he needed to be a part of.

"My baby is out there somewhere with God only knows who. Why the fuck are you standing in my house right now talking about *ifs?*" Eason boomed.

"Just breathe," I urged, stepping into his side. His heart was beating so fast that I could feel it pounding against his ribs. "Just let him talk, okay?"

He stabbed a hand into the top of his hair and the muscles on his neck strained, but he closed his mouth long enough to let the detective continue.

"What I was trying to say was we have an entire team working on finding your daughter. I know Agent Garrett was here earlier from the Bureau and spoke with both of you separately about possible suspects and the hazards of paying the ransom."

I closed my eyes and stared down at the floor, Luna's honey browns on the backs of my lids. For Luna, I would have paid any amount of money in the world to end the nightmare. Neither of us had five million just sitting around. But, with enough time, I had faith I could gain access to it. I could sell the house, clear out every bank account, retirement account, and investment portfolio I had. Selling Prism alone would have netted me ten times that.

But with our chances of finding her after the twenty-four-hour mark dwindling by the second, time was the one thing we did not have.

Even if we could come up with the money, Agent Garrett and his team were strictly against paying the ransom. They said there was no guarantee the abductors would give her back and sometimes it just made them greedy and violent, demanding even more.

So Luna was gone.

Someone had taken her.

And we were at a stalemate with no way to get her back.

I would have rather been back at the fire.

I would have rather been back *inside* the fire.

I would have rather been *on* fire than not knowing if we would ever see our little girl again.

And based on the agony carved in his face, Eason would have said the same.

"So, what do we do now?" Eason asked, his anger ebbing into helplessness.

Detective Hoffman hitched up his navy slacks, his badge showing on his hip. "We are working closely with the FBI to bring your daughter home. But I'm going to be honest with you. We don't have a lot of information to go on here. We have a couple theories we're looking into though. The first being that this is something related to your newfound celebrity status. Maybe a stalker or someone of the likes. The fact that the note was left on your piano is telling. And if both girls were asleep in the same room, it would definitely explain why they only took your daughter and left the Winters girl behind."

"A stranger wouldn't know which one was my daughter," Eason snapped. "I'm not famous. I played the Grammys once and had my photo snapped a few times with Levee Williams, but my daughter's picture isn't slapped all over the internet. Nothing more than what the few people had dug up from when she was a baby." He walked over to a table against the wall and snatched up a framed picture of Madison and Luna posing in front of the Christmas tree. "Look at them. Tell me in a dark room, two beds side by side, that you could pick out who is who."

He definitely had a point there. There was a reason we'd spent so long questioning Luna's paternity. Roughly the same age, same size, same hair color, different shades of brown eyes, but not enough for an outsider to be able to tell them apart.

"Okay," the detective conceded. "That theory also doesn't explain how this person got into your home. There is no sign of forced entry, and according to your security company, your alarm was disengaged with a preset code. Which has me thinking we're dealing with someone who knows you."

"Nobody has *our* code though," I argued.

He quirked a furry, gray eyebrow. "Take a minute and really think about this. Babysitters, maids, house sitter? *Nobody* else has a code to your home?"

"No," Eason stated firmly. "You guys have already cleared our babysitter, Evelyn. She's the only person allowed in our house and even she has her own unique code. That wasn't what they used to disarm the alarm."

I didn't want to say it. I would sound ridiculous, and it felt even worse than that, but I'd take the humiliation any day of the week if it got Luna back. "What about Rob?"

Eason's gaze swung down to meet mine, his mouth an angry slash, but he didn't utter the first objection, which made it all too clear he'd been thinking about it too.

The detective let out a throaty rumble and cut his gaze over my shoulder. "Listen, speaking from almost forty years of experience, kids aren't the best eyewitnesses. When traumatic things happen, their minds struggle to look past the fear, so their brains fill in details in an attempt to make sense of a situation. It is not uncommon for children to—"

I took a step toward him. "But this would make sense."

He slanted his head. "A dead man coming back to life to kidnap a child that is not his own? That makes sense to you?"

"Hey," Eason growled, all patience with the entire day gone. "Watch your fucking tone."

He lifted his hands in surrender. "No disrespect intended. Just trying to be real with you."

"None of this is fucking real!" Eason boomed.

"Look." I stepped in between the two men, resting my hand on Eason's chest, which was rising and falling at a marathon pace. "It sounds insane. And impossible. But just for the sake of covering all bases, let's think about it. Rob knew where every single camera on this house is. He had the security company install them himself. The code on the alarm hasn't changed since he's been gone. And Eason swears he locked the doors, but the back door was unlocked, and the pool house was standing wide open. Someone must have had a key." I swallowed hard and shook my head. "Rob's keys were in his pocket the night he died, and as far as I know, they were never recovered."

Detective Hoffman inhaled deeply, a calm that had been evading Eason and me all day washing over him. "Again, Mrs. Winters. I mean this with the utmost respect. We are not in the business of chasing a dead man."

"And neither am I," I sniped. "But my kid isn't a liar. He's been shaking and crying all day, thinking a ghost took his sister. I think we can all agree this was not Rob, but what if it was somebody close to him? My ex-husband was not a faithful man. We have proof he was sleeping with Eason's wife…in my bed. What if he had someone else too? What if, before he died, he'd given someone a key to the house, a code to the security system, a pattern to avoid the security cameras—and not because they were planning to kidnap our child, but because they were trying to avoid being caught having an affair in my home?" Tears I should have long since run out of filled my eyes. "I don't know who Asher saw, okay? But I am begging you not to rule out the idea that he could still be responsible for this." A sob tore from my throat as I finished.

"Come here," Eason whispered, draping his arm around my shoulders and curling me into his chest.

I always felt safe in Eason's arms. But this wasn't something that could be soothed or quelled.

We'd already lived through hell, but there we were, our nightmares coming true faster than our dreams ever could.

"We just need her back," I told the detective, my cries muffled by Eason's strong chest. "Please, just help us find her."

CHAPTER TWENTY-SIX

EASON

NUMB YET SIMULTANEOUSLY FROZEN IN A STATE OF MORE pain than I had ever experienced, I spent the rest of the day on autopilot.

My heart beat.

My lungs expanded.

But my mind was lost in a sea of what-ifs.

Not the kind of what-ifs that could ever be spoken out loud for fear the universe would hear me and take them as a challenge. The world was full of sick and twisted people.

And now, one of them had my baby girl.

Bree had called a locksmith to change every lock in the house. The garage door had been reprogramed, and the security company was coming out the next morning to install new cameras inside and outside the house.

But until that was done, and maybe not ever, neither of us felt safe staying in the house. We also didn't want to go far though. I'd spent the day staring at the door as the police took pictures and examined every square inch of our home. I was hanging on the edge of a cliff, knowing that someone had taken her, but there was still a part of me that hoped she had just wandered away and at any minute would come back home.

She wouldn't. I knew that. But hope was my drug of choice at the moment.

Thankfully, Evelyn lived just down the street and reached out to us that afternoon. She'd spent the day with officers combing her house, and the minute they cleared her as a potential suspect, she opened her doors to us.

It was closer than a hotel on the off chance we needed to get back home quickly, and Asher and Madison adored her, so they would feel comfortable there as well. The police thought it was a good idea to leave for a few nights too, so with a gaping hole in my chest, we packed bags and left the last place I'd kissed my daughter goodnight.

Bree and I wouldn't let the kids out of our sight, but Evelyn took over cooking dinner, passing out snacks, even luring Madison, who hadn't stopped asking for Luna all day, into a game of hide-and-seek.

Asher wouldn't budge though, and when it came time to tuck them into bed that night, he was no less anxious.

"I'm not lying!" Asher cried, clinging to Bree's neck.

"I know." Bree stroked the back of his dark hair.

"Can people come back from heaven?"

I sank down on the edge of the bed, put my elbows to my knees, and hung my head.

"No, baby. They can't," Bree replied, resting her other hand on my bouncing knee.

"Then how was he there?" His head suddenly popped up, a new round of panic showing on his face. "Oh no. What if he took Luna back to heaven with him? Maybe Aunt Jessica missed her."

That thought lodged a boulder in my throat, causing me to

nearly suffocate, and I had to stand up and walk to the door or chance breaking down right in front of him.

"That's not possible, baby," Bree whispered. "Look at me, Ash. We believe you. You saw someone, and I know you would never lie about that. But they had a mask on, right? Maybe it was just someone who looked like—"

"It was Dad!" he shouted, frantic desperation thick in his voice. "I looked right at him before he ran away. I remember what he looked like, and I know it was him."

I sucked in a deep breath, holding it until my lungs ached. The pain in my chest had been so excruciating all day that the momentary burning from oxygen deprivation felt like a reprieve. Turning on a toe, I looked him straight in the eye. "I believe you, Ash."

I didn't. But he needed to know we did.

That kid.

That kid, with a heart of gold who would forever own a piece of my own, looked me dead in the eye and then absolutely slayed me. "I'm sorry, Eason. I'm sorry I didn't stop him. I got scared because I thought he was a ghost."

I had him in my arms in the very next second. Like a baby, he folded his arms around my neck and his legs around my waist, sobbing into my shoulder for something that never should have been his to bear. I knew all too well what it was like to fail someone you loved. And to carry the guilt for something completely out of your control. That kind of regret was not something I ever wanted my boy to experience.

I held him tight, my forearms crossed over his back. "You did everything right this morning. You're seven years old. It is not your job to stop an intruder in our house. Do you understand me? You did the right thing. You came and woke us up. Knowing that he took her as quickly as we did is really going to help the police find her. You did good, buddy. Really good."

He continued to cry, the sobs ravaging his small body cutting me to the quick. Bree stood across the room, tears streaming down her cheeks, but neither of us knew what to do.

And quite honestly, the hardest part was that there wasn't actually anything left to do at all.

We just had to wait and pray they found her.

After a few minutes, Bree took him from my arms, and together, they lay down on the bed. Evelyn had set up two of her guest rooms for us, and originally, I was going to bunk with Asher while Bree was going to take Madison. But he needed his mom for a little while.

And I needed a quiet moment to remember how to breathe.

I stopped at the other guest room and peeked inside. Madison was already out, sprawled out across the bed. She was old enough to realize her best friend was gone, but she was oblivious to the fear and panic that was circling like a vortex around us all. As I watched her sleeping, not a worry in the world, I was enormously grateful that at least one of us could rest.

Ever so quietly, I closed the door to her room, pulled my phone from my back pocket, and then sank to the floor. I must have had a million text notifications. Word had gotten out when police had activated the Amber Alert and everyone from old bar buddies to Levee and Sam had been texting me, offering any assistance they could provide. I'd replied to none of them. I didn't need a casserole, a beer, or, in Levee's case, a bodyguard.

I just needed Luna. I had no idea how I would survive the night without her.

Clicking the green call button twice, I lifted the ringing phone to my ear. I didn't even have to dial his number. He was the only person I'd called all day. Detective Hoffman and the members of the APD who were hanging out at our house in case the asshole tried to come back were great. But I knew that the FBI task force was hard at work across town.

"Agent Garrett," he answered.

"Please tell me you have something new?" I begged.

He sighed. "How ya holding up, Eason?"

"I'm not. You gotta give me something here. I'm falling apart."

After humming sympathetically, he said, "We haven't found Luna. Let me just start by saying that." Another rusty knife of reality stabbed me in the gut. "But I was actually just about to head your way. We got a hit on that number from the note. It's not a banking account number. It's to a private cryptocurrency account. Anonymous owner, virtually untraceable."

"Fuck," I breathed.

"But, while we can't track down the owner, we did run it through some of our databases and got a lead on another cryptocurrency account who received funds from your guy's account a while back."

My heart stopped and I sat up straight. It wasn't Luna, but it was at least something. "That's good, right?"

"It's a jumping-off point, that's for sure. Do you know anyone by the name S. Barton?"

"Doesn't ring a bell. Why?"

"Because less than twenty-four hours before your house exploded, the man who kidnapped your daughter sent him half a million dollars."

My heart stopped and a cold chill rolled over my body. "What the fuck did you just say?"

"You heard me right. I've got guys on it. I'm swinging by the police department to pick up the fire inspector's report and then I'm on my way to you. Hang tight. I'll see you and Bree in thirty."

He hung up, but my mind raced faster than ever. It could have been a coincidence. People all around the world had been living their lives, making transactions, buying and selling anything and everything under the sun both before, during, and after the fire.

But what were the chances those people would later kidnap my daughter?

I paced the hallway for what felt like an eternity but probably measured closer to ten minutes before Bree finally came out of the bedroom.

One look at me and she went on alert. "What's wrong?"

I stopped and gripped the back of my neck. "Agent Garrett is on his way."

In the narrow hall, she rushed the few steps toward me. "Did they find her?"

I shook my head, unable to even say the single syllable of truth. "They were able to find someone who had received money from the ransom account. Half a million dollars within a day of the fire."

"What?" she gasped. "That's—"

"Suspicious as fuck," I finished for her. "Some guy named S. Barton."

"Who's that?"

Unable to stand still, I resumed my pace up and down the hallway. "Hell if I know. Garrett said they are looking into it but—"

"Wait." She narrowed her eyes on a blank space above the door. "Barton."

"That's what he said."

She snapped her fingers twice and then, without another word, barged into the room Madison was sleeping in.

I followed after her, whisper-yelling, "Hey, shhhh, she's asleep."

Once she'd grabbed the computer bag she'd brought from the house, she silently slipped out of the room just as quickly as she'd entered it. She made fast work of pulling out her laptop and then passed the bag to me. "Find me my external key."

She sank down on the top stair, typing in passwords and booting up her computer. I dug to the bottom of the bag, finding the small flash-drive-sized device she used to securely access Prism from home. "What are you doing?"

"We had a Barton at Prism. I don't remember his first name though."

With my heart pounding in my chest, I passed her the digital key and wedged my large body beside her at the top of the stairwell. "You think it could be him?"

"I don't know. He's the only Barton I know though." She continued staring at the screen, her fingers flying across the keyboard. "Do you remember when I first went back to work after the fire? There was a maintenance guy who no-showed for an entire month before anyone noticed and cut him from the books."

I did not remember this in the least. I was, however, hovered over her screen as if I could magically unlock the universe and I prayed with my entire soul I could.

Suddenly, her back shot straight, and she leaned in close to the screen. "Steven Barton. S. Barton—he used to work at Prism."

She turned the screen my way and there he was. A man I didn't recognize with dark-brown hair and a thick beard. Steven Todd Barton in the fucking flesh who possibly knew who had taken my daughter.

I shot to my feet. "What's his address?"

She continued frantically clicking around on the screen.

"Bree, what the fuck is his address?"

"I don't know. I'm looking. He doesn't seem to have one. The address section is all blacked out." She shook her head. "That's not possible. Get Jillian on the phone. Everyone has an address on file. It's policy."

It took one ring for Jillian to answer the phone. "Hello?"

"Why doesn't Barton have an address?" I snapped.

"What?" she asked, thoroughly perplexed.

Bree reached up and took the cell from my ear. "Hey, Jill, it's Bree. Listen, I'm looking at a file for a former employee. His address is all blacked out though. Why?" She hit the speaker button and then set the phone beside her so she could use both hands.

Jillian's voice filled the hallway. "A lot of times, when employees just up and quit or get fired, they forget to send us their new address. When tax season rolls around, we send everything out *do not forward*. That way, the post office will send it back to us with the correct address and we can update it in the system. If you hit the yellow arrows, it should take you to the newest address we have on record."

"Yeah, I see the yellow arrows." Another click. "Yep. Okay. I got it."

I read over her shoulder—the three-line address branded on the backs of my lids.

"Any word on Luna yet?" Jillian asked.

"We're working on it." Bree ended the phone call, but I was already halfway down the stairs. "Where are you going?"

"Eight-ninety-one Richmont Way."

"You can't go there," she hissed, her feet pounding the stairs as she hurried after me, but I didn't slow. "You don't even know if it's the same guy."

"I'll take my chances being wrong." Each step toward the door made me more determined than the last.

"Eason," she called. "Wait, let's call Agent Garrett."

"Happy to as soon as we get on the fucking road." I paused as I passed Evelyn, who was sitting in her recliner. "Can you watch the kids for a few?"

She sat up and kicked the footrest closed, her eyes wide. "Of course. What's going on? Did they find her?"

"Not yet." I snatched my keys from my pocket and shoved my feet into a pair of boots by the back door, not bothering with the laces. "But we're working on it."

Bree chased me all the way out to my Tahoe, and even though I loved that woman, my already thin patience was waning.

"Eason, stop," she ordered, jumping between me and the car door.

"I can't fucking stop. Do you understand me?" I seethed. "Someone has my daughter. Someone I do not know. Someone who could—right this very second—be hurting her, abusing her." I leaned in close and added through clenched teeth, "Killing her. Stopping is no longer an option. This Steven Barton ends up being the wrong guy, then I have not one fucking thing to lose besides a trip across town. Though, he ends up being the right guy…" I lifted my T-shirt to reveal my moon-covered pec. "I have the entire fucking world to gain. So either move and let me go or get in the fucking car, but one way or another, with or without you, I'm going to find my daughter."

She stared deep into my eyes, searching for the right thing to do. I was past all that. Bree wasn't rash or reckless. She was too evenly measured to be fueled by desperate emotion. She was, however, my soul mate, the mother of my child—DNA be damned—and the smartest woman I had ever met.

Proof being: She got into the car.

CHAPTER TWENTY-SEVEN

BREE

"**D**ON'T YOU FUCKING DARE GO OVER THERE!" Agent Garrett yelled so loudly that I wasn't even holding the phone and heard it clear across the Tahoe.

"Too late. I'm already here," Eason said, no fucks left to give. He ended the call and dropped the phone into the cupholder. It immediately lit with an incoming call, but it was safe to say Eason was done talking.

I reached across the center console and gave his thigh a squeeze. "Eason, honey. Can we just take a breather for a minute? It's completely possible this guy has nothing to do with Luna."

"This look like the neighborhood of an entry-level maintenance man to you?" he asked, following his GPS through manicured streets and charming boulevards we raced by.

No. It was safe to say it did *not*. This place was gorgeous, everything spread out unlike some of the newer neighborhoods in the suburbs of Atlanta where the houses were practically on top of each other. Large homes with sprawling, green lawns were set back from the street. Old-timey streetlights illuminated sidewalks and even a bike path disappearing into a wooded area. The houses weren't quite as big as ours, but the neighborhood itself was impressive.

"Maybe his parents live here or—"

"Or maybe he bought it with the half million he got paid for lighting my house on fire and killing two people."

My stomach wrenched. This was a theory he'd brought up while weaving through traffic on the way over, and I had to admit the timing of the payment seemed suspect as hell, but the police had never once considered the fire arson.

He was teetering on the edge of sanity, adrenaline spinning his mind in every possible direction. I understood. I was desperate too. But if I couldn't make him wait on the police, I could at least talk him off the ledge of doing something that might drive us even further away from finding Luna.

"We don't know that," I told him. "And if you walk up to that door, slinging accusations, we may never know. I am behind you one thousand percent here. But emotions are high, and we can't lose our focus. Steven Barton received money from the man who has Luna. All we need is a name, Eason. Save the rest of the interrogation for the cops."

The hinges of his jaw ticked, and his eyes remained fixated on the road, but even with as pissed off and scared as he was, he knew I was right. "Look for eight-ninety-one," he said, and it wasn't an order or said with a bark, so I assumed I'd gotten through.

We pulled into the driveway of a brick two-story at just past ten. The porch light was on as well as several inside both upstairs and down, so if Barton was in there, we weren't going to have to wake him up.

Eason was out of the car first, and I had to jog to keep up with him. He stomped his way up the stairway leading to a massive wraparound front porch. At least half a dozen white rocking chairs and hanging plants lined the front. Such a normal house to be standing in front of under such horrific pretenses.

My heart was in my throat as Eason rang the doorbell. I tried to play it cool, but his adrenaline spread to me as we stood there, impatiently waiting, hoping and praying this man could lead us to Luna.

After several seconds of nothing, Eason knocked hard with his fist.

"Easy," I whispered, walking around the rocking chair to peer inside a window. Modern dark leather furniture decorated the living room as the local news flashed across a large flat screen mounted above the fireplace.

"Do you see anyone?" he asked.

"No, but the TV's on."

"Then someone's got to be in there." He rattled the doorknob, groaning when it didn't give. "Fuck it. I'm going around back."

"Eason—" I started to scold, a whole lecture about trespassing poised on the tip of my tongue, but it died before it ever made it out of my mouth.

Suddenly, a sharp cry sounded from the inside of the house, and I felt it hit my body with the force of a sledgehammer.

It wasn't Steven Barton.

It wasn't a man at all.

But there was no mistaking it. I would recognize that voice anywhere.

And I wasn't the only one.

"Luna!" Eason bellowed, ramming his shoulder into the door.

A man's broad back appeared as he ran down the hallway with our little girl dangling in his arms. Her honey-brown eyes collided with mine over his shoulder. I couldn't hear her muffled voice, but the sound of her sweet "Bwee" played in my head all the same.

"She's in there!" I yelled, panic consuming me. "I think he's taking her out the back."

I took off around the side of the house. Eason was faster though, sprinting past me, his feet hammering on the wooden porch. With two hands on the railing, he propelled himself over it and disappeared from my sight.

"Hey!" he boomed. "Stop right fucking there."

Blood thundered in my ears as I rounded the corner to the back steps, skipping every other one on my way down. I made it to the bottom just in time to see Eason dive and tackle the bearded man holding Luna.

Luna flew from his arms and landed hard in the grass, a pained wail tearing from her throat.

"Get her!" Eason yelled at me while clinging to the man, fighting beneath him to get away. Punches were exchanged, grunts and cusses echoing through the otherwise silent night.

With my heart in my throat, I bolted to Luna. Her arms were already stretched as high as she could get them, reaching for me, twin rivers dripping off her chin. Mid-stride, I scooped her up, planting her on my hip, but she crawled up my front, shaking as she hugged my neck.

"I want Daddy!" she cried.

"Shhh. It's okay. I've got you," I soothed, stroking a hand down her back.

The right thing to do was to take Luna and leave. Eason could handle himself. I told my feet to move. My brain all but screamed it. But for some reason, I couldn't stop staring at the man Eason was fighting to restrain.

I wouldn't recognize Steven Barton. I'd never seen more than the one picture of him on my computer. The dark-brown hair matched. So did the thick beard.

But none of that explained why the hairs on the back of my neck stood on end.

"You motherfucker," Eason snarled, rolling on top of him and wrapping a hand around his throat. Using his knees, he pinned him to the ground, reared back his fist, and then stopped. Completely. Head to toe. His entire taut, rage-filled, adrenaline-ravaged body just...

Froze.

Just like my heart, as the entire world once again caught fire around us.

His name slipped through my lips on a violent whisper. "Rob?"

CHAPTER TWENTY-EIGHT

EASON

"WHAT THE HELL?" I BREATHED, THE FIST AIMED at my former best friend's face dropping limply to my side.

My *dead* former best friend's face.

"Get the fuck off me." He bucked beneath me, blood dripping from his lip into his beard.

I shook my head, seeing but in no way believing that the man breathing in front of me could actually be alive.

I couldn't lie. I hated Rob for so many things I'd learned since his death, but there was still a tiny part inside me that sparked, almost *happy* at seeing the man I had considered my brother for so many years with a pulse again.

Until I remembered he had taken my daughter.

With both hands wrapped around his neck, I cracked his head against the ground, roaring, "You're dead! We buried you!"

A sinister smile curled the corners of his mouth. "No. You buried Steven. That dumb fuck deserved to die. Setting off the explosive in the basement too soon. Fucking amateur cost me my whole damn life."

I blinked, literally nothing about the moment making sense. I had so many questions, but my mind couldn't steady on one long enough to ask any of them. It was Luna's cry from behind me that finally broke through my shock.

I looked up and found my woman holding her a few yards away, her face pale, as though she'd seen a ghost. Which, in reality, she had. But she had my daughter, my baby, safe in her arms, out of reach of whoever this madman was beneath me. Even with the utter shitstorm brewing all around me, I managed to let out a sigh of relief.

Bree started to take a step forward but froze, the shock leaving her unable to get any closer. "How did you get out?" Her voice shook, but her words were clear. "No one could have survived the second explosion."

Rob sneered, "No one should have survived the *first* one. And yet here we are."

I didn't want to take my eyes off Luna, afraid that, if I looked away, I'd be thrust back into the nightmare of not knowing where she was. But it was Rob's maniacal laughter that sent chills down my spine, forcing me to focus on him.

"God, this is so damn poetic. Eason, you should write a song about this shit. Maybe it'll actually be good for once."

A low blow from the man who'd spent years encouraging me to pursue my dreams. But the more words poured out of him, the more he told me that that man no longer existed.

Maybe he never had.

"Do you have any idea how hard it was to find someone willing to kill you two? I spent months siphoning money from Prism. I plotted out every fucking detail, right down to how Jessica would spend her time lounging by the pool—or better yet, on her knees, treating me like a fucking king." Even with my hands still wrapped around his throat, he managed to turn his head to look at his wife.

No, fuck that. *My* woman. "Your life insurance policy was going to allow us the life we *both* deserved. Half a million fucking dollars wasted on Steven Barton, and in the end, she was the only one who died." He let out a low growl filled with pain.

The air around us went static, and in that moment, pinning him to the earth, which he should have been six feet deep under, I could feel the fire licking at my neck all over again.

The fear as I woke up covered in rubble.

The pain as I sliced my hands, searching through the wreckage for Jessica.

The unrivaled agony as I stood outside, knowing I had failed my wife and best friend.

"You did this?" I seethed, the pieces of his deception clicking into place almost as fast as my fist came down on his face. "You tried to have me killed?"

He grunted under the force of my punch, but his slimy grin grew. "Well, technically, it was only Bree who was supposed to die. Jessica was the one who threw you into the deal. God, she hated you."

I wanted to choke the life out of him. My vision tunneled as blood roared in my ears. With his vile confessions slamming into me over and over, I could have done it without the first ounce of guilt.

You couldn't kill a man who was already dead, right? But I was so damn confused; I needed answers more than I needed revenge.

"What the fuck, Rob? You sleep with my wife, fall in love, or whatever the hell you two were doing. Then you fake your own death *and then* kidnap my kid? Who in the fuck are you?"

"I wouldn't have needed Luna if that bitch over there hadn't fired my cash cow."

Bree gasped and I wanted to go to her, hold her and Luna in

my arms as we tried to piece this sick, twisted puzzle together, but I couldn't risk giving Rob a chance to escape.

"Bree, get Luna out of here!" I shouted at her, my eyes still boring into a face that was both familiar and foreign. I could hear her footsteps, but instead of moving away, they grew closer.

"Who the hell did you have on the inside at Prism?" she asked.

"Oh, don't look so surprised. There was probably a line of people who would have been happy to help me destroy you. Doug was just the one I caught stealing money first. And now there's not a snowball's chance in hell he's not going to flip on me as soon as his trial rolls around. Five million was my last chance at a one-way trip to Mexico." He squirmed beneath me. "Get the fuck off. I can't breathe."

I leaned into his face, a bead of my sweat dripping onto his forehead. "Good. Welcome to the hell we've been living for the last two years now." Although I briefly wondered if it had been hell at all. I had the best family, the best woman, and now a career I'd always dreamed about. The heartache had been worth it.

"Oh, come on. It hasn't been that bad," he laughed. "You didn't waste any time slipping into my life—or my wife." He tore his eyes away from me and that slimy motherfucker *winked* at Bree. "I figured she'd still have you out in the pool house, but after that Grammy performance, I guess she moved you right upstairs." He laughed before spitting into my face. "I never thought you'd make it, much less with my wife's ice-cold pussy on your arm."

"What?" Bree breathed.

"I said, your ice-cold—"

He didn't finish the sentence before I popped him in the mouth again. I wasn't a violent man, but damn it felt good to feel the bones of my knuckles cracking against his face.

"Stop fucking punching me!" he barked as he bucked his hips. "Or I swear to God I'm going to snap your neck."

It was my turn to smirk, although I didn't hold half of the disgusting smugness his did. "You already tried to kill me once, asshole. How'd that work out for you?"

Bree once again waded into this clusterfuck conversation. "You had Doug embezzling money for you?"

Rob laughed. "He'd been doing it for years. When I got fucked at the fire, I told him if I was going down so was he. *Then* the money became about me."

"Why?" Bree asked, the hurt so clear in her voice it made my blood run hot.

"Why what? Shit didn't go as planned. What do you want from me? The fucking house exploded too soon. It isn't rocket science. I got out the back, but my life was over the minute I saw you two out front. I was not going to let all the work I did be for nothing. With Steven dead, I went back to his place and decided to start over. I used the money to get something that wasn't a piece-of-shit dilapidated cabin and stayed close to keep an eye on Doug. The last thing I needed was that bastard growing a conscience."

"You know they make this little thing called divorce, right?" she snapped.

"Right. So you could take my company and use the kids to lead me around by my dick for the rest of my life? Fuck that. Married or not, I'd rather be dead than live another fucking day where I had to hand over my balls to you. And surprise, surprise. Here you are, fucking me all over again. I just needed a way out."

"No. You needed a way out without looking like a failure!" she hissed, cradling Luna's face in the curve of her neck. "Your poor, precious little ego. Prism was in the red. Your plan to off me and

Eason backfired. You killed your own girlfriend. Everything you've ever touched has been one failure after another."

"Shut your fucking mouth!" he roared, fighting beneath me, but I kept him pinned.

"I'll shut your fucking mouth for you," I rasped, my throat feeling like I'd swallowed a razor blade. "You thought, now that I got a little money, kidnapping my daughter would be your ticket to freedom?"

"Oh, Eason. You always were so fucking gullible. You honestly think that kid over there is yours? You and Jessica were fucking how often? Once a month? I took her daily. A few times when you were just in the other room. Why do you think Luna looks so much like Asher and Madison? I hate to be the one to break it to you, but Luna Maxwell is actually Luna Winters."

It was my turn to offer a smug smile. "Oh, Rob," I mimicked. "You always were so fucking egotistical. Jessica may have told you Luna was yours, but you never did a DNA test, did you? You call me the gullible one, but all it took was a woman to put her mouth on your cock whenever you wanted and you just believed any line of bullshit you were fed. We found your extra phone. The texts, the fucking pictures. We knew about the affair and how you thought Luna was biologically yours. Only I wasn't so stupid to blindly believe something I was told."

I flexed my fingers around his throat as I brought my face so close to his that our noses were touching. With more pleasure than I'd ever experienced before, I told him the truth.

"Luna is *mine.*"

His eyes widened, and for the first time since this insane scenario had started, he looked shocked. "You're lying."

"Sorry. Unlike Jessica, DNA doesn't lie. And you want to hear my favorite part? Now, Bree is mine too. Your boy Asher?

Mine. Madison? Mine. A life free and easy, not rotting in a prison cell?" I dropped my voice low and declared, "*Mine*. So tell me, Rob. Who's the fucking winner in this situation?"

With all the adrenaline that had been pumping through my veins, it wasn't the satisfying sound of flesh on flesh as I punched the man who had turned our world upside down that set me free. It was the way Rob's face ran through the gamut of emotions as he realized he'd thrown away his life for a woman who had done nothing more than manipulate us all.

I might have wanted to kill him a few minutes earlier, and if I were being honest, the urge still burned at the edge of my mind. But the sweet victory of knowing I'd been able to deliver the news that rocked him the hardest was all the justice I needed.

Bree and I were silent after that. She finally took Luna around the front of the house and waited for the police. Rob yelled a lot as we waited. Screaming and cussing. Slinging insults and death threats like they were his second language. But none of it mattered anymore.

Because once and for all, Rob Winters didn't matter anymore.

Agent Garrett and his team arrived shortly. As soon as I was able to release my hold on that delusional psychopath, I took off around the house to find my daughter.

Luna dove into my arms, still quietly crying. Her warmth immediately thawed the ice that had formed in my veins the second I'd found out she was missing. "Shhh, Daddy's got you. It's over now."

Even from the front, we could hear Rob continuing to struggle with the officers, yelling at me and Bree as if we had somehow caused his fall from grace.

Right after the fire, I'd spent too long blaming myself for the things I couldn't control. I'd grieved the loss of a wife who had never loved me and a man who had posed as my best friend but had been ready to kill me to seize some bullshit idea he had about the perfect life.

Too many nights, I'd lain awake in bed, replaying the fire in my head over and over, the sour of guilt churning in my stomach because I'd thought I'd saved the wrong woman.

But with my daughter on my hip and Bree at my side as we headed home to our family, I knew I'd saved exactly the right one.

CHAPTER TWENTY-NINE

BREE

"Hey, Sug, have you seen my keys?" Eason asked, his broad shoulders filling my doorway.

I rolled my eyes at his incessant use of the silly nickname. He only called me that when he was trying to wind me up. And with Eason, as soon as he got the reaction he was hunting for, he'd lean in and kiss me breathless. Being called Sug was a small sacrifice to make.

I peered up at him from the ground, where I was taping up a box of my panties. "Check on the hook by the back door. I had to move the Tahoe to the garage when the packers got here." I paused and tried to suppress a smile. "And stop calling me Sug."

"You know I can't do that." Grinning from ear to ear, he prowled over to me. Cupping the back of my head, he folded at the hips and dipped low to make good on his Sug routine.

I nipped at his bottom lip, asking for more, and Eason was never one to deny me anything. His mouth opened, his tongue snaking out for an all-too-brief tangle with mine.

On a low growl, he asked, "They aren't taking the beds tonight, right?"

I let out a laugh and rested my hand on the side of his face.

"No, just packing things up. Movers will be here tomorrow. Though our best bet is going to be a shower after everyone passes out."

It had been two weeks since Rob had been arrested.

Two weeks of trying to figure out why he had done the things he had done.

Two weeks of trying to relax without the memories of those hours while Luna was missing ravaging our thoughts.

The betrayal of finding out that your husband was in love with your best friend was a dagger through the heart. The reality that they hated you so much they were willing to have you killed was more like being hit by a train.

With Rob in custody, Doug sang like a bird, throwing my ex-husband so far under the bus it hit him with every single wheel.

Based on Doug's statement to the police, he confessed to introducing Steven Barton to Rob but maintained his innocence about anything that had happened after that. Though the fact that he had still been sending a supposed dead man money every month said otherwise.

If Rob hadn't been such a greedy, power-hungry maniac and gone after Luna, he probably could have gotten away with all of it too.

It still boggled my mind that he'd chosen to take her. Not Asher or Madison—the children he'd raised from birth. But then again, he'd thought Luna was his daughter with his darling Jessica.

It was purely speculation, since Rob had refused to cooperate with the police. But I thought there was a part of him who just wanted to punish Eason. Seeing him succeed on that Grammy stage, knowing his dreams were coming true while Rob sat alone in hiding, his good name on a tombstone, had to have ignited him into a jealous frenzy.

Rob had always seemed so supportive of Eason's music, but

looking back, I was starting to think that their friendship had only existed because Rob had always expected Eason to fail. Rob got to play the part of the hero, encouraging Eason, preaching to him that the world was at his fingertips, meanwhile finding peace in his assumption that Eason would never be able to best him in any aspect of life.

Until he did.

And Rob went off the deep end.

Honestly, Rob's inferiority complex made up the bulk of his issues. He'd hid it well, but he couldn't stand the idea of his wife being more successful than him. Before I'd stepped down after having Asher, I made more money than he did. Held a higher position than he did. Prism was mine, and while I viewed our work together as a partnership, clearly he did not. I never once asked Rob to stand in my shadow, but he proved to be just an insecure man, scared of the darkness cast by his wife.

Eason and I still had a lot of questions. Most of which started with *why*. But regardless of how many answers we got or, as it turned out, didn't get, the insane and deranged actions of Rob and Jessica would never truly make sense.

Together, Eason and I could accept that. We were adults with extreme therapy bills. The kids were having a rougher go at things. Luna was experiencing nightmares to the point that Eason had moved her into our room. Deep down, that had as much to do with his fears as her own. But again, together, we were working our way through it.

While Asher was relieved to find out that he hadn't seen a ghost and seemed to accept our profuse apologies for not taking his accusations more seriously, he struggled with the truth about what his father had done. We told him as gently as possible after consulting a child psychologist, but there was no way to sugarcoat that kind of depravity. His deluge of questions switched from those about heaven to ones like if Daddy was going to come back and take him or Madison in the middle of the night. Or if Rob could make our house catch fire from jail. We assured him that none of those things were possible, but he asked if he could sleep in our room for a while. And while Madison seemed to be coping pretty well, we were not about to leave my baby girl out.

Every night, the five of us piled into that bed. There was little sleep to be found, with elbows in my ribs and, on more than one occasion, Eason catching a foot in his nether regions. However, we were together and safe, so the few minutes of rest we did catch were the most peaceful of all.

I had always been adamant about giving the kids a sense of stability after Rob died. But when that stability became tainted by fear and trauma, it was time to go.

I had no intention of ever going back to work at Prism. And only part of that was because of the role it had played in Rob's attempt on our lives. The biggest reason was: I just didn't want to.

After everything we'd been through, my family needed me more than ever. And truth be told, I needed them a hundred times more.

The minute the FBI closed its audit, I was selling the company. Business was good, though news of Rob's return from the dead had hit the media and soiled our good name. But we still had plenty of offers rolling in from around the world.

Without anything else holding us in Atlanta, Eason and I had a long talk. His career was just taking off, and for that, he needed to be in LA. We just needed to be with him.

And thus, the decision was made. In less than twenty-four hours, our little family was off to California.

The man of my dreams smiled down at me. "Mmm, I could

go for another shower with you." He pecked my lips again and then stood up. "If we have packers here, why are you sitting there packing your stuff?"

"Oh, right. Why don't you just go grab one of the guys and tell them to come box up my underwear?"

He let out a horrified gasp. "No way any man is touching my woman's Hanes Her Ways."

I barked a laugh. "Hey! I have some sexy stuff too."

"Yeah, but you know what those white cotton granny panties do for me." He bit his bottom lip and waggled his eyebrows.

God, I loved that ridiculous man.

I swatted at him, but he jumped out of my reach, laughing.

When he finally sobered, he planted his hands on his hips. "I see you still haven't cracked into my red M&M's yet."

I followed his gaze to the nightstand and shrugged. "I haven't been much in the mood for candy recently, I guess."

"Hmmm." He turned his sexy gaze back on me. "You planning on doing that before we leave tomorrow?"

I eyed him suspiciously. "I hadn't planned on it."

"Kids, Mom has candy!" he yelled while staring right at me. "What about now?"

"Eason! It's almost dinner time. And if you have any hope of them falling asleep tonight for you to get that sexy shower, I'm not sure candy is the way to do it."

"Hmmm, guess I didn't think that through. Too late now though." He shrugged nonchalantly as the sound of a stampede raced up the stairs.

Asher got there first. "I want candy."

Madison was next, her hands raised high above her head. "Me. Me. Me."

Luna pulled up the rear. "I *need* candy!"

Eason grabbed the jar of M&M's off the nightstand and brought them over to me. Four eager hands extended out in front of me. Yes. *Four*. Eason had his stuck out front and center.

Unscrewing the top, I shook my head. "Two each."

"Two!" Asher complained. "Eason promised us ten!"

He bumped Asher with his hip. "Boy, don't you get me in trouble."

Asher giggled, falling over to the side, his hand still outstretched as he climbed back to his feet.

"Psh. Ten? Eason was telling stories again." The lid released and I lifted it off. "Because there is no—"

And just like that, there were no more words left in the English language.

Okay, well, maybe one. "Eason!" I breathed, tears welling in my eyes as I stared down at a gorgeous emerald-cut diamond solitaire.

"You hid it in the M&M's?" Asher asked, clearly somewhat in on the plan.

My head snapped up and I found Eason on bended knee in the middle of the kids. Their little hands never lowered even as he started speaking.

"I have loved you since before I knew I loved you. I have loved you since before I was supposed to love you. And I will continue to love you every single day for the rest of eternity. I cannot tell you life will always be easy. Let's be honest, I'm still going to call you Sug sometimes."

I laughed and a tear rolled down my cheek.

He wiped it away before continuing. "But I can tell you that I will always be here for you in any and every way you need. I'll be your best friend. Your biggest fan. The man who drives you crazy in both good and bad ways. I don't care how you need me or even if you need me at all—I'll still be here, considering myself the luckiest man on the planet as long as we do this life together." He lifted the diamond ring from the jar and held it out in front of him. "Bree, will you do me the biggest honor of my life and marry me?"

This.

Man.

I'd thought my life was over the day of the fire, but little had I known, as I'd woken up in his arms outside that raging inferno, it was only the start of forever.

It was by far the easiest question I would ever answer.

"Yes," I breathed. Rising to my knees, I threw my arms around his neck, repeating, "Yes, yes, yes, yes."

He slid the ring on my finger and then let out a loud laugh, standing up with me in his arms.

"She said yes! That means they are getting married," Asher explained to the girls.

A round of cheers and giggles broke out around us as Eason peppered kisses all over my face.

A thought struck me and I leaned away to catch his eyes. "How long has that ring been in that jar?"

He beamed with pride. "Since I brought it home from California."

"Were you ever planning on telling me?"

"Well, I do know how you love a surprise."

I laughed. "I liked this one."

"Good. I don't want to hear a single peep about me eating your red M&M's from now on. I'd have finished the jar by now."

He could have every M&M in the world for all I cared. He could even call me Sug, though I wasn't about to tell him that.

"I love you so much."

He smiled the most beautiful grin I had ever seen, and because it was Eason, that was saying a lot. "I love you too."

EPILOGUE

EASON

Two years later…

"AND THE NOMINEES FOR ALBUM OF THE YEAR ARE…" a man announced, but I was too busy staring at my wife to focus on the stage.

"Talk to me," I whispered.

Bree blew out a controlled breath and gripped down on my thigh painfully tight. "Relax. The camera's about to come to you."

"I don't give a shit about the camera if—"

The opening notes of my number-one hit played through the Staples Center as the presenter, who I belatedly recognized as Shawn Hill, announced my nomination, "*From the Embers*, Eason Maxwell."

Straightening in my seat, I slapped on a smile that I prayed looked more genuine than it felt.

Levee turned around in her seat in front of us and shot me a beaming grin. "You got this."

I wasn't so sure she was right. Then again, I wasn't sure it mattered, either.

After moving to Los Angeles, life had changed completely. And thank fuck for that. Not that I didn't have fond memories in Atlanta. Playing with the kids in the backyard. Falling in love with Bree around the firepit. The kids giggling as Oreo climbed the curtains like a cat on crack. But none of that had to end based on our location. Every one of the people I shared those memories with were with me—crazy feline included.

It took about two weeks for us to find our dream house in California. It cost a damn mint compared to the Georgia housing market, but my advance from Downside Up more than covered things. Bree fell in love with the security gate across the driveway and cameras on every corner, and the kids fell in love with the pool—or, more accurately, the waterslide leading into the pool. I just fell in love with the fact that they had fallen in love. Win-win all the way around.

As soon as we got the keys, I hired a company to build us a bigger and better firepit—mainly because it didn't include fire at all. Twin curved couches surrounded a brick circle, but the burn basin was the center of an inverted water fountain. It was quiet enough that I could still hear Bree's content hums but relaxing enough that we could sit out there for hours on stressful nights, lost in our thoughts alone—together.

Even after we'd moved, it took a while for the kids to adjust to life after Rob's dramatic return. Slow and steady, Luna had re-emerged as the sassy, wild child she'd always been. Madison smiled and giggled with her every step of the way. Asher's emotional recovery was slightly more of an uphill climb. He trusted no one. Questioned everything. Just acclimating to a new school almost broke him. Watching my outgoing, lovestruck boy withdraw into himself made me hate Rob Winters that much more. And it should be noted that I'd already hated that asshole with the wrath of a rabid tiger, so that was really saying something.

It wasn't until six months later, when Rob accepted a plea deal for a life sentence in order to avoid the possibility of the death penalty, that Asher seemed to finally relax. Before we'd left Atlanta, the courts had approved Bree's petition to have their marriage dissolved—immediately. But in an even bigger move, as a part of Rob's sentencing, the judge stripped him of his parental rights too.

That was the day everything changed for Asher. Knowing Rob was in jail was one thing, but knowing he would never get out was another. However, the tears in his eyes and the relief on his face as we explained that Rob would no longer legally be his father healed wounds inside me I hadn't even realized I was still carrying. Knowing Asher had felt that fear, had been worried he'd have to go visit the man who had kidnapped his sister and terrified that he'd somehow come back for him, shattered me in so many different ways.

Though, when he looked at me and asked, "Does that mean you can finally be my real dad now?" all the pieces of my heart clicked into place.

I couldn't say yes fast enough, but then again, I couldn't really say anything past the emotion lodged in my throat. I gathered *my son* in my arms and nodded at least a dozen times. Bree quickly excused herself, and a little while later, I found her sitting on the floor in the pantry, crying and separating the red M&M's from her secret stash.

"You can have every red M&M for the rest of our lives for that," she croaked.

I didn't give a damn about red M&M's—I stole them all anyway. But adopting Asher and Madison was not a favor or a good deed that deserved a reward. They were *my kids*. Period. Full stop. End of story.

Bree and I hadn't been married yet. We were planning a small destination-wedding-slash-family-vacation to Jamaica in the spring when my schedule opened up. However, as soon as the courthouse opened the next day, we were standing on the front steps. If we were making our family official, I wasn't about to half-ass it in any way.

In front of a county clerk, wearing a white sundress while I sported a pair of jeans and a pale-blue button-down—sans a tie—Bree Winters became Bree Maxwell. And then, four months later, after a mile-high stack of paperwork, a judge granted our adoption request, making me the legal father to Asher Maxwell, Madison Maxwell, and of course, their glowing and giddy little sister, Luna Maxwell.

However, at the current moment, I was more worried about our fourth child making its debut in the middle of the Grammys.

As quickly as the camera shifted to the next nominee, my smile fell and I turned back to Bree. "You gotta give me something here. How close together are your contractions?"

Her lips thinned. "Do you mean the ones this morning or the ones now?"

"You were having contractions this morning?" I hissed. "Jesus, Bree. What the hell are we doing here, then?"

She crossed her arms over her chest, resting them on top of her round stomach, and shot me my favorite glare. "I don't know about you, but I'm about to watch my husband win a Grammy." She paused, screwing her eyes shut, before sucking in a sharp breath through her teeth.

Any other day when the birth of my child wasn't at risk of being a televised event, I would have been moved by her support. On that day, with her being thirty-eight-weeks pregnant and having contractions, I was just moved to get the hell out of there. "That's it. Let's go. I'm taking you to the hospital."

Tugging her arm out of my grip, she slanted her head. "Would you stop? I'm fine. The contractions aren't regular yet. But even if

I was crowning, there is exactly a zero percent chance of me letting you miss this. So sit back, relax, smile, and enjoy the moment you've worked your ass off for."

I gritted my teeth.

Bree was the most stubborn and fiercely independent woman I had ever met. And while those were usually qualities I admired, with nerves churning in my stomach, they weren't my favorite of her attributes at the moment.

"I swear, if you go into labor and Shawn Hill gets to look up your dress while I'm forced to deliver our child, I'm never forgiving you."

She let out a quiet laugh. "Great. Well, now you've ruined my plan. Everybody knows there is nothing sexier than childbirth."

No less nervous, I grinned over at her. "I've got my eyes on you, Maxwell."

She laughed again, but it ended with another wince.

"Not regular, huh?"

Clamping her jaw shut, she shook her head. So. Damn. Stubborn.

Only a year earlier, we'd sat at the same awards show with three nominations under my belt for Best New Artist, Song of the Year, and Record of the Year. I hadn't won any of them, but with my music on every station across the country and a headliner tour selling out as quickly as dates went up, it was hard to feel anything other than grateful.

For Bree and me, having another baby was an easy decision. I'd always wanted a whole herd of kids, and while sometimes it'd felt like just that with the three we already had, the idea of adding another had been more tempting than either of us could resist. With my tour winding down and work already starting on my next album, it was perfect timing.

Though our current predicament was less than stellar.

"And the winner is…" Shawn Hill's voice boomed, forcing my attention back to the big stage.

After my first loss of the evening, I'd told myself a win didn't matter. I got to make music for a living. It was a job that more than supported my family, and my career had grown to levels I hadn't even known to dream about. I had a gorgeous wife who loved and supported me wholly and with her entire being, three beautiful, healthy kids at home and another who, with any luck, would hold tight until we made it to the hospital.

Despite the chaos and tragedy of my past, I had a life I loved. Winning a Grammy wouldn't change any of that.

But it still sounded like the sweetest melody when I heard, *"From the Embers, Eason Maxwell!"*

A wave of emotion crashed into me, pinning me to my seat, so I turned into Bree as she threw her arm around my shoulders. The biggest names in the entire industry clapped and cheered. Levee and Sam stood up, shouting my name and patting me on the shoulder, but it was Bree's voice in my ear that made my throat get thick.

"This is all you. Even when people told you to stop and the world quite literally caught fire around us, you kept going. And *you* did this, Eason. All of this."

When all other words failed me, I managed to whisper, "I love you."

"I love you too," she said before releasing me. "Now, go get your Grammy."

With shaking hands and breathless lungs, I stood up, pressing a kiss to her lips before heading up to the stage. Shawn handed me my award and I took a moment just to admire it, absorbing the weight of it in my hands. I'd seen them a dozen times in studios and at Levee's house; there were even replicas sold in gift shops around the city.

But none of those had been mine.

Swallowing hard and praying that my brain found words, I looked out at the crowd. My gaze zeroed in on where Bree and Levee were still on their feet as my producer, Lincoln, joined me on stage. We did the whole handshake-hug-back-pat routine before I passed off the golden gramophone to him and stepped up to the mic.

"I, um, have made a living for the past decade writing lyrics. But I was too worried I'd jinx it if I wrote anything down for tonight." I rubbed my sweaty palms together, not having the first damn clue what to do with my hands without an instrument to fill them. "I'm kinda regretting that now."

The crowd laughed and I took the moment to clear my throat.

"I want to start out by thanking my wife. I know a lot of you have heard bits and pieces of our story, but for those who haven't, I'll give you the abridged version. Some years back, there was a fire at my house. It was horrific. Lives were lost. Paths were forever changed. But the media reported that I saved the life of that beautiful woman over there." I locked my eyes on Bree, pouring every ounce of love into my words. "But the truth is: She saved me."

Tears filled her eyes as she blew me a kiss.

"Without that woman, there would be no Eason Maxwell." I smiled and swayed my head from side to side. "There might be an Easton Maxwell, but that's a story for a different day."

The tears finally escaped her eyes as she laughed.

"I guess I just want to say thank you. To my old record label, who shall remain nameless, for dropping me all those years ago. To Levee and the entire Downside Up team for taking a chance on me. To Asher, Madison, and Luna, you three are the biggest dream

I've ever had. Thank you for letting me be your daddy. It has been a wild ride, and now, if you'll excuse me, it's about to get a whole lot crazier. My wonderful, supportive wife neglected to mention that she's been having contractions all day. I should probably get her to the hospital."

My producer handed the award back to me and I hefted it into the air and finished my totally unscripted-but-straight-from-the-depths-of-my-heart speech. "So, thank you. Also, I wasn't supposed to tell anyone, but it's a girl." I grinned and shot a wink at Bree, and even though she was glaring, the smile on her lips told me I wasn't in too much trouble.

The crowd roared, everyone standing on their feet, all eyes aimed at Bree. Just as they should be.

I might have been the one who created the music.

But Bree would forever be the star of our show.

Eight hours later, Ava Grace Maxwell was born looking just like her sisters and completing the family we had forged from the embers—the way it was always supposed to be.

OTHER BOOKS

Release

Reclaim

THE RETRIEVAL DUET

Retrieval

Transfer

GUARDIAN PROTECTION SERIES

Singe

Thrive

THE FALL UP SERIES

The Fall Up

The Spiral Down

THE DARKEST SUNRISE SERIES

The Darkest Sunrise

The Brightest Sunset

Across the Horizon

THE TRUTH DUET

The Truth About Lies

The Trust About Us

THE REGRET DUET

Written with Regret

Written with You

THE WRECKED AND RUINED SERIES

Changing Course

Stolen Course

Broken Course

Among the Echoes

ON THE ROPES

Fighting Silence

Fighting Shadows

Fighting Solutude

CO-WRITTEN ROMANTIC COMEDY

When the Walls Come Down

When the Time is Right

ABOUT THE AUTHOR

Originally from Savannah, Georgia, *USA Today* bestselling author Aly Martinez now lives in South Carolina with her husband and four young children.

Never one to take herself too seriously, she enjoys cheap wine, mystery leggings, and baked feta. It should be known, however, that she hates pizza and ice cream, almost as much as writing her bio in the third person.

She passes what little free time she has reading anything and everything she can get her hands on, preferably with a super-sized tumbler of wine by her side.

Facebook: www.facebook.com/AuthorAlyMartinez

Facebook Group: www.facebook.com/groups/TheWinery

Twitter: twitter.com/AlyMartinezAuth

Goodreads: www.goodreads.com/AlyMartinez

www.alymartinez.com

Made in the USA
Las Vegas, NV
02 May 2023

71336033R00157